West of the Sea

STEPHANIE WILLING

VIKING

VIKING
An imprint of Penguin Random House LLC, New York

First published in the United States of America by Viking, an imprint of
Penguin Random House LLC, 2023

Visit us online at PenguinRandomHouse.com.

Library of Congress Cataloging-in-Publication Data is available.

ISBN 9780593465578

10 9 8 7 6 5 4 3 2 1

Printed in the United States of America

BVG

Design by Lily K. Qian
Text set in FS Brabo

Dedicated with love to

Theodore and Ezra. Y'all are my every heartbeat.
And to Kimberly, for cottonwoods, wheat fields, and stars.

1

COUNTRY GIRLS DON'T GET SCARED when things go thump in the night. There's always some critter out there making noise and trouble. So when I heard the scratching out back, I didn't think too hard on it.

A low rumble, a *scrrritchy* sort of sound, and my brain put two and two together: there was an owl with a tummyache scratching at my window. It made perfect sense.

Scrrritch.

Wait, no, it didn't.

Thump. Scrrrritch. THUD.

I shoved myself upright and rubbed the sleep grit out of my eyes.

There was a face at the window. It had a long, snaky neck and a sharp, pointy beak. Looking at me.

My heart jumped up past my throat and choked off a scream.

But then I slumped against the headboard. I knew that face. It was Harry. My dang peacock. Presumably hoping for breakfast in the middle of the night.

He had no sense of time. He had no sense period, but then, neither did I.

Moonlight spilled over the bed, illuminating me and the fossil I'd fallen asleep holding. I'd scooped this stony relic off one of Mama's cairns in the weak hope that she'd come looking for it.

I'd actually thought stealing a fossil would do something, like get a reaction.

Mama could smell a fossil five feet out of the ground, so it stood to figure she'd be drawn to this one too, and then I'd get to say goodnight to her before she locked herself in the bathroom to soak in the tub for hours. *Again.* If I got really lucky, maybe she'd even smooth my hair, or sing me our old lullaby, or scold me for messing up her stack of stones. I wasn't picky. I'd take anything other than how I became invisible to her at night.

Scritch. Thump.

A draft of cold air rustled the room, and I pulled the quilt up around me. I was almost twelve, not a little girl anymore. I shouldn't need Mama to come say goodnight to me. It would be better if I learned to not need her, like my big sister, Margie, had.

Scritch scritch SCRATCH.

"Ugh, I'm coming," I said. Keeping the quilt, I scooted out of bed and stomped over to where my peacock watched me through the window. I pushed the pane up until there was only the screen between us.

Harry scraped and rustled inside a decrepit old wheelbarrow that Mama had parked under my window and made into a flower box. She was always taking broken things and turning them into something beautiful. At least, she used to.

"Harry, it is not breakfast time," I told him.

He clucked and spread his fan of tail feathers. He was only one year old, so it wasn't impressive, but I never let on. There was a lot he didn't know. He'd been born in the drought, and if it ever rained, he'd probably think the sky was falling.

"Yes, you're very handsome, but not even the handsomest birds get fed before six a.m."

I scolded him, but I wasn't *really* mad. I got it. Sometimes I woke up lonely too and went hunting for a snack.

The night air smelled warm and dry. I wasn't sure why I'd felt such a chill in the room when I woke up. I let the quilt fall to the floor.

I looked past Harry to our wheat fields. They rustled in endless silver waves under the moon. But the stalks were weak and not as tall as they should be. If the drought didn't break, we'd be out a year's harvest, and the lines in Papa's

3

face would get deeper. Mama would sink even quieter, Margie would get angrier, and I'd . . . I'd be fine.

Harry pressed his face against the screen, and I pushed my hand against the shape of him. He chirruped.

The house was silent. I listened for the soft splish-splash sounds of Mama soaking in the tub down the hall, but she must've gotten out while I was asleep. Or maybe she'd dozed off in there. It wouldn't be the first time.

Thunder rumbled, and I realized I was squeezing the fossil tight in my right hand. I hadn't noticed I was still holding it.

I frowned. If there was thunder, there should be clouds. And if there were clouds, the moon wouldn't be this bright.

"Go back to the coop, Harry," I said. "Papa's gonna feed you in a few hours."

Harry closed his fan, bobbed his head, and jumped to the ground.

And that's when I saw the dimetrodon in the vegetable garden.

2

I DROPPED DOWN AND PRESSED my back against the wall. My breaths came fast as I tried to understand what I'd seen, but there was no making it make sense.

Turning around slowly, I inched back up until my eyes were just above the sill.

Yep.

There was a reptile the size of a full-grown alligator with a large sail on its back and four stumpy legs standing in the middle of our tomatoes.

It was a dimetrodon. No question. The sail was a dead giveaway. I'd scribbled in enough dinosaur coloring books to know it on sight by age three, and by age five I'd known it wasn't a dinosaur at all.

I stared at the rest of it: the long tail, the legs thrust out to the side like our modern-day reptiles, and the long beak-looking jaw. The only thing that had me doubting myself was the fact that dimetrodons hadn't walked the earth since the Permian period 270 million years ago.

The dimetrodon ambled behind our leaf-littered trampoline toward the fields. A moment later, it slipped through— *through???*—the fence posts and disappeared into the wheat.

I stayed there, frozen, as the old clock down the hall ticked out the seconds and minutes. The longer I stayed put, the less real what I'd seen felt. After enough crickets had sung through their symphonies, I figured it was safe to move.

Grandma West, rest her soul, used to make up her own homespun wisdoms, and she'd pretend folks had been saying them for years. It was her voice I heard in the back of my mind just now.

Haven, she'd said, *trouble's like a fly ball—you catch it best with your eyes and hands open.*

I couldn't explain the dimetrodon, but I'd seen what I'd seen. And there was only one thing to do now. Investigate.

I pulled on my boots—they pinched my baby toes, but I hadn't grown into Margie's next biggest pair yet—and pulled my hair back into a ponytail. My pajamas were just some old gym shorts and a hand-me-down Texas A&M sweatshirt, so, count me dressed for adventure.

I took the fossil with me. For luck. I glanced outside, but there was no sign of the dimetrodon.

As I stepped out into the hall, the house made strange

sounds. The clock seemed louder at night than it ever was during the day, and the floor creaked beneath my boots.

But first, I needed to get backup.

I pushed Margie's door open. "M? You awake?"

The room was lit in purples and greens by the revolving geometric colors of her computer's screen saver.

She didn't answer, and when I spotted her under her rumpled plaid comforter, I saw the big headphones over her ears and the bug-eyed sunglasses on her face. She'd fallen asleep wearing her sensory armor again. Together, the headphones and glasses blocked out the whole world—including me.

I could go wake her, but I wanted to live to see my twelfth birthday. I'd have to go this one alone.

I left the door cracked and tiptoed past the bathroom. Empty. Mama had gotten out of the bath after all.

The clock chimed one. I jumped, and the fossil clattered to the floor somewhere in the dark.

I swore under my breath. I'd have to find it before Mama did and figured out I'd snatched it, but it was too dark to look for it now. Besides, I had a dimetrodon to find.

The kitchen had a wide view of the backyard, and there was nothing out there but the shadowy silhouette of Harry slowly making his way back to the chicken coop.

Guilt needled me. He'd be an ideal snack for a dimetrodon, and I'd forgotten all about him the moment I saw the reptilian creature. I watched Harry bob across the lawn, looking like a cross between a perfume bottle and a dino-saur, and for a moment, I wondered if I'd just gotten con-fused in the moonlight.

I shook my head. Harry might be a very distantly evolved relative, but I knew I wouldn't mistake a peacock for a Perm-ian predator.

I stared out the window at the fields and waited for some-thing to move. My throat felt as parched as our wheat looked.

I grabbed a purple plastic cup from the drying rack and moved to the sink. Just as I was about to fill it up from the tap, I heard my parents' voices drifting from the screened-in porch.

That was odd. They were never up this late, especially Papa. He was an early-to-bed, early-to-rise farmer type. Mama's sleep was super erratic, but I didn't think she was typically up at this hour either.

Maybe they'd seen the dimetrodon! I started toward them, but their words stopped me in place.

"No, Zeke! We *can't*. The bungalow is the only connec-tion I still have to them." Mama.

"Exactly. That's why I think it would be best if we sold it," Papa said. "For everyone, but especially you."

Turning back around, I eased the faucet on and drowned out whatever they said next.

If I never heard another word about Grandmer and Grandpepper's old off-the-grid bungalow again, that'd be fine by me. It had a mildew problem and no electricity.

The only nice thing about it was that it was built on an inlet right on the Gulf of Mexico, so it had a pretty view, but we couldn't even swim there because of bacteria in the salt marsh. Besides, the bungalow was nearly five hundred miles away as the crow flies.

As I shut the water off, I heard Mama make the gaspy sound she did when she was trying not cry. I hated that sound. I'd heard it too much in the year since her parents had died in the car crash.

But what she said next confused me enough to pause my quest for the dimetrodon.

"Just, let me keep trying." Her voice quivered. "If I can do it, then we won't need to sell it for the money, right?"

Try to do what? I was raised better than to eavesdrop, but that didn't stop me tonight. I leaned against the counter and took a big gulp of the tap water. It was cool and comforting as I hoped to hear something that might help me understand why Mama couldn't do anything but sleep and sit and mope.

I also kept a weather eye on the wheat fields in case el Señor Not-a-Dinosaur chose to prance across the lawn again.

With my eyes adjusted to the darkness, I could see Papa's outline as he continued. "Maureen, I see you out in the field every day. I know you're trying to fix things, darlin', but you're just wearing yourself out. And, let's be honest. You've never been able to do what your parents could."

Well, that was clear as mud. I had no idea what he could be talking about. Grandpepper had spent all his time sunbathing, and Grandmer's activities included staring at the sun, watercolors, and odd conversational segues. I knew Mama wasn't painting out in the fields. I wish she was. That would be so much better than what she actually did out there.

Mama's gaspy sounds got louder.

He continued. "If we sell the bungalow, we don't have to pay the taxes, we get a boost financially, and the most important thing: Maybe it'll help you finally let go. You know? You can say goodbye and really be here with us. I miss my wife."

"I miss me too," she said.

I was surprised when tears pricked at the back of my own eyelids, and I brushed them away. "I miss you too, Mama," I whispered into the safety of my cup.

Her words bumped like a plow over rocky ground. "Do you even . . . Can you understand . . . how lonely it is? To be the only one? The only one left."

Papa's voice softened. "You're one of a kind, Reenie. It's just another reason I love you so much."

She cleared her throat. "If we sell it, I will have lost everything."

"If we don't sell it, we might lose everything else."

Mama was crying for real now. "Maybe we should tell them?"

Papa shook his head and rested his hand on the top of her head. "You know it's better if they don't know."

As if it was some big secret that the farm was in trouble. It wasn't like the thought of it made my stomach curl into knots when I tried to imagine what would happen if we lost the only home I'd ever known.

Oh wait, yes, it did.

Quietly as I could in my boots, I retreated down the hall. My foot hit the fossil I'd lost in the dark, and I heard it skitter through the doorway into Margie's room.

I thought about leaving the vertebra until morning, but when I imagined Margie stepping on it and raging through the house about who had left a fossil in her room, I got down on my hands and knees and crept in after it.

The worn carpet zinged me with static as I swept my hand across the floor. My fingers brushed against the fossil, and I grabbed it and stood up.

My heart jumped into overdrive again.

The dimetrodon was outside her window now. It had gone round front.

With my pulse going at NASCAR levels, I ran across the room to the window. I'd seen it twice. I couldn't be imagining this.

"Margie, wake up!" I said. She'd forgive me once she saw this, I was sure. But Margie didn't move.

I pressed my nose to the glass. It had disappeared again.

I fingered the fossil, letting its familiar grooves occupy me.

Clawed feet appeared on the windowsill, and the dimetrodon pulled itself up to eye level.

For one moment, I stared into the creature's cold gaze, and when it swung its head in the other direction, as if to look at me with its other eye, I yelped and stumbled backward.

Something tangled around my ankles—a backpack?—and I flailed onto Margie's bed.

"What the—?" she screeched as she pushed me off her. I toppled onto the floor, pulling her comforter with me.

She flipped on the side lamp, and when I emerged from the blanket, the dimetrodon was gone.

I popped up and pressed my face against the glass, shielding my eyes from the lamp's glare to stare through the window. The dimetrodon was lumbering away through the neglected flower beds in front of the house.

"Margie, look, you have to see!" I cried.

A terrifying figure reflected in the glass from behind me, and I realized my groggy teenage sister was the more immediate concern. I turned my back on the window.

"What the heck is wrong with you?" Margie exploded, shoving her sunglasses and headphones off. Muted emo rock spilled out, and her typically green eyes blazed fiery orange.

3

"SUNGLASSES OFF AT THE TABLE," Papa said. There was dirt in the lines of his face, but his hands were clean. He'd been in the fields before sunup and had stopped back in for some breakfast.

As Margie pushed them back, Papa frowned. "You look tired. Were you up late?"

Margie shot me a withering look. "Bad dreams."

He poured half a cup of coffee into his emptied mug and slid it across the table to her, winking. "Don't tell your mother."

Her eyes briefly shifted to a light blue as she wrapped her hands around the mug—a blip of happiness—then slid right back into annoyed green. Blink and you'd miss it, but I knew Papa saw it too 'cause his smile perked up.

He popped another microwave biscuit in his mouth and headed for the back door. "Y'all be good now."

Once we'd heard the door slam on his pickup and the engine start up, Margie turned full body to face me.

"Heyyyyy," I said. Cranky sisters weren't the most predictable creatures.

She held out her hand and dropped the fossil on the table. "I stepped on this when I got out of bed this morning. So, *thanks* for that."

There was no use telling her I'd only gone into her room because I was trying to avoid that very scenario. She always assumed all I wanted was to hang out with her and make her life harder.

Which wasn't entirely wrong? But not the making-her-life-harder part. There just weren't that many kids around. Harry was great, but he wasn't much of a conversationalist.

I ran a finger along the vertebra's grooves before slipping it into my jeans pocket. "Yeah, sorry. I must've dropped it last night when . . ." I didn't want to say it aloud again. She already thought I was ridiculous.

Margie's green eyes darkened to hazel. This was her skeptical look. "You saw a dinosaur?"

"Dimetrodons are synapsids," I corrected.

She crossed her arms at my technicality. "True, but you and I are also synapsids."

"Fiiiine. A nonmammalian synapsid."

Thanks to Mama, we were all prehistoric experts in this house whether we wanted to be or not.

She took a sip of the coffee and grimaced. Papa always sugared his up, but she and Mama liked to drink it black.

Last night, when I'd finally convinced Margie to look outside, there was nothing left to see. She'd sent me away with grim threats that I was pretty sure she'd pulled from Edgar Allan Poe stories. Mama and Papa never even heard our ruckus. I'd fallen asleep with a hollow feeling in my stomach that was caused as much by my parents' conversation as the mysterious sighting.

At a glance, Margie looked so much like Mama they might've been twins, except twenty years apart. They both had red springy hair and pale skin that rusted under the Texas sun. Their edges were soft and generous as vanilla custard, while I was scrawny and sun-toasted like Papa.

And she had Mama's eyes. They literally changed colors with her moods. She wore her sunglasses a lot now, but at the table I could watch her go from a happy pale blue to anxious gray to irritated green to curious brown.

Her eyes hadn't always been that way. They'd changed around puberty. When I'd gotten my period two months ago, I'd stared in the mirror and waited, but nothing happened. My eyes stayed the same denim blue as Papa's. Honestly? I was relieved. I didn't want to be special—at least, not like that.

To look at us, the only thing Margie and I had in common were the silver bracelets we both wore all the time.

Mama gave us each one on our tenth birthdays, and once I'd put it on, I'd never wanted to take it off. Margie usually hated everything, but she wore hers too. I'd see her playing with it when she did her deepest thinking.

Like she was right now. She dragged it across her wrist in an endless loop. "It wasn't a wild pig?"

I rolled my eyes. "Since when do those have sails on their back?"

She argued, "But it sounds like it could be the same size."

I scratched at a stain on my jeans. "Yeah, I guess."

"What about an alligator?"

"From where? There's no alligators around here."

"What if it escaped from the zoo?"

"In Abilene? That's a hundred miles away! Also, they don't have sails either."

"I don't know, Haven, it just doesn't make any sense."

"I know, okay?"

I gnawed on my rubbery freezer waffle and chewed on the question that had been nagging me since last night.

"Has Mama ever mentioned seeing things?" I asked without looking at my sister. "Like, things that aren't there?"

She squeezed the mug and snapped, "Stop it. Don't even think it. You are nothing like her, okay?"

I flinched. "Okay."

I knew Margie had the same fears as me—that whatever was wrong with Mama would be wrong with us too. At least

I didn't look like her. Margie saw her every time she looked in a mirror.

When I was little, I'd wanted to be just like my mama. She loved to play games, and she could tell a story so good it seemed better than TV. She was pretty, and she smiled all the time, and she smelled like flowers and coffee. That Mama, and that me, seemed as extinct as the creature I'd seen last night.

Margie took another long sip. "I mean, it was probably a pig, you know? You probably saw a dimetrodon just 'cause you really like dinosaurs."

Synapsids, I corrected again silently as I fiddled with the fossil. "Yeah, I guess. That makes the most sense."

It was easier just to agree with her. But I'd never mistaken bird poop for chocolate, and I definitely hadn't made a dimetrodon out of a pig.

4

THE CEILING OVERHEAD CREAKED, AND our faces turned up. Margie and I went silent as we listened to Mama's slow footsteps crossing the floor. When she walked, the whole house felt heavier. My breaths got tighter. The world compressed to listening.

The tense quiet reminded me of the conversation I'd overheard last night. "Margie, what do you think it means if someone says they're the only one? And they're, like, upset about it?"

Margie fidgeted with her sunglasses. "The only what?"

"I don't know." If I told her Mama had said it, Margie wouldn't even consider the question. She had no patience for puzzling out Mama's reasons anymore.

She squinted at me with purple-gray eyes, then said, "Maybe they feel like no one understands what they're going through, and even if someone tried, they wouldn't get it, or would judge them."

That made me sad. I loved Mama the way she was, warts and all. Maybe if she'd talk to us, things wouldn't feel so hard for her.

Margie's eyes returned to their normal grouchy green. "Look, don't tell Mom about what you think you saw out the window last night, okay?"

"Well, duh. I don't want to worry her." Either about the creature, or that I might be seeing things that weren't there.

Margie's eyes flared orange. "She's not worried about us. She doesn't even think about us."

"That's not true—"

She interrupted. "I just don't want her to go looking for whatever you saw. She's so out of it, she could walk to Oklahoma and never even notice."

The footsteps arrived at the top of the stairs, and Margie sprang into evasive action. She tugged her headphones back up and vanished inside her bedroom.

Last summer, everything had been different. Mama would be up in the mornings with Papa, and she'd go out to her vegetable garden before it got too hot. I'd wake up to the sound of her laughter outside my window as she watched a barn cat do flips trying to catch the grasshoppers she threw off the plants.

Sometimes I'd hear Margie's voice out there too, telling

her all about some new poet she'd found online or a classic Russian novel she'd read for fun. Margie never wore her sunglasses at home then, and I could watch her eyes kaleidoscope all day.

I'd roll out of bed to join Mama on her nature walk just as the world was really warming up. We'd walk around the property and hunt fossils, take them back to the table, and spread them out to identify them. I'd look them up in the fossil books we'd gotten from a library discards sale, while she'd whip up something fast and tasty in the oven for brunch. The recipe was usually just a box of cheap cake mix, some pineapple juice, and canned fruit, but it was the best-tasting thing you could imagine. That, paired with the aroma of fresh coffee brewing, was what summer smelled like.

I took a tiny sip of Margie's abandoned coffee.

Blech. It was cold. If I needed sugar and caffeine, give me a Dr Pepper any day. I took the mug to the sink and dumped it.

This summer smelled like unwashed clothes, a musty bathroom, and burnt crumbs in the toaster. I took the final bite of my freezer waffle and waited for Mama to appear.

5

MAMA'S SEAFOAM-GREEN TERRYCLOTH ROBE HUNG loose around her hips and swayed with every step like it was underwater. Her red hair ran long and lank down her back. It looked greasy, even though I knew she soaked in the tub every night.

"Hey, Mama."

"Morning, sweetheart." She gave me a small smile as she took out the mug I'd emptied from the sink, wiped the drips on the edge of her robe, and filled it with the leftover coffee in the pot.

She opened the fridge door and stood in front of it for a long minute. Too long. My shoulders began to hitch up toward my ears.

"You want a waffle?" I suggested.

She shut the door. "I'm not really hungry."

"You should eat. You're getting too thin."

"Isn't that my line?" She smiled at me again, and my heart lifted a little. She banged through the kitchen, opening and shutting different cupboards.

"What are you looking for?" I asked.

"I think I want something salty," she said.

My shoulders relaxed. She'd smiled at me, she was making little jokes, and she was gonna eat something. This was one of the good mornings.

But I knew it wouldn't last. As the day ticked on, she'd drain quicker than an old phone battery.

Still, this was why I hung around in the mornings. Sometimes the real Mama would show up.

Other times, she appeared puffy eyed and silent, and those mornings were bitter as unsweet tea. Margie didn't wait around to see what we'd get. She'd rather skip the whole thing.

Mama's hand snaked into the back of the cupboard and pulled out a tin. Leaning against the counter, she pulled the tab. A nasty, fishy smell filled the kitchen.

She held it up to her face and sipped it like soup.

I nearly gagged. "You're having sardines for breakfast?"

"Yep." She dropped into the chair across from me with the coffee and half-empty tin. "God, I'm so tired."

"But you just got up."

She nodded, her eyes distant again, and sucked out another fish.

I knew nobody was happy all the time, but Mama seemed like a mood ring stuck on the blues.

Last night's conversation was echoing inside my head, and I wanted to ask her about it, but I didn't want her to know I'd been eavesdropping. I had to be subtle.

"Hey, Mama?"

"Yeah, hon?"

I tried to ignore her fishy breath. "You ever feel alone? Like, maybe you're the only one in the whole world like you?"

For a moment, her focus landed on me. She reached out and took my hand and squeezed it. "You *are* the only one like you, sweetheart. You're so special."

I groan-laughed. "Thanks, Mama."

"And besides, you're not alone. You've got Margie. You're so lucky to have a sister like that." She almost sounded envious, the way she said it.

"And you," I pressed. "Right? I'm lucky to have you too."

She avoided my eyes. "Sure."

This conversation was only making me sad, so I stopped digging.

She slurped her last sardine and pushed up from the table. "What are you up to today?"

I put on a big smile for her when she glanced at me.

"Gonna read my library books, watch some *Star Trek*." I watched her walk past me. "Maybe go look for a wandering dimetrodon."

I waited for a response as she walked toward the back door, but nothing. I heard Margie's voice in my head again. *She doesn't even think about us.*

"Get outside a little, okay?" Her hand lingered on the doorframe.

"Okay."

She cinched her robe tighter, slipped on her Crocs, and moved outside to the deck. My smile slid off my face and into my socks, where I'd keep it until the next time I had to pull it out.

I watched her waver on the edge and then step out. No hat, no sunscreen, no boots.

If I'd done that a year ago, she would've tackled me before I could take another step. As beautiful as our land was, it was still wild. From scorpions to rattlesnakes to feral pigs, we had critters big and small with nasty teeth, tusks, venom, and stingers.

Not to mention whatever I'd seen last night.

Mama was too vulnerable out there in her clogs and no pants, but I knew where she was headed, and I didn't want to follow.

Fortunately, I had my very own rattlesnake hunter to send with her. So far, he hadn't killed anything, but he came from an ancestral line of royal snake hunters. Probably.

He was waiting for me on the back porch. Papa had already given all the birds their breakfast, so Harry was sun-ning himself beside a donkey-shaped terra-cotta planter.

I gently tapped his beak. "Harry, go after Mama. Keep an eye out for rattlers."

He tilted his head at me and squawked.

"It's literally the only job you have around here. Go be the great snake hunter you were born to be!" I threw my arms up to cheer him on.

He tucked his head under his wing. Apparently he preferred naps to a future of glory.

I bent down next to him and whispered the few words I figured he knew. "Mama. Chicken feed. Food. Mama."

He gently nipped my toes as if to say *nice try* and went back to his sunbath. Maybe he was onto my schemes.

But also, I really shouldn't leave Mama's safety up to a bird. I grabbed my boots and slipped them on.

After looking left and right for rogue synapsids, I headed for the bone garden.

6

A WIND PICKED UP AS soon as I got outside. With a glance at the sky, I plunged across the open backyard and into the overgrown field behind our house. It used to be a working wheat field, like most of our land, but that was before Mama took it over for her bone garden.

One summer ago, after Grandmer and Grandpepper died, she'd gathered up all the fossils we'd ever collected, even the most special ones I'd kept in my room. She took them all and brought them out here.

I'd been so angry when she took my favorites, but Papa said it was her way of grieving. I'd tried to imagine she was planting the fossils, and that one day we'd have a garden full of fossil trees.

Some she stacked in little towers. Similar to cairns, Margie had told me. I hadn't known what those were, but I looked it up, and historically they were a way of marking a path. But Mama's cairns didn't lead anywhere. They sprang up like bony anthills in all directions.

She spent hours out here, burying the fossils, digging them back up and rearranging them, stacking them. Like an endless, impossible game of solitaire.

Papa had let this field go to seed, and now wildflowers were breaking out everywhere. Red-and-gold firewheels, paintbrushes, and purple thistles pushed out between the golden shafts.

Trampled wheat stalks made a path I could follow, and I walked it with my head down as it wound snakelike all the way to the corner of the field where two lines of fence met behind a cottonwood.

When I stepped into the shade and looked up from my feet, I was in the bone garden, and it was snowing.

I blinked. No. The cottonwood tree was shedding its fluffs, and the air was full of soft seed packets floating in the wind.

Then I saw Mama.

She was by the tree trunk, on her hands and knees like a dog, surrounded by cairns of fossils. Her fingers clawed into the dirt. Her eyes were wide and staring as she sang something in slippery, breathy words I didn't know.

My own breath stopped for a few long seconds. The wind dropped off, and the fluffs wafted down to the dirt.

Goose bumps pimpled my skin. She looked familiar but wild, like a lost pet gone feral. Horror closed my throat.

Papa had told me not to show when Mama upset me. He said it would make her even sadder. I was glad I didn't have Margie's color-changing eyes—they would've given me away in an instant.

I couldn't quite pull the smile back out for her, but I could keep my face neutral. Stone. Like the fossils all around us. *Be stone.*

Mama growled in frustration and leaned back on her heels.

I cleared my throat. "Mama? You okay?"

She pushed her limp hair behind her ears. "I'm calling to her, but she never answers me anymore. She's too asleep here."

My goose bumps grew goose bumps. "Who are you calling?"

"The sea." Her eyes were sad and far away.

The sea? Or something only she could "see"?

I shivered. "Oh. Right. Okay."

Not okay.

"My shape is trapped in the rock. What we need is in the air, but my power is in the water." She held up some dirt and let it fall through her hands. "And there's no water."

She started digging with her bare hands and muttering again. "Tree at the center, rings around, from oldest to youngest . . . maybe the trilobite, it must be older than I thought . . ."

28

Frustration and panic donkey-kicked inside my chest. Usually I was glad when Mama said anything at all, but not this kind of scary talk.

I stuffed my emotions down until I couldn't feel them anymore. The numbness was a relief, but there was also something about feeling nothing that was very, very scary.

I dropped the boots. "Put 'em on," I said. I didn't recognize my own voice. It was flat and expressionless.

Mama stared at me, then reached a dirty hand for the boots.

I didn't wait to see her put them on. I backed away, and as soon as I was out of earshot, I turned and ran back the way I came.

The lid on my feelings didn't last much longer. Tears welled up and ran down my cheeks, and I brushed them off along with the questions piling up inside me. *What is she looking for? What did she mean? Why isn't Papa doing anything to help her get better?*

But there was one question I couldn't push away.

What if I'm like her?

Last night I'd seen something I couldn't explain, something that people might call me crazy for if I told them.

Margie was the only one I'd told about the dimetrodon, and it was gonna stay that way. And if I saw it again, I'd just pretend I didn't. I never wanted someone to look at me the way I'd just looked at Mama.

With horror.

I glanced back toward the bone garden, where Mama was now hidden by long stalks of scraggly wheat. I hoped she found whatever she was looking for soon. Maybe then Mama could stop staring at the ground and finally look up at me again.

7

GRANDMA WEST USED TO SAY to me, *You can count on two things. Sisters and sunrises.*

I didn't actually remember Grandma West. Not really. She was Papa's mother, and she died of breast cancer not long after my third birthday. But she'd watched me a lot while Mama was busy taking Margie to see specialists in Wichita Falls for her sensory issues, and Grandma had a phone. She'd made a ton of videos of us together, and like any kid, I'd rewatch videos of myself on repeat.

Haven, she'd say and snuggle me. *You're a West girl, like me. And us West girls, we don't come two of a kind. But we're like the land round here, tough, strong, and*—she'd boop me on the nose—*pretty as a wildflower.*

I missed those phantom arms. And I felt guilty that I missed her more than Mama's parents, who I did remember.

When they'd passed, Mama had been devastated.

The rest of us, well, we'd been shocked and sad, of course, but we weren't destroyed like she was. We just weren't all that close. They never came to visit us here, and when we drove all the way to them, they barely talked to us. Their deaths didn't change our lives very much, until it changed Mama.

Margie was sitting on the back porch with her headphones and a KN95 mask on while she painted her nails. Harry preened himself beside her. We had a bunch of extra masks, and she'd figured out if she wore one and sat outside until the polish dried, the fumes wouldn't give her a headache.

Using the barest bit of her fingertips, she turned the page of a paperback tome. Her toenails glittered sparkly black in the sun.

As I got closer, I heard, "Spend less time with nightingales and peacocks. One is just a voice, the other color." She paused. "That's Rumi, so you know it's true, but don't worry, it's probably a metaphor."

Ugh. If Margie thought her color-changing eyes were the oddest thing about her, she was wrong. Reading Sufi wisdom to a bird was stranger.

Margie saw me and slipped her headphones down around her neck. Faint classical music leaked out.

She didn't wear headphones just so she could tune us out if she wanted to. She did it to block everything out. For Margie, everything was extra sensitive. Sounds, sights, tastes, touch, smells. All of it.

Because of her, I had to use unscented deodorants, and I couldn't wear perfumes. When all the girls in my class bought the same cherry vanilla lotion, I couldn't because it would've given Margie a migraine. That turned out to be a blessing, though, 'cause that scent worked like a blood drive for the local mosquito population.

She looked me over as I walked up. I rubbed some snot on my shoulder sleeve and tried to look like I hadn't just been crying.

"You okay?" she asked, then turned her attention back to her hands.

I sat down on the step below her and ignored her question. She'd painted each finger a different pastel. "Oooh, rainbow colors. Pretty."

Margie didn't look up as she carefully dragged lavender over her pinky nail. "Thanks."

The fossil in my pocket from breakfast dug into my thigh, and I pulled it out and set it on the porch.

I thought about how Mama's fingers clawed into the ground and the dirt caked around her cuticles. No wonder she took so many baths. She was practically coated in it.

I shuddered. "Can you do me next?"

I expected her to say no, so I was surprised when she nudged her canvas bag toward me.

"Sure. Pick one."

"But you did rainbows."

"*One.*"

I dug through her collection, enjoying the clink of the glass bottles, and pulled out a glittery blue. "Can we do toes too?"

"Are you gonna stomp around barefoot and ruin it in like five minutes? I don't want to waste my time."

"No. Cross my heart."

"Fine. Wash your feet off first, though."

I walked over to the hose, turned the spigot, and slipped off my boots. The water was sun-warmed, then chilly. I rinsed my feet and walked across the prickly grass with my toes flexed away from the ground.

She shook and uncapped the bottle while I spread my fingers wide and held them out for her.

"Hold still," she said, and flattened the brush against my nail and drew it down slowly until there was a smooth, sparkling sheen across all of them. I loved it.

I hugged my knees so my feet were flat on the ground, and she dabbed the same glittery blue all across.

She capped the bottle and said, "Now hold them out in the sun. They'll dry fast."

I stretched my hands and legs out and watched the sun glint off the glitter in the polish. I felt fancy and clean and nothing like the woman out there in the field. "Preeeeetty, thank you."

We sat with our hands and feet in the sun, our faces in shadow, as Beethoven's *Pastoral*—according to Margie—played dimly through her headphones.

Our spines both straightened at the same time when we saw Mama stand up under the cottonwood tree an acre away.

Margie tapped the enamel on her nails. "I'm dry. You wanna go dinosaur hunting? Kidding. Synapsid hunting?"

"There's no dimetrodon."

She frowned. "But—"

"It was a bad dream. I woke you up for nothing."

She banged her fists on her knees. "Di-no hunt. Di-no hunt. Di-no hunt."

"Uggh, and what, you think I should just wander around and see if I run into a large spiny synapsid?"

"Sounds like a good time to me. Why, you have somewhere else you need to be?"

I didn't, and she knew it. I tapped on my toenails. They were done.

She hopped up. "C'mon, I'll go with you."

I waited for the punch line, but she seemed serious. "Why?"

She quoted, " 'The peacock has a score of eyes, with which he cannot see.' Rossetti."

"What?"

"I'm bored, Haven. It's not that deep." She held up a mini backpack and threw her *The Essential Rumi* inside. It barely fit. "I already have water bottles and everything. Let's go for a walk."

She cast one more glance over her shoulder at Mama, who was standing stock-still.

I gingerly slipped my socks and boots back on. "Which way?"

West were the pastures and the river; east was the stone-fruit orchard. Maybe hallucinatory dimetrodons liked desiccated peaches.

"I don't know, you're the dino seer." She stopped and chuckled. "Dinoseer. That's funny."

I groaned, but my smile started feeling safe enough to come back.

Getting into the act, I said, "Shhhhhh. I'm gonna listen for it. I need absolute quiet to sense the presence of the dinosaur ghost."

"Synapsid ghost," she whispered.

"Shhhh!"

"Sorry."

I grabbed the fossil and lifted it up toward the sky like an offering and closed my eyes.

It was just a joke. It was. But then, I felt something from the west. A breeze, and an itchy, tugging feeling and a murmur, like a shushing kind of whisper.

When I opened my eyes, Margie was looking toward the sound with yellow eyes and a strange look on her face.

Behind her, Mama's face was turned toward the west too.

"Let's go that way," I said.

"Yeah."

Toward the Brazos River.

8

IT WAS A HOT HALF mile to the river. We followed the
county road past sun-blasted fields and limp-leaved trees
toward a horizon that was more sky than land.

Folks think the color of drought is brown, but they're
wrong. It's blue. It's the brightest, clearest, most endless blue
you've ever seen.

I took big gulps from the water bottle Margie had
brought for me. The wheat seemed to lean toward me, it was
so thirsty.

"You see anything?" Margie asked.

From her tone, I couldn't tell if she was teasing me or if
she really believed that I'd seen something last night. I figured it was the former, and that was fine. I was ready to forget all about it. But the way the river was pulling me—I was
curious about that.

I shielded my eyes as we got close to a faded red farm-house. It sat about an acre off the road, and it was the only other house near us.

"There's a boy on that roof."

Margie stopped and turned to stare with me. "Whoa!"

The house hummed with air conditioners, and sitting on the apex of a dormer window was a boy holding a bright blue umbrella, looking west toward the river.

"Why does he have an umbrella?" I wondered aloud.

"That's your most pressing question?" Margie said. "How about, what the heck is he doing up there?"

His head swiveled in our direction, and we went silent.

I waved.

He waved back.

"That must be the Wilson-Ruiz kid," I said. He looked about my age.

In a small town like LaVerne, news traveled on the wind, and we'd heard about the Wilson-Ruiz family as soon as they'd rented the place. They'd moved in right after school ended, but I hadn't met them yet. Maybe if Mama was feeling better, we would've already stopped by with a pie or a jar of peaches from the last good harvest, but she didn't, and we hadn't.

The river still tugged. "Let's keep going," I said.

Another quarter mile and we stood on the bridge looking at the Brazos. It was a shallow, glistening brown ribbon of water that carved through farmland like ours, but it was too salty to use for irrigation.

Without a word, Margie and I turned off the road and trudged into the shade under the low overpass that connected the red banks. The river had never been very deep around here, except for the one shadowy part under the bridge where Margie and I used to dunk each other, but the drought had shrunk it even shallower.

Hshhhhhhhshhhhhh, the river said. *Innnnnnnn.*

I dug my heels into the red dirt. The pull was so strong it felt dangerous, like an undertow.

My brain flooded with images of being under the surface and staying there, down in the mud, for hours.

Wanting to get in the water on a hot day? Very normal.

Wanting to throw yourself in and sink to the bottom and never come back up? Not normal! I tried to think about my birthday coming up, or the books I needed to return to the library, anything to get these river thoughts out of my head.

It reminded me of Mama climbing into the bath and refusing to come out all night.

I wanted it *too* much.

Hssssshhhhh innnnnnnn.

I wouldn't be like her. I dropped down on the ground and tried to distract myself by throwing small rocks into the water.

Plop.

My sister clearly didn't feel the same thing I did. She

slipped her sunglasses on top of her head and sat down to tug off her boots. Dusting red dirt from her pants, she stood up and waded into the water barefoot.

She glanced at me over her shoulder, and I almost jumped. Her eyes were an electric blue I'd never seen before. "You coming in?"

I shook my head. "Nah. Don't want to mess up the pedicure."

"Oh shoot, you're right," she said, but she didn't get out of the river. Instead she closed her eyes and took a deep breath. "It's so much quieter when I'm in the water."

"What is?" I threw another stone.

She shrugged. "Everything."

". . . Like?"

"The sounds, the itchiness, the colors. All of it. It goes far away."

I listened to the low-level whine of gnats and the chirp of grasshoppers. Peaceful earth sounds.

Not that I felt calm.

Innnn, the river beckoned.

Stop it, I thought back at it.

Margie opened her eyes again and stared at me with her unnerving blue irises. "Did I ever tell you I can hear your heartbeat?"

"What? No. That seems . . . intense."

"Yeah." She cocked her head and stared at me harder.

"But you've been sounding different lately. Maybe it's 'cause you got your period."

"Eww, why are you so weird?" Talking about stuff like that made me uncomfortable. It was too private.

She winced, and I really wished I hadn't said it that way. She was sensitive about, well, her sensitivities.

The sunglasses went back on. "I *am* weird, Haven. No point in pretending I'm not. I might as well try not to be . . ." She trailed off.

"Be what?"

"Never mind."

I traced a circle on the ground with a bit of rock. Thunder rumbled.

The water looked so good. My resistance was dissolving like sugar in hot tea, and I was just about to take my boots off when I heard a strange sound. A trickling water sound that was completely different from the slow lapping of the Brazos.

"You hear that splash?" I asked.

"Probably a fish," Margie said.

"No, like a tiny waterfall."

She laughed. "Ha, good one."

"Wait, you *don't* hear it? You're the one with supersonic hearing."

She kicked the water at me, but it fell short. "Did it sound like that?"

Ignoring her, I walked up toward the road. The trickling sound got louder with every step.

It led to a patch of ground that looked just as plain and brown as the rest. Tentatively I put one hand down; the earth moved slightly beneath my fingers, and I snatched my hand back.

When nothing emerged, I pushed the dirt away and found purple-blue rock underneath.

The trickling got quieter as I revealed more and more of the stone. There was a shape there. I started digging, and the dirt gave way.

The water sound was almost gone, but the rock had revealed a boomerang shape. I stared at the fossil and pulled my hand back to cover my mouth.

This wasn't a small trilobite, or a shark tooth, or a prehistoric fern. All of which would be awesome, but this was a freaking diplocaulus skull.

There was no mistaking that shape. This extinct amphibian was more than 70 million years old. Older than dinosaurs. It was incredible.

"What's wrong? Are you having a heat stroke?" Cold bottled water poured down my face.

I gasped, and with the water in my eyes, I saw it.

The diplocaulus.

It swam away from me in a sea that stretched all around us. I grabbed Margie's arm before we got swept away.

We were in the middle of a flood.

9

I BLINKED THE WATER OUT of my eyes, and the sea disappeared. Spinning around, I looked for the water that had vanished. "I saw—a flood. Or the sea, or something . . ."

Margie lifted both eyebrows. "The water is literally six inches, except for the deep spot. Maybe the sun really is getting to you." Her smile turned wicked. "You want me to dunk you?"

I jerked away from her and kicked some dirt over the diplocaulus skull. So far, every time I'd seen something strange—something that couldn't possibly be real—I'd been touching a fossil. Lesson learned. I could see the pattern, even if I didn't understand why. No matter how cool a discovery the skull was, it wasn't worth the hallucinations.

I walked away from the river toward home. "I'm not in the mood."

Turning my back on the water was physically painful.

My hands were trembling. I dug them in my pockets, but then I felt the vertebra that had sent us toward the river. I jerked my hands back out.

Still, it burned beside my thigh. I was aware of it every moment.

Margie jogged up beside me. "Hey, you wanna—?" She gestured in sister shorthand for me to tell her more.

"No."

She shrugged. "Okay."

No, I did not want to talk about it. I was getting more freaked out every second. Bones shouldn't broadcast their location, but I'd heard that sound and felt its pull, like it wanted to be found.

Like it was waking up.

I just wanted to close my eyes to all of it. Instead I tilted my head back and walked without watching where I was going. I knew my feet would find the ground.

We walked for five minutes in silence until Margie said, "I don't know, Haven, if all you found is an ocean, I think this dino hunt is a bust."

A loud voice startled me. "You're on a dino hunt?"

We looked up the long driveway to the farmhouse, where the roof kid was now on the front porch and dragging a garbage bag out the front door. He had dark brown skin and tightly coiled hair, and his jeans looked a lot newer and nicer than mine or Margie's.

An older male voice yelled something indistinct, and the boy shouted back into the house, "I'm taking it, Dad."

He leaned his blue umbrella against the front of the house and hoisted the garbage bag onto a furniture dolly. He pushed it down toward the road where we were standing.

"That's creative," I said, just to have something to say.

"You know, work smarter," he said. He thrust open the plastic garbage can near the ditch and tossed in the bag. "Save energy."

Margie frowned. "You left the front door open. That's not very energy efficient."

"Oh, shoot. My dad's gonna yell." He sounded annoyed more than worried.

"Rye!" A tall, slender Black man was silhouetted in the doorway. "What did I say about—?" He stopped when he saw us.

I'd gotten a whiff of food garbage when the garbage can opened, but it was replaced moments later by a heavenly aroma coming from the house. It smelled like birthdays and Christmas cookies and warm bread all at once.

"You smell that too, right?" I asked Margie. My senses were no longer to be trusted, especially when the vertebra in my pocket felt like it was vibrating against me.

Margie nodded. "Mmm, yeah. Vanilla, cinnamon, yeast, and . . . lavender?"

Rye's dad smiled and stepped out into the sunlight. "That's right! Lavender-vanilla donuts. I'm experimenting."

In a low voice, Rye muttered, "He had the best burger stand in Austin, but he's a baker now, apparently."

"That's a bad thing?" I asked.

Rye kicked the trash can and didn't answer, then tried kicking it again but missed and got dirt on his pants.

Maybe I was rude? I wondered as he stayed silent. Ugh. I scratched my shoulder and a strip of skin peeled up, although I didn't remember getting a sunburn.

Without thinking, I pulled on it, but now what was I going to do with it? No one wants to meet someone literally peeling dead skin off their own body. I shoved it in my pocket and hoped no one had noticed.

Rye's dad walked down the long driveway toward us. "Rye, introduce yourself!"

"You just said my name for me!" he yelled back, then looked down and muttered, "God."

His father's face creased in annoyance.

Margie jumped to fill in the gap. "I'm Margie, and this is Haven." She pointed down the road. "We live at that house over there."

"Neighbors! Wonderful." Rye's dad looked genuinely delighted as he stopped beside his son and clapped his shoulder. "Isn't this great? Only a month here, and you're already making friends."

Rye and I frowned at each other. Friendship took more than proximity.

"How old are you?" I asked him out of politeness.

"Almost twelve," he said. "My birthday's next month."

"Mine too," I said, looking at him with a little more curiosity. "What day?"

"When?" he asked at the same time.

"Sorry, you go," I said.

"No, you asked first."

Our words jumbled and bumped against each other like sharp elbows.

"Uhh, the seventeenth," I said.

"The nineteenth," he overlapped.

"Ha, I'm older!" I punched the sky.

"By just two days," he shot back.

We trailed into silence, and I scratched at the peeling skin on my shoulder again. "Doesn't matter," I said, gracious in my victory. "We'll be in the same class at school."

He looked confused. "How do you know which class I'll be in?"

Margie laughed. "'Cause the whole grade is in the same class. Last year's graduating class was seven kids."

Rye looked horrified, but his dad didn't seem to notice. "Small classes, gotta love that. I'm Marcus Wilson-Ruiz, and you've got a great nose," he said to Margie. "ID'ing lavender? Incredible. I bet you're a super-taster too. I should hire you to test my recipes."

Margie's smile was warmer than I would've expected for

a stranger, but then I realized, this was probably one of the first times her sensitivities singled her out in a good way.

"I'm not cheap," she warned. "I require at least five donuts per tasting, minimum."

He chuckled. "Don't worry. Haven—great name, by the way—I'll send Rye to school with extras for you. Any friend of his gets donuts for life."

"Used to be french fries," Rye said. He squinted at his dad. "Not that it worked, Dad. It didn't make me popular there either."

Rye accidentally caught my eyes, then looked down and away, and I looked away too, feeling embarrassed for him.

Mr. Wilson-Ruiz brushed away his son's comments like an irritating fly. "Now, let me ask you, since y'all are locals— gotta do some market research when I can!—what does absolutely everyone, no exceptions, not even the most pickiest person, *every*one love in the morning?"

The man was like sunshine in a human body. He was almost too bright to look at, but I liked his warmth, and I didn't want to disappoint him.

"Umm . . . coffee?" I guessed.

Rye threw his head back like this conversation was causing him physical pain.

"Excellent suggestion! And yes, we will have coffee. We will have hazelnut, vanilla, dark roast, medium roast, all the roasts. I'm a tea drinker myself," he interrupted himself to say, "but there will be coffee, absolutely, and a lovely array of artisanal teas. But what can nobody, and I mean nobody, say no to?"

"Fresh donuts?" Margie guessed.

He pumped the air. "Yes! Donuts! And breakfast burritos. It can't lose. I got a brand-new coffee truck"—he gestured behind the house, where a gleaming vehicle sat parked beside a white car—"so now I'm just working out the menu."

I stared at the coffee truck. It looked like an old UPS delivery van painted silver. "I've never heard of anyone moving to LaVerne to open a coffee and donut business."

I replayed that sentence in my head immediately and wondered again if I'd been rude. Maybe Mama had the right idea hiding away from everyone—it was like I didn't know how to be with people.

"Life's an adventure, Haven—" Mr. Wilson-Ruiz started.

"He always says that," Rye grumbled.

"—and I'm excited to be here," he finished with a frown at his son.

Margie's nose twitched. "I think the donuts are burning."

Mr. Wilson-Ruiz looked stricken. He turned and ran back inside without saying a word, and the door slammed behind him.

"He's fun," Margie said, sounding amused.

Rye winced. "Yeah, everyone likes him."

Margie asked, "So he just one day woke up and decided to open a business here because . . . ?"

Rye laughed without joy. "Yeah, no. We moved for my mom. She got this promotion for WindAir Energy, and now she's based out here to set up turbines."

"Wait—wind turbines?" I interrupted.

The "damn pinwheels," as Papa called them, tore up the horizon. We'd driven past them in other towns, and there was a hum in the air that you couldn't get away from until you left the blades in your rearview mirror. I'd hated it, he'd hated it, and we'd turned up our noses at the farmers who'd leased their lands to the wind companies and chosen money over tradition.

Rye was still talking. "She'd been wanting to do field-work, so yay. Here we are."

"In the fields," I said dryly.

"One could say she's having a field day," Margie punned.

"Margie!" I flushed at the terrible joke.

Rye groaned, and for a moment, he and I were united.

"You sound thrilled to be here," Margie said, her sarcasm cruising along undeterred.

"Who wouldn't want to move from Austin"—he made it sound like the capital of the world, instead of just the state—"to the middle of nowhere?"

"Some of us call it home," I said and, unable to resist the scrap of skin, peeled another strip off my shoulder. Why was I shedding?

Rye swatted at a fly that zoomed too close to his face. "And now I do too. Ugh."

I scowled, and he added, "Not ugh, your home, but ugh, the bug. Sorry."

I didn't want to sympathize, but I got it. I'd feel the same way if someone uprooted me and took me far from home. And as much as I loved LaVerne, Texas, it had lots more cows than it did people, and it was always eleventy billion degrees in the summer, with nothing but a Dairy Queen to cool you off.

Rye brushed sweat away from his forehead. "You know, I've done a dino hunt. Back in Austin, there's a park where you can go dig for fossils, and then when you got sweaty there was a nice, like, splash pad to jump around in."

"They had real fossils?" I asked.

He shook his head. "No, they were casts, I think. You could play on them." In a fast voice, he added, "I haven't been in a long time, though, 'cause it's mostly for little kids."

Sounded like a waste of water and time to me, but I didn't say that. "Well, there's no splash pad here, but there's fossils everywhere if you know where to look."

I reached into my pocket to pull out the vertebra, relieved to have something to do with it. I wiped it on my shorts to make sure my clammy hands hadn't made it gross and then dropped it in his palm.

"Here," I said. "Welcome to the neighborhood."

"What is it?" If there was any hand sweat, he didn't seem to notice. He held the fossil up between his fingers. "You know what, don't tell me. I want to figure it out. I love puzzles."

"Great."

He tossed it from hand to hand, and I hated how my eyes followed it. Any minute I'd start calling it "my precioussss."

He missed the next toss, and the vertebra tumbled to the ground. "Whoops."

Before I could stop myself, I was on all fours like a coyote, my hands in the dirt, scrabbling for the fossil.

As soon as my fingers touched it, the dimetrodon was back. It materialized beside Rye. I automatically dug my hands deeper into the ground, and the synapsid's form became more solid.

My heart stuttered. I could see through the sail on the dimetrodon's back to the house behind it, but it seemed to look right at me.

I turned my head and locked eyes with Rye.

He was staring at me. "Sorry, I didn't mean to drop it. I mean, it's not like it's fragile, right? Pretty sure it's just a rock."

And there it was. The look I was so scared of. A mix of confusion and horror.

I looked like *her* with my hands in the dirt.

I jumped up fast, and if the dimetrodon were actually

real like, say, a cow, it would've startled and run away, or if it were a wild pig, it would've attacked.

But it just looked at me from the distance of hundreds of millions of years.

I threw the vertebra at Rye's chest, brushed my hands off, turned, and ran.

10

OUR LANDLINE PHONE WAS RINGING as I burst inside the house. Margie was five steps behind me. "Haven, you're starting to scare me. What's going on with you?"

I answered the phone, mostly to avoid talking to Margie. She'd pushed her sunglasses up to pin me with a determined navy-blue stare.

"Hello?" I tried to catch my breath.

A low, raspy voice said, "You didn't have to race to the phone. I know how to leave a message."

My shoulders dropped back below my ears. Our godmother, Dr. Kay, had a knack for calling at just the right time. "Hi, Dr. Kay."

Margie's eyes lit up light blue. "Oooh, I want talk to her."

"Shush, I'm talking to her now."

Dr. Kay said, "I'll make this easy on y'all. I need to talk to Maureen—she around?"

"She wants to talk to Mama," I told Margie.

"So go find her."

"You do it! I have the phone."

"Ughhhh, fine." Margie sauntered away.

Dr. Kay chuckled. "So, how you doin', kiddo? You good?"

For a moment, my stone-self cracked open and threatened to spill everything. She was Mama's best friend from a long time back, and she'd known me my whole life. She never judged, just listened and observed. It was part of what made her such a great veterinarian.

But I sealed myself back up. If I didn't talk about the strange creatures I'd been seeing, maybe they'd go away. Talking about it made it feel even more real.

Instead I swallowed and said, "You know me. I'm a West girl. I'm always good."

"You don't need anyone's help," she said, but there was a tone that made me wonder if she thought that was a good thing.

"That's right," I said, a little doubt creeping into my voice. "Tough as nails."

The line went quiet.

I heard Margie stomping around upstairs, then hushed conversation.

"What've you got in your lap right now?" I asked.

Dr. Kay sounded indignant. "What are you, a mind reader? How do you know I've got anything in my lap?"

"'Cause you always do."

Dr. Kay's ranch was part veterinary clinic, part hobby farm, and 100 percent animal rescue central. Critters stuck to her like barnacles to a boat.

She huffed. "Well, little miss know-it-all, it's a domesticated chinchilla named Blue who needs some dental work, and she's about five months old that I can tell."

"Awwwww! Send us a picture."

"Hang on, lemme try to . . . Lynne? Can you come take a photo of this fur girl? You know I can't walk and chew gum at the same time," she said with an awkward laugh.

When Dr. Kay laughed, her lungs rattled with the ghost of cigarettes past. She'd given up smoking a few years ago when she'd gotten a roommate on the ranch—she said Lynne wouldn't move in otherwise—and I figured it had probably saved her life.

Mama's cell phone buzzed from under a magazine, and I snatched it up to unlock. Dr. Kay always called the landline 'cause half the time Mama forgot she even had a phone. She was as bad at technology as Grandmer and Grandpepper had been.

A photo of Dr. Kay in the afternoon sunlight greeted me. Her dark graying hair was braided into two plaits, and she wore her trademark wide-brimmed straw hat. She held up the fat squirrel-looking rodent beside her face, and her grin creased into fine wrinkles around her eyes and mouth. *Ho-*

rizon lines, she'd called them once. *You look at enough sunsets, you'll get 'em too.*

"So cute! And tell Lynne nice photo."

"She's an artiste, that's for sure. She just repainted my clinic sign—I'll try to get you a photo of that too."

I saved the photo and favorited it so it would be easy to find again. There was a click, and Mama's breathy voice came on the landline. "Kay?"

Dr. Kay's voice went soft. "Hey there, Reenie. How's it goin', girl?"

"I've got it, Haven," Mama said.

Resentment flared for a moment, but I doused it. Maybe this call would make Mama feel happier.

"Bye, Dr. Kay," I said finally.

"Bye, darlin'."

I set the phone on the hook and thought for a moment about how nice it would be to just call Mama and get her to talk to you, instead of living with her and wondering if and when she would.

I went back to the cell phone and brought up Dr. Kay's photo again, then scrolled back to look at other favorited photos. An orange-pink sunset over the wheat fields. Papa laughing next to his tractor. A shot of Margie's eyes up close, turning from violet to turquoise. Me holding Harry when he was a fluffy brown chick.

I paused on a photo of the Gulf of Mexico that I didn't

remember seeing before. I could tell by the handrail in the shot that it was taken from the deck outside Grandmer and Grandpepper's bungalow.

Tag this person? the app asked.

I frowned. Stupid tech. It was just a pretty picture of a sunrise.

But I zoomed in on the corner the photo indicated, and chills ran up my back.

There was a face in the water. Looking up at the camera.

It didn't look human.

11

THE BACK DOOR CREAKED OPEN.

Papa stepped in caked in dirt and sweat. "Hey, sweetheart. Could you grab me a glass of water? I don't wanna track in any more dirt than I have to."

"Sure thing, Papa," I said without taking my eyes off the photo. I quickly sent it to myself as an email so I could have a copy, then set the phone down.

Papa felt like chatting, so I got stuck on the back porch while he drank his water and had a sandwich, and by the time he went back to work, Margie had scooped the phone up. Our internet was pretty spotty since we weren't close to any big towns, and we relied on the phone data to do most internet things.

"Hey, I was using that," I said.

She held it up to show a Pinterest page of recipes. "I'm sorry, were you using it to research the best way to feed and nourish the family you didn't choose but was thrust upon you, along with the age-inappropriate responsibility of dinner whenever Mom is indisposed?"

"Technically, no, but—"

"Then you'll have to wait."

I looked over her shoulder. "Can we have burgers? That Rye kid talking about his dad's burger stand made me want some."

"Is that an offer to help make dinner?" Margie asked pointedly.

"Nooo."

"Then your cravings are irrelevant."

She settled back into scrolling through recipes, and I resigned myself to looking at the photo again later.

The weight of everything I'd experienced in the last twenty-four hours hit me like gravity on Jupiter. I dragged myself to the couch and wrapped up in another of Grandma West's intricate quilts.

A quilt is a couch cocoon, she'd said once. *Crawl in cranky, emerge a better butterfly.*

Chrysalis, I mentally corrected her idiom. Moths made cocoons, not butterflies.

I gave up for now on solving the great mysteries of moms and prehistoric reptiles. From deep inside my chrysalis, I tried to stream a cartoon on Netflix about a dragon war, but our internet signal was too weak. Per usual.

Instead, I pushed play on one of my dad's *Star Trek: Deep*

Space Nine DVDs and let myself get absorbed in the future concerns of our galaxy.

I must've drifted off around the third episode because a door slam woke me up, and I heard Papa's tired but cheery voice in the kitchen. Something smelled delicious.

The quilt fell off as I sat up, but I didn't feel like a butterfly or even a moth. I was sluggish. I'd devolved.

"Where's Haven?" Papa asked.

"Asleep on the couch," Margie said.

"I'm awake," I said loudly to be heard.

Papa walked in the living room. "Hey, sleepyhead. You didn't watch TV all day, did you?"

I shook my head and tried to clear it.

"Good, 'cause look what I've got."

He held up an ugly yellow-and-black DVD with a library sticker on the side. "Draack-yuuu-laaa," he said in a terrible attempt at an eastern European accent.

"Haven't we already seen that one?" I squinted at the familiar cover.

"Have we?" He turned it over to read the back.

Papa loved everything sci-fi and horror, and he had the worst memory for movies, which meant he could enjoy them again and again. It was fine with me—I liked knowing how things ended.

"Well, it's Christopher Lee, so you know it's good," he said. "I mean, I guess we could watch something else. Like a romance or a Western."

I gave an obligatory chuckle. We only had specific genres of movies in this house—sci-fi, horror, fantasy, and musicals. Star Wars, Star Trek, star-anything—we had it. We had a movie or series for every day of the week. Literally.

Monster Mondays, Trekkie Tuesdays, Wizard Wednesdays, Thrilling Thursdays, Freaky Fridays, and Surreal Saturdays. No horror or sci-fi on Sundays. On church days we watched musicals 'cause that seemed more respectful.

"Pretty sure it's Monster Monday," I said.

Papa knelt down in front of the TV just as Margie walked in with loaded plates. "I need surfaces."

I pulled out the TV trays, and she set dinner down in front of me. It was gooey and cheesy with bits of tomato and hamburger meat, plus a little salad drowned in ranch dressing.

"It's not a burger," she said, "but it's cheeseburger casserole."

"Awww, you love me," I said, and wrapped my arms around her waist.

She pushed me off her, but she was smiling. "Whatever, it was a good idea. Just eat it."

Margie dropped off plates for her and Papa, then went down the hall and knocked on the bathroom door.

"Mom? Dinner's ready."

I went stone still and waited.

"You need to eat," Margie said. I heard a gentle thud,

and I could picture Margie leaning her forehead against the door. "C'mon, it's a new recipe. It'll be good. I made it a little salty, the way you like."

"Maybe later," Mama said, her voice strange through the door.

Margie stomped back into the living room and threw herself on the couch beside me. She began shoving the casserole into her mouth.

"She's already in the bath?" I said in a voice that was smaller than I liked.

"Yep," Margie grumbled.

Papa pushed play.

Forty-five minutes later, I'd gotten bored and sprawled out on the floor. I contemplated Margie's socked foot hanging over the edge of the couch where she was sulking.

I reached out my hand to tickle her heel—

"Don't you even," she said.

I pulled my hand back behind my head. Mondays were the worst. I tried not to think of what they were like before, but my mind was wandering.

Mondays used to be when Grandmer and Grandpepper would call. They didn't have a phone in their bungalow, so they'd drive into town and make a call from Randy's Tackle, Bait, and Candy Shop.

We'd pause the movie long enough for each of us to say hi to them on speakerphone, and then Mama would take the call to the back porch. My grandparents never asked to speak to me or Margie, not even on our birthdays, just to her.

Mama would always start with "How's Freddy?" and laugh. I asked her once who Freddy was, and she just said an old friend.

Then she'd switch to the Orkney dialect that none of us spoke a word of, rock in her rocking chair on the porch, and watch the fields. We'd hear the airy, slippery language behind whatever movie we were watching.

It hurt a little that they didn't seem to care about getting to know me or Margie much—weren't grandparents supposed to be nuts about their grandkids?—but it made her happy to talk to them, so I got over it.

Then one Monday night the phone never rang. When it did, hours after they were supposed to call, it was Randy saying that there'd been a terrible accident and he was so very, very sorry. A week later we spread their ashes in the gulf.

Even if we'd never been close, I missed their calls and the way Mama lit up when the phone rang. There was a hollow space to the evening, like an empty chair, that would always hold the memory of their shape.

The vampire on-screen whipped around with the cape over his face, and I yawned. Again contemplated the foot. Considered the pros and cons.

Went for it.

"Haven!" Margie shrieked. She kicked both feet at me

and fell off the couch tangled in the quilt. Grandma was still watching out for me. Papa burst out laughing, and I dashed for my boots, shoved them on, and ran outside to escape any looming retribution.

I turned around laughing and stared back at the illuminated house. My breaths slowed and went quiet as I watched Margie storm around until she settled back down in the living room.

A low rumble of thunder surprised me, and I looked up at the sky. There were no clouds blocking the millions of stars. The moon was half-full, bright enough to hang shadows across the limbs of trees like laundry, but not so bright it dimmed the starlight.

It was a slow-breathing, stargazing kind of night.

So why was my heart about to beat out of my chest?

Slowly, I turned my back on the house.

The fence separating our yard from the wheat looked like bleached bone floating in the night, and behind it stretched fields of total darkness.

I shivered. There was nothing out there. Nothing to see.

Except the bone garden.

"Catch trouble with open eyes," I said, arming myself with Grandma West's words. I slipped over the fence.

The bone garden was even darker under the limbs of the tree than the rest of the field. Mama's cairns looked alien in the gloom. I tried to dodge the piled rocks that dotted the ground everywhere.

A bird flushed out of the tree with a loud caw, and I about near jumped out of my skin.

The darkness was thick enough to swim through. I didn't know what I was looking for out here. I hated the bone garden during the day—in the dark, the cairns were extra disturbing.

I didn't like this. Time to go.

I turned around fast and knocked straight into a cairn. The rocks tumbled invisibly to the ground.

"Oh, crapadoodle." Mama would be upset.

I dropped to the ground and felt around for them. My search yielded a few orphaned rocks, and I quickly stacked them on top of each other and hoped for the best.

Whoooosh. A tingling feeling passed from the stones to my fingers, and I jerked my hands away.

Too late.

All around me, the forms of reptiles, water creatures, and bugs were beginning to glow. I pressed myself against the trunk of the cottonwood and tried not to see what I was seeing.

Luminous flying bugs darted through the air at my face. At my feet, millions of trilobites swam around me, under me, *through* me.

A dimetrodon's sail peaked above the wheat and strode in my direction.

A massive shark circled the tree. A diplocaulus sidewinded through the air as if it were swimming.

"Go away!" I yelled at them.

But instead, more appeared.

A two-foot-long lizard thing brushed past my ankle, and I screeched. Without thinking, I kicked at it, and my foot collided with a cairn. The lizard flickered and disappeared. Maybe the cairns were connected to the ghostlike creatures somehow?

Maybe—

I knocked over another one, and a diplocaulus vanished mid-swim.

Instinct took over.

I smashed one cairn after another, and the glowing creatures dimmed and disappeared.

In a terror, in a rage, I knocked over cairn after cairn until the swarm was gone and the only creature watching me was the dimetrodon.

"Please," I gasped. "Leave me alone."

The dimetrodon turned around and walked away into the wheat fields until it faded completely.

I was alone again in the dark, surrounded by lifeless stones. Walking quickly, I set my eyes on the light above the kitchen sink inside the house, and I didn't look away once.

But chasing me was the horrible realization of what I'd destroyed.

Mama's bone garden.

12

MARGIE WAS TOWEL-DRYING DISHES WHEN I shoved the back door shut behind me. Without setting the spatula in her hand down, she turned and flicked the dish towel at me.

"Ow!" The seamed corner stung my thigh.

"Gotcha." She grinned and held the towel over her head like a banner. "I have avenged mine own tickling."

When I didn't smile or fight back, her blue eyes shifted to spearmint. "What? You look like you've seen a ghost."

I turned to look back at the field, as if my cairn crimes or the creatures had followed me, but outside was a curtain of black.

"Triceratops this time?" she said with a sprinkle of sarcasm.

"Ha ha," I forced myself to fake laugh. "Yeah, just barely survived a stampede of woolly mammoths."

She snorted, and I rubbed my face with both hands—

being haunted by prehistoric creatures was exhausting.

Papa's snores emanated from the living room.

"He slept through the ending." Margie rolled her eyes in Papa's direction. "So we can look forward to an encore performance of *Dracula* later this week."

I felt too unbalanced to banter with her right now.

"I'm gonna go to bed," I told her, and headed toward the hallway. "Is the bathroom . . . ?"

"Ocupado," she said.

So Mama was still in there. I paused in front of the bathroom door with my hand lifted to knock, but I chickened out at the last second. I'd tell her about the cairns after Margie went to bed.

Instead I got in my jammies and slipped up the stairs to the half bath. Margie and I kept an extra toothbrush up there for nights like this when Mama set up camp in the tub.

Coming back down, I paused halfway on the stairs to listen. Dishes still clinked in the kitchen, the TV muttered in the living room, and the bathroom was silent. Nothing had changed. *Nothing ever changes*, a bitter part of my brain said.

Every day I hoped Mama would get better, but she didn't. And every day I moved through the house like it was booby-trapped, trying to avoid triggering more tears, or avoiding her if she was already mid-breakdown.

Sometimes I wondered if there was something wrong with me. I mean, Grandmer and Grandpepper hadn't wanted to be in our lives, and Mama seemed miserable, so maybe it was me. Mothers were supposed to like being with their kids, right?

I slipped down to my bedroom and crawled into bed. My stomach still felt sick when I thought of what I'd done. Sure, it had been self-defense, sort of, against the creatures I was seeing in my mind (it was in my head, right?).

But if I was being bare-bones honest, it had felt good to knock down those cairns. Mama gave them more attention than she gave me. But at least they made her happy, unlike me. So smashing them probably made me a pretty terrible daughter.

I rolled over to face the wall. Mama spent almost every waking hour out there. I'd ruined her, I don't know, her memorial.

I flopped to my other side. I should tell her. She'd be even more sad, and Papa would probably take away my TV privileges for the summer, but that way she wouldn't be surprised when she went outside and saw her fossils strewn everywhere.

Or—or—or maybe I could say that Harry had done it? Or a pig!

But I already knew that wouldn't work. There was no getting away with it, so I should probably just get on with it.

Hours went by as I dozed and tossed in the dark. Until finally, the floor creaked as wet footsteps slapped down the hall.

I pushed up on my elbow. "Mama?" I called.

The footsteps stopped in the kitchen, then slowly tracked back toward me.

My bedroom door whined open, and my heart lurched. I had to do this.

She swayed in the doorway. She was wearing her bathrobe with the hood over her head, which made her look like a Jedi. Or a Sith.

"You should be asssleep," she scolded. Her voice had a hissing sound that I'd never heard before, and her feet shifted like she wanted to be somewhere else.

"Yeah, I know. I just . . . I couldn't sleep until I . . ." I took a deep breath and braced myself to tell her that I'd destroyed her cairns. "You know how sometimes you do something, and you feel bad about it, but, like, it's hard? And you didn't mean to, but you also kind of *did*—"

Mama sighed and stepped inside. "Close your eyessss," she ordered.

I jumped at the chance to change the subject. "Are you cold, Mama? You sound like you're shivering."

"Shhhhh." Her face looked odd in the shadows as she sat down on the edge of the bed. "Eyessss. Shut."

She reached out a hand and smoothed my hair, and my eyes closed on their own as her fingers threaded again and again though the strands. The memory of the scattered fossils made me restless, though. I forced myself to stay still.

"*Tara, my daughter, come in from the water,*" she began in a low voice, and all my plans to confess drifted away as she sang my favorite of her many lullabies.

Nighttime is breaking,
The ssstars are all waking.
Drift off to sssleep now,
Ssswift off to sssleep now.
Dream in the ssstarlight
And sssleep through the long night.

Her fingers kept up their weaving as she sang through the other verses until she reached the end of the song and went quiet.

I floated half-asleep under the spell of her gentle touch until I felt her gathering herself up. I murmured, "Stay with me."

She set her hand on my face, and I grabbed it with my own. Her skin felt clammy and ridged. She was still pruny from her bath.

"I have to go." She sounded sad.

"Sing it again," I yawned. "Stay."

She squeezed my hand and said, "I want to. I love you sssso much."

I started without her. "*Tara, my daughter . . .* "

She stood, and with a pang, I realized this was it. My last chance to warn her about the garden before she saw it for herself.

I took a breath, my stomach clenched, and the sky rumbled. It felt like the sky was echoing my nerves.

"Mama, I need—"

My words faded away as a flash of lightning from outside illuminated the room. Mama turned to look at the window, and for a moment she was completely lit.

I wanted to scream—my hands covered my mouth—but I couldn't make a sound.

Her face looked like it was split in half. As if someone had taken a knife and cut her lips from ear to ear. Like a puppet.

Her eyes were in the wrong place. They were globes on the side of her face.

And was that a tail peeking out from under her robe?!

Her eyes shifted to me just as the light disappeared. I shrank back into my covers.

"Mama???" I squeaked.

"It's jusssst thunder," she said. "Don't be ssscared. Go to sssleep."

"But—your face—"

The thunder boomed and swallowed my voice. The bedroom door closed on the sound of her footsteps racing down the hall.

My heartbeat roared in my ears.

This was just like that one movie we watched on a Freaky Friday where aliens slipped inside human bodies and no one could tell who was human and who was alien. What if . . . ?

I waited for my heart to slow down. This was my *mother*. There was no way something could take her place without me noticing it. And besides, no one else knew our lullaby.

The storm door slammed open and shut, and I knew Mama had gone outside. Hopefully she'd worn real shoes this time.

This was just a dream, right? I'd been seeing weird things all day.

But it didn't feel like a dream. It felt as real as the quilt I held in front of my chest like a shield.

Her skin felt so strange.

I pushed the window by my bed up a few inches. Just enough to let in the outdoor sounds and smells.

I watched the flashes of lightning and listened for her footsteps to return until I drifted into an uneasy, watery sleep.

13

"HAY-ULPP!"

Harry's scream jolted me awake. I glanced at my bedroom door as Mama's deformed face loomed in my memory,
but it was shut. *It was just a dream*, I told myself.

"Ouch." My tailbone hurt when I sat up, which was
weird. I hadn't fallen down recently.

I ran my tongue over my lips and tasted salt, as if I'd
sweated in the night. My throat, my mouth, my nose, my
skin, my everything felt like I'd been fried up along with a
batch of okra to be served for supper.

I shut my window firmly to keep the heat out.

A piece of skin between my fingers was peeling off. I
tugged on it, and a long strip pulled off. So gross.

Harry screamed again. He must be hungry. That was
odd, 'cause Papa normally had all the birds fed by sunup.

Well, Harry wasn't going to shut up until someone fed him, so I pulled my boots on.

My heart sank as I remembered all over again that I'd destroyed Mama's bone garden. I wondered if she'd seen it yet, or if she was still in bed. I tiptoed down the hall and hoped she'd sleep in nice and late today.

"Thirst things first," I said, and thought Grandma West would've liked my invented saying. In the kitchen, I filled a purple cup with tap water, dropped in some Texas-shaped ice cubes, and chugged it down. Better.

The hallway creaked behind me, and I jumped, half expecting to see a monstrous face lunging at me. Cold water spilled on my pajama shirt.

Nobody there, but I heard a low murmur. I peered down the empty hall and pushed the bathroom door open. "Mama, you in here?"

Empty. Damp-looking towels hung on the racks. A bag of Mama's bath salts perched on the edge of the tub where she'd left them. *Hssssssssshhh*.

Nope.

I closed the bathroom door. It was impossible to hear the river from here. Maybe the pipes were acting funny.

The sun was already baking the ground when I headed toward the chicken coop. Harry usually slept in the apple tree above it, but he ate with the chickens.

"Hay-ulpp!" Harry ran past me in a blue-and-green blur.

That was normal, but he was going in the wrong direction. His tail was low to the ground, and his head pointed forward as he raced along the edge of the bone field fence. At the far end, he turned around and ran back.

"Harry, stop being a weirdo," I said. "Your food bowl is over here."

He didn't stop, or even slow down.

"Look, Harry," I called to him. "I'm feeding you. Just like you want." I poured him the mixture of chicken scratch, cat food, and pellets that made up his daily feed.

When he didn't come, I walked over to the field. He made another turn and slowed down to approach me.

"Hey, buddy." I knelt down. "Why are you acting so strange? Did you see a snake or something?" I tried to stroke his head, but he was bobbing up and down too fast.

The patio door slammed, and Harry streaked away toward the pasture. I hooded my eyes with my hand and watched him until he disappeared into the underbrush.

I turned, expecting to see Margie or Mama, but Papa stood there instead. That was strange too. He should've already been in the fields.

"Maureen!"

I jumped as Papa bellowed Mama's name.

"Maureen!" he yelled again. There was a scratchy, scary sound to his voice that made my arm hairs stand up.

There is an ocean of difference between calling for someone you know is nearby and shouting in hopes that they'll hear you. One is like, X marks the spot, and the other is a fishing line. Papa's voice sounded like he was casting a net as wide as the whole world.

"Mama?" I called, trying to sound casual, but my voice pitched too high and came out like a second reel of fishing line.

No reply but insect sounds and birdcalls.

My hands felt icy even though it was hot as blazes. Maybe she was in the bone garden and just so shocked by the destruction she couldn't even respond.

Papa must've had a similar thought 'cause he strode past me to the field. He hopped the fence and landed in the uneven wheat with both feet, then took off.

I clambered over and followed him.

The bone garden looked even worse than I'd seen in the dark last night. It was the wrong kind of chaos, the opposite of Mama's artful erratic sculptures. The dirt was torn up, and the fossils looked like the leftovers of a massacre.

Worst of all, she wasn't here.

The tree flung its cotton around like a thousand dandelion clocks. A deluge of wasted wishes.

"Papa?" I said. "Where's Mama?"

Cold fear slithered into my gut. I tried to push away the feeling that something really, *really* bad was happening.

Papa's hands were shaking like a laundry line in the wind. That scared me as much as anything else.

"Where's Mama?" I repeated. A numb kind of horror spread through me.

This was my fault.

"She's not here," he said.

I darted a glance toward the driveway. "But her car is here."

Papa dug his trembling hands into his pockets and looked out at the sun. "Yep. But she's gone."

"But . . . but," I argued, "where would she go?"

Papa's chin was tucked to his chest as he walked out of the bone garden and mumbled, "Why would she do this?"

I stood in the middle of my destruction. The weather turned as stormy as my mood. The sky began to cloud, and gusts of wind rattled the limbs of the cottonwood.

I felt my life separating into canyons. On one side, life as it had been. *You wanted things to change, didn't you?* my inner voice mocked. On the other, impossible side of the canyon, everything was upside down and terrifying.

I searched my memory for any Grandma West words of wisdom that might apply here, but I came up empty. Just like the garden.

14

I STUMBLED TO CATCH UP with Papa. He was walking fast through the peach tree grove, looking side to side, but he kept breaking out of the walk and into a trot like a horse fighting its bridle.

"Did she leave a note? A message?" I asked.

"No," Papa said.

I tried to recall what all she'd said to me. "When Mama came to say goodnight last night—"

Papa stopped where he was and whipped around to look at me. "You saw her after her bath?"

"You didn't?"

He gave a short jerk of his head. "What did she say?"

The snake in my gut twisted. That meant Mama had been gone—or at least been outside—since last night.

The words rushed out. "She came in and sang me a lullaby, and then it was thundering, and she went outside, but I thought she just sat on the porch."

"How did she look? Did she seem upset?" he asked.

The memory of her distorted face flashed again. My voice cracked. "I—I don't know? It was dark. But she looked different."

Papa went still. "Different how?"

"Well, her face . . . was all . . . messed up." My shoulders hitched up.

"Messed up," he repeated.

"Like . . ." It felt like a betrayal of Mama to say it out loud. No one should think thoughts like this about their mother.

"Like what?" he prompted.

"Like a monster." I couldn't meet his eyes. "She didn't, you know, look human."

He let out a long, long breath. "She's not a monster."

I wrapped my arms behind my back and fidgeted. "Yeah, I know, I must've been confused, it was just, it was a dream, I think. That's what I saw."

Papa said a really bad swear word and kicked the peach tree.

I flinched. He never swore in front of us.

He covered his eyes with his hands and sat down hard against the tree. "That's that, then." He cursed again.

I toed the dirt. "What's what?"

"Maybe if we'd gotten some rain, she could've . . . *Damn* it."

Now Papa wasn't making sense. It made me even more uneasy. Was he crying? I'd only ever seen him cry once, when McMurtry, his ancient dog, got hit by a truck.

He said slowly, as if trying to make the pieces fit together, "So she took her salt bath, broke down the cairns, and left."

Guilt rattled inside me, leaving me no choice but to tell him what I hadn't been able to tell Mama.

"It was me," I whispered.

Papa wiped his eyes and squinted. "What did you say?"

I took a shuddering breath. "I did it. I knocked it all down. Not Mama."

The look on his face made me want to bury myself under my covers, but all he said was "Why?"

Because sharks were coming out of the ground and trilobites were swarming my feet and I got really scared and kicking the cairns made them go away.

I tried to shrug, but it came out as a shiver. "I never liked them."

Disbelief etched his face. "You knocked them down because—"

Footsteps in the grass stopped our conversation.

Margie stood there in sneakers, her green eyes almost neon in her pale face, wearing her maroon-and-white high school sweatshirt and shorts. "What's going on?"

"Mama—" I choked saying it and started over. "Mama's missing."

"She left us?" Margie's mouth trembled.

"She's missing," I insisted. "She could—she could be anywhere. It doesn't mean she *left*."

Her eyes shifted shades so fast it was like watching a pinwheel. When they went solid gray, she pressed her lips and said, "I'll make more coffee. We'll need coffee, right? I'll make coffee."

She walked away fast.

My hands and feet tingled with the need to move, to run, to go after Mama.

"We need to call 911!" I said, tamping down the sobs I could feel building up. "Let them know she's missing. Papa."

He just sat there, cradling his head in his hands.

"Papa," I said louder. "We have to call 911. We have to *do* something."

"There's nothing to do," he said.

I stifled a frustrated scream. I felt trapped, my feelings all tangled up and pointing in different directions, like a weather vane in twister season. If I didn't move, I was going to explode.

Hsssssssh, the river called.

From out of sight, Harry screamed.

I turned and ran toward the sounds. The cottonwood, the wheat fields, the pasture all blended together in a canvas of panicked brown.

Grasshoppers jumped out of my way as my boots

crushed the stiff, weedy grass. One flew at me and clutched the edge of my collar. I grabbed the scratchy body in one hand and tore it off my shirt.

The horizon had a break in it at the edge of our property where the Brazos River wrapped its long arm around our fields. That's where Harry stood crowing.

My heart tightened, and my feet slowed.

Harry strutted around a blue robe on the ground. *Mama's robe.*

I couldn't speak, or breathe, or anything. I could only stare. Then I found my voice.

"Papa!" I yelled. "Papa, come here!"

My heart pulsed against my ribs, and not from the running.

In a half minute that felt like an hour, Papa stood beside me. "Oh, Maureen. What have you done?"

We stared at the wide, shallow river. Our breaths were loud in the quiet. The worst question I could imagine pounded inside my head.

Finally I said it out loud. "She wouldn't have gone in the water, right? What if she drowned or something?"

Papa laughed. It was a bitter sound. "That's the one thing we don't have to worry about. My girl can swim."

"She can?" When we'd visited her parents on the gulf, she'd always stayed on shore, her feet tucked under her, watching us while we played with Papa in the water.

"Why is her robe here?" I persisted. "Where'd she *go*? She has to be somewhere."

I rubbed my low back where it ached.

"I don't know." He put a hand on my shoulder. I leaned into him; he leaned into me. We watched the river like it could tell us what to do next.

"C'mon," Papa said at last. "Let's call the police and let 'em know she's missing."

We left the robe where it was. We figured the cops might want to see it.

Papa's hand fell on my shoulder. "Haven."

"Yeah?"

"Don't mention what your mother looked like when you saw her, okay? Don't tell the police about the monster."

My heart raced. "My nightmare."

"Right."

"Why not?"

He grimaced and scratched his head. "You're the last one who saw her, and they might think you dreamed the whole thing if you say something like that."

"Oh, okay."

It made sense, but I got the feeling there was another reason he didn't want me to talk about it. Like I was now part of keeping a secret. "Can I tell Margie about my dream?"

He frowned. "If you want to. Just keep it quiet, okay? Keep it in the family."

"Okay. I probably won't, 'cause she already thinks I'm super weird," I only half joked.

Papa didn't laugh. I followed a step behind him in his shadow as we walked away.

The river tugged at my attention, and I couldn't resist looking back as we walked. *Shhhhhere.*

15

THE SHERIFF'S OFFICE TOLD US over the phone that they recommended waiting twenty-four hours to give folks a chance to turn up on their own, but since they had an officer in the area already, he'd swing by and get some info from us.

Ten minutes later, the doorbell rang. I lunged for it, expecting the police officer—but instead, it was Rye, leaning against the front porch railing with his blue umbrella and a plastic container.

"Hey there. You're Haven, right?" He did a slow, awkward point at me.

"Hey. Yeah, that's me, I mean, I'm me, I'm—" I couldn't make sense of him being here. He belonged to the before side of the time canyon.

He thrust a Tupperware container at me. "My dad wanted to send this over for y'all to try. My mom wants the container back, though. She didn't say that, but trust me, she does." The words "trust me" came out weirdly louder than the rest of the sentence, and he flushed and shrank back against the railing.

"Oh, okay, sure." On autopilot, I took it from him.

He popped his blue umbrella open and leaped off the porch into our sunbaked yard. "Okay, bye."

I stared through the plastic container at the tiny frosted squares inside. "Cakes?"

He turned back. "He's experimenting with petit fours," he said, and added grudgingly, "They're pretty good."

"I've never heard of those." I studied the squares. "What makes them different from cake?"

He twirled the umbrella restlessly. "Almond paste or something? But you're right, it's cake. Fancy cake."

"Tiny fancy cakes," I said. "I bet my mom'll like it. She likes to bake."

I said it without thinking, 'cause for three and a half seconds, I'd forgotten that she was missing. The pain of remembering was such a shock that I stumbled forward.

Rye lurched onto the shady porch with the open umbrella and one empty hand. "You okay?"

I was very not okay, but I barely knew this kid, and I wasn't about to tell him what was really going on.

"Bet you've never met someone who has trouble standing and talking at the same time," I said, trying to play it off.

"Do you always have that umbrella with you?" I was determined to change the subject.

He closed it. "Only if the sun's out."

"That's—that's so strange."

He looked pained. "I know. I just don't like getting too much sun."

Margie appeared beside me. "Not here yet?"

Rye's mouth and train of thought dropped. Instead he was staring at my sister.

I glanced up at her and realized the problem.

"Margie. Sunglasses," I said quickly.

Her eyes had been cycling gray to green to purple, but then they flushed to light brown as she pulled her sunglasses off her collar and popped them on her face.

I felt my cheeks heating up. Margie's eyes might change colors, but I'd have to wear a mask to hide my blush. We'd met Rye less than twenty-four hours ago, and he was already getting a front-row seat to almost everything that made me and my family unusual.

"What—why do your eyes—" he started.

I interrupted. "Why were you on the roof yesterday?"

It was his turn to look self-conscious. "That's just me being a nerd. I told you I like puzzles, right?" His voice squeaked a little at the end.

As if to emphasize his point, he pulled out a Rubik's Cube keychain and fidgeted with it. "There's this, uh, this game you can play online? Where you get a photo of a location, and it can literally be, like, anywhere in the world, and you have to figure out where it is from the street signs or the kinds of plants and stuff, and it's really tough, but I'm getting pretty good at it."

He tucked the Rubik's Cube back in his pocket. Without anything to do, he began tapping his knuckles on the porch railing, which was littered with lots of little treasures I'd left there on display, like an abandoned mud daubers' nest.

"So you climb on roofs to . . . what, practice?" I asked.

"Exactly." A quick catlike smile stretched across his face, and a springy curl fell over his brow. When he smiled, he didn't look bored or like he hated everything about my hometown.

My traitorous heart thumped for a brand-new reason. It felt strange to be noticing it right now, but he was really cute. Like, *pretty*, with burnished brown skin, wild dark curls, and eyelashes so thick and long, a butterfly might mistake them for flower petals.

He picked up the mud daubers' nest and lifted it to one of his eyes like a telescope. "I try to see everything from a different angle."

Margie was looking past him at the road, but she asked, "Do you win anything if you solve the puzzles?"

He wandered down the length of our porch, touching all the stuff I'd left out there. It was nice, actually. I used to share my collections with Mama, but now she never noticed them.

He rattled my bucket of coins, marbles, and snail shells. He picked up and set down a piece of pottery I'd found weeding in the garden, then he traced the serrated edges of a small aloe vera plant I was trying to keep alive. "No, just bragging rights. Oh, hey"—he turned around quickly—"I, uh, I brought this back for you."

He pulled the fossil I'd launched at him from his pocket and held it out to me.

My chest tightened. My fingers itched to wrap around it, but I knew if I touched it, I might start seeing creatures that weren't there again.

"You can put it on the rail," I said. "Add it to the collection."

He set it down and patted it. "Good rock."

To my surprise, a tiny laugh escaped me. "Did you figure out what it is?"

Was I sweating? I was.

He shook his head, and another lone curl bounced over his eyebrow. "Nah, just that it was probably Permian, based on the coloration."

"Not bad," Margie said, sounding impressed.

He shrugged. "I can google. Didn't take much to figure out this is the red dirt river basin. Lots of Permian fossils around here."

He gestured toward all of LaVerne.

"There used to be a sea here," I said, and then stopped, chilled. I didn't know where the words came from. They weren't mine. I'd never been told that before, but deep in my bones, I knew they were true.

The *shhhhhhhh* in my ears roared so loud that I missed what Rye said next.

When I could tune back in, Margie was diplomatically getting rid of him. "I know it's hot out, so please thank your dad for the"—she tipped open the lid and took a sniff—"vanilla almond, chocolate cream, cherry coconut, and . . . is that pineapple sunshine cake?"

He thumped the umbrella on the wooden floor. "Nailed it."

"They're petit fours," I corrected her.

"Oooh la la." Margie dripped sarcasm. "Is this an add-on to your dad's donuts-for-friendship exchange program?"

Rye laughed, but it seemed a little forced. His eyes cut to mine and then dropped to the ground.

A long, painful silence stretched like a hand waiting to be shaken.

"Umm, you should climb our, uh, windmill sometime," I said. "So you can see the view from there. I like to go up there and watch for storms. Maybe it'll help your puzzle game thing."

He nodded. "Sounds cool."

"No donuts required," I added.

The quicksilver smile he shot me made something in my tummy go flip-flop.

A white car turned onto our stretch of street, and for a moment I thought the police were already here. "Is that—?"

Rye's face relaxed. "Oh, that's my mom. She's home early." He jumped up and down and waved to get her attention.

Papa must've heard the car too, 'cause he came outside. He stared in surprise at Rye on our front porch.

"Dad, this is Rye," Margie said. "He and his family moved in across the street. Rye, this is our dad, Ezekiel, but everyone calls him Zeke."

"Nice to meet you, Mr. Zeke," Rye said politely.

"You too," Papa said with a distracted smile. Then he focused on the vehicle. "Is that from one of those pinwheel companies?"

Rye snickered at Papa's word for the turbines. "Yeah, my mom gets a company car because she has to drive around and talk to people about setting them up. You know anyone who wants to lease their land? They get paid and stuff."

"I don't." Papa frowned at the car, but he didn't say anything else about it. He went back inside and left us with Rye.

The WindAir Energy car slowed down at the end of our drive. It was hard to make out details, but I could see the woman's dark curly hair and the great big smile that spread over her face as she waved back to Rye.

Mama hadn't smiled like that in a long time, not at anything, and definitely not at me.

"You're so close, you could just walk home." I tried to keep the jealousy out of my voice. Probably failed.

Rye jumped off the porch and waved the umbrella. "Yeah, but she's gonna wait for me no matter what. And it's got air-conditioning! See ya."

I waved for ten seconds too long and then stuffed my hands in my pockets.

My eye caught on the vertebra he'd brought back for me. I tried not to think about how he'd held the fossil in his hand, and what would it be like to hold his hand.

Probably sweaty and fidgety, a reasonable voice in my head said.

Trying to avoid touching it, I held open my pocket and scooped the vertebra inside to keep a little bit of Rye close to me.

Brains were so odd. This was not the right time to be thinking about a cute boy! *Especially* a nerdy city boy who didn't appreciate the raw beauty of my favorite place on earth.

But all thoughts of Rye were gone minutes later as Officer Bryant took his cowboy hat off and entered the living room. He was noodle thin, but his face looked like a Sunday special at the T&D Café: sunny-side-up eyes, fat sausage smile, and cheese grits for stubble.

He moved a couple embroidered pillows out of his way and sat down on our couch before starting with the basics: driver's license, recent pictures, stuff like that.

I watched him from the computer chair, spinning a little left, a little right, as I pushed from foot to foot.

He nodded toward me. "You sure you want your daughters here for this?" the officer asked Papa. "These things tend to get . . . personal."

Papa was perched stiffly on the edge of his recliner. "Haven was the last one to see Maureen, so you're gonna want to talk to her."

The officer switched his cowboy hat from hand to hand. "Go on, then. Tell me what you remember."

I looked to Margie for reassurance where she stood just inside the kitchen, but she wouldn't look at me. She still wore her sunglasses, and she'd added her headphones, as if she wanted as little to do with this reality as possible.

Without Mama here, without Margie's encouragement, I felt more alone than I ever had in my life. My throat constricted, but I managed to tell Officer Bryant about the night before. Like Papa told me to, I left out the bits about the monster face. And what I'd done to the bone garden.

"Did she say goodbye?" he asked.

"Ummm, no." Hugging myself, I thought back to those last sleepy moments before I saw the scary face. "I tried to get her to stay longer with me, but she went outside anyway."

"Interesting." He scribbled in a small notebook before he turned his questions to Papa.

Papa kept his answers short. He seemed calm, but if you knew what to look for, you'd see the way he held his jaw rigid, like these questions might break his teeth.

No, she didn't have a boyfriend. No, she didn't sneak out at night regularly. No, they weren't fighting. No, Papa had never hit her.

"Any unexplained mood or behavior changes?"

Papa cleared his voice. "She's been, uh, depressed for, uh, for a while," he admitted.

"At least a year," Margie said, speaking for the first time.

Goose bumps ran up my arms. We'd been tiptoeing around that word. I'd read about it online when I tried to look up Mama's symptoms, but we'd never put a name to it before.

Depressed. It took Mama disappearing for anyone to say it out loud.

Officer Bryant said, "So, assuming she left of her own free will, where do you think she went?"

Papa sighed. "I think she's headed to the gulf."

The officer raised his eyebrows. ". . . Of Mexico?"

"That's where she's from."

Margie rubbed her forehead and nodded like this was all making sense. "Near Galveston. She's been missing it." Her voice was soft and hot, like water just before it boils.

Surprised, I looked around at everyone. Wasn't anyone else concerned that something had, I don't know, *happened* to her? Why did everyone assume she'd left?

"But she loves it here too," I said. The evidence was all around. Like the octopus welcome mat that said NICE TO SEA YOU! She'd picked that out special and waited until she had a coupon to buy it. And the officer was sitting in Mama's spot, right where she liked to be on our sci-fi movie nights. Even the hand-painted water glass we gave him that sat untouched on the coffee table—that came from a rummage sale where she'd let me pick anything I wanted. *And she loves us*, I added silently.

The officer's eyes flicked to me, then away, as if nothing I said mattered.

He asked, "When was the last time she was there?"

Papa cleared his throat. "A year ago, for her parents' funeral. Before that, about three years ago. We tried to go more often, but what with the price of wheat going south, and the cost of gas . . ."

"Of course." The officer scratched his head with his pen. "Have you called your wife's family?"

Papa shook his head. "She's the only one, since her parents passed. Car accident."

The only one left. Mama's words echoed suddenly.

My fingers twisted around each other until my bones hurt with remembering. The funeral had been really private.

Mama had kept looking around like she'd hoped other people would be there, but it was just us, Dr. Kay, her roommate Lynne, and the minister. I think that was the moment that all the lights inside her began to go out one by one.

The officer scowled, his sausage lips curling into a frowny-face breakfast platter. "But you think your wife is headed to the Gulf of Mexico by herself with no car, phone, or wallet?"

When he put it that way, it didn't make much sense.

Papa shrugged. "Yes. That's what I think."

"Well, you know her best. But in my experience"—he avoided Margie's and my eyes—"when an unhappy or mentally unwell woman abandons her family, she doesn't do it alone. Most times it's with a"—he paused and scratched the back of his neck—"it's with a romantic partner, or if not, another family member. But you said they're all dead."

Papa finally looked mad. He pushed up to standing and said, "Look, I didn't call you 'cause I need you to play detective. I think my wife left for reasons that make sense to her, and I think she's coming back. But I figured y'all should know."

Officer Bryant put his hat back on. "Yep, no, you're right. It's good you have this on record, should you want to pursue sole custody."

Margie gasped. I froze in my chair.

Papa looked like he'd been slapped. "We're not—she didn't—my wife's coming back, Officer."

Officer Bryant closed his notebook. "I've got a few more questions. But first I'd like to see the robe."

I moved to go with them, but Officer Bryant said, "Just me and your dad, if you don't mind, ladies." When the storm door slammed behind them, silence settled over the house.

My eyelids were two heavy feedbags, even though I'd only been up a few hours. "I wish I could just go to sleep, and when I woke up, she'd be here," I said.

Margie took off her glasses to rub her eyes. "Yeah. Me too."

As I sat rooted to the chair, I wondered if this wasn't so different from the way Mama felt after Grandmer and Grandpepper died. Maybe she'd slept so much 'cause she hoped that when she woke up, things would feel different.

16

ABOVE OUR HEADS, THE CEILING fan whirred, and I watched it like it was television. The fan moved fast, but it didn't go anywhere. Like me. I felt as useless as a watering can in a hurricane. At least the ceiling fan cooled the room off.

Margie sighed and sat down hard on the couch. "This suuuuuuucks."

From behind her in the spinny chair, I said in a low voice, "I think it's my fault Mama left."

"No," she said without a moment to consider it. "It's not your fault."

"But I knocked down all her cairns," I confessed. "Last night, when I was outside."

She turned around and pushed her sunglasses up to stare at me. But instead of looking disgusted, like I expected, she looked . . . impressed?

"Wow. Good for you," she said.

I shook my head. "No, if I had just—"

"Listen to me," Margie interrupted to glare at me with fierce yellow eyes. "We did *everything*. We were quiet when she slept in; we basically stopped using the bathroom so she could have it whenever she wanted a bath; I've been cooking all our meals for months; when our clothes got gross, we washed them; you packed your own lunches—"

"Yeah, I was such a big help," I said, feeling irritated with myself.

Margie's eyes were so yellow now they looked golden. "You never should've had to do anything, Haven," she said. "Besides be a kid."

She dropped the sunglasses back on her nose and flopped to face forward again. "This is all on her."

Everything my sister said made sense, but it didn't feel true. I knew I'd done something terrible when I messed up Mama's bone garden, and I hadn't apologized when I had the chance. And now she was gone. Tears threatened at the corners of my eyes, and I fought them back. I told myself I wasn't allowed to cry until I could tell Mama I was sorry. We needed a plan, not a crybaby.

Papa came back in and tossed the officer's business card on the coffee table. "He said to call if we hear anything from Mom, and if not, he'll put out a missing person bulletin tomorrow."

"Okay." I watched him for signs of what to expect, but it didn't seem like he was going to say anything else. "So. What's next? What do we do now?" I asked.

Papa looked lost. He said, "I guess we just stick to the routine."

Margie gasp-laughed. "The routine? Like we have for the past year, pretending nothing's wrong? Hoping Mom would just get better? Where did that routine get us?"

Her face was as red as her hair. Tears simmered behind her words.

The sound of my big sister trying not to cry got me moving. If she broke down, then I'd break down.

"I'm gonna check on Harry," I said, and pushed off the chair.

"Don't be out long," Papa said. "The weather is changing."

The storm door swung shut behind me with a bang. Outside, a ragged wind scrambled across the wheat like it wanted to escape, just like me.

I ran a pasture away to our old windmill. Maybe it was because I'd brought it up, or Rye's influence, but I found myself climbing to get a different angle.

Gusts of wind tugged at my clothes and my ponytail with invisible hands. Beam by beam, joist by joist, I pulled myself toward the top.

I stopped and straddled a beam just short of the old

blades circling in the air. With one arm hooked for safety, I twisted around until I could see the road that ran to town. If Mama had driven, she would've gone that way. But there wasn't a car in sight, except for Mama's parked right in our yard. She hadn't driven it in a couple weeks.

Turning back around, I let out a slow breath and stared west toward the horizon. Overhead, the windmill's blades sped up in the rising wind. I wasn't much higher than the scrubby trees that dotted the pasture, but the land was flat, and I could see for miles. Wheat fields, patchy pastures, and red cliffs.

Harry screamed somewhere nearby, and a few dark birds were flying above the next pasture. But where was Mama?

The Brazos River caught my eyes, a snaky line of gold in the red clay, and I traced it south until it curved out of sight. There was movement everywhere if I let my gaze go out of focus, but nothing that moved like a person.

I tried to reason through it. We knew Mama had gone to the river. The river went to the gulf. Theoretically, a person could get themselves there if they floated all the way through the heart of Texas and out into the ocean.

But if Papa was right and that was where she was headed, how would she get there—by boat? I almost laughed. You'd look as foolish as Noah to have a boat out here where water was as scarce as profits.

I watched big clouds gather on the horizon and tried to

hope. If it rained, it would be a sign that our luck was turning. But my hope felt like a dollar-store kite. It was hard to get off the ground and even harder to keep it up there.

"Cumulonimbus." I sounded out each syllable as if I could call them, and they'd come. It was like incanting a spell. Haven West, weather witch.

Nothing happened, of course.

I slumped with my arms around the beams and closed my eyes. The wind moved around me, and I wished with every cell in my body that I could bring Mama home. I hummed the first line of our lullaby, but I changed the words in my mind. *Tara, my mother, come in from the water.*

I opened my eyes to see the clouds billowing larger and traveling fast across the fields. There was another blast of storm air, and I pivoted ten degrees to face it. Had I done that?

Delusions of grandeur much? More like Haven the weather vane as I twisted around to look everywhere at once.

"Mama," I whispered into the wind, in case I could pull her home instead.

Movement caught my attention. I straightened, then slumped. It was Rye setting up a ladder on the side of his house. He climbed to the top rung and carefully shifted to sit on the roof's edge. I watched his head turn slowly as he looked across the land, and I wondered what it was he was really looking for.

His gaze stopped when it got to me.

I waved.

He waved back.

It was gonna get awkward if I kept looking in his direction. I turned away and latched on to the birds flying nearby so I wouldn't be tempted to glance back at him.

Realization slowly dawned.

The birds—they were vultures. And they weren't just flying.

They were circling.

17

I BARELY FELT THE BEAMS as I clambered down, and as soon as my feet touched dirt, I ran toward the next field.

Vultures meant something was dying or dead. My eyes stayed on the birds as I tracked them. A vulture swooped down and stayed down. Then another.

My breath came short as the brown grass blurred beneath me. My thoughts ran in opposites: *Don't be Mama. Please let me find Mama. Don't be Mama.*

The circle of naked heads turned to look at me as I sprinted toward them. I didn't stop running.

The vultures flapped off into nearby trees, hissing and shaking their red necks.

I came to a slow, halting stop.

Ants were already crawling over the carcass.

The six-foot-long body of a rattlesnake curved in lifeless loops. Bits of flesh were missing from its body.

It was fresh.

I was gonna be sick. My hands dropped to my knees, and I fought to keep my roiling stomach from vomiting up bile.

Not Mama. Thank goodness.

"Hay-ulpp!" the snake killer screeched.

Harry leaped to the ground from the low limb of a black locust tree.

My stomach settled enough for me to straighten up. "Good job, Harry."

His head perked up. Unfolding like a jeweled fan, he displayed his almost fully grown tail feathers. He shook them at me, or maybe at the vultures.

"Such a good snaker," I praised him, and tried to calm my racing heart. There was no reason to think anything bad had happened to Mama. Not yet.

The ants moved over the snake like a pixelated wave. Before I could stop myself, I saw in my mind how Mama might look if we found her like this.

Then I did throw up. More food for the ants. I wiped my mouth with the back of my hand.

Hsssssheeere.

I looked up. The Brazos was only fifty yards away.

I'd always loved the sound of water—sleeping out on the deck at Grandmer and Grandpepper's bungalow had been the best part of those visits—but this felt different.

I cocked my head to listen. This felt like a song fading in and out on an old radio, or that strange thing where I'd swear I'd heard someone say my name in an empty room.

It made me want to listen closer.

What if—my heartbeat increased—what if this feeling was actually coming from Mama? She was part of me, and I was part of her. I knew it wasn't a scientifically grounded theory, but what if I was *feeling* her out there?

And what if I followed her?

Papa had said to stay close, but it was only a few more steps to the red riverbanks.

Innnnnnnn. Hsssssheeeeere.

I'd just walk beside it a little ways to see if there were any clues to where Mama went.

My feet turned south toward the overpass and the Wilson-Ruizes' land. "Harry, go back home."

He listened to me as much as always, which is to say, not at all. He held his tail off the ground and zigzagged behind me in sudden darts. Clouds tumbled overhead as Harry filled the air with his eerie screams.

I scanned the riverbanks, looking for any footprints or shoe prints, but I didn't see anything. As I walked, I tried to fit all the pieces together like Rye's Rubik's Cube, but no matter how I turned them around, they didn't make sense.

Mama's monstrous face in the moonlight. Her cairns.

The only one left.

I tried a different angle.

Margie's eyes. My dinosaur ghost visions. The photograph of the inhuman face in the water.

Another angle.

Mama's depression. Papa pretending everything was fine. Margie shutting everyone out.

The answer was in there somewhere, but I couldn't see it. What it all came down to was that Mama wasn't home with us, and that was the strangest and most terrifying thing yet.

A trickling water sound made me look down. Without realizing it, I'd walked toward the diplocaulus skull. The dirt was still disturbed from where I'd kicked it the day before.

It couldn't be a coincidence that I'd started seeing dimetrodons right before Mama disappeared, right? No one loved prehistoric fossils more than her. Maybe the dimetrodon had been a warning—*pay attention, mother on the edge of breakdown!*

Or maybe I was the one breaking down.

I knelt beside the diplocaulus. Harry clucked and sat beside me.

I reached my hands out, then hesitated. I didn't want to stand out, like Margie, and I didn't want to be obsessive, like Mama.

But I did want to find her. And maybe there was something in me, in the visions, or the voices I was hearing in the water, that could help.

Even if it was scary. I brushed the dirt away and pressed both hands against the fossil.

18

I WAS UNDERWATER.

The sea was warm, but the sun was too far above me. I couldn't swim fast enough. I'd drown!

I pumped my arms to swim up, and the watery world vanished. My arms swung in the air. Not underwater after all, but still on land.

Well, that was embarrassing.

Harry clucked and moved several feet away from me.

Just. Breathe. `

I tried again.

I closed my eyes, pressed my hands against the dry rock of the fossil, and focused on that sensation. The rock. The ground. The dirt. Then I let myself look around.

I was underwater.

The sea was warm.

Dark shapes moved between me and the surface. The sun was far above me, but I could breathe.

There were no words for this.

It was almost like a movie was playing on top of another one. I could see Harry beside me, the river behind me, and Rye's house half a mile away. But I could also see a diplocaulus swimming up toward the water's surface. When it broke through, I saw it use its boomerang-shaped skull to stay on top of the water. Now that I was calmer, it was actually pretty cool. No, it was amazing.

Fish darted overhead, and huge shadowy figures swam south, out of sight. The big ones made me nervous, even though nothing I'd seen so far had been able to touch me.

And still that sound, so close to a voice, calling, *Shhhhhh heeeeere.*

I strained to listen for Mama, or any clues as to where she'd gone, but her voice was still too far away.

I stood up and dusted the dirt from my hands. The world went brown, dry, and hot again.

A grin stole across my face. I'd seen a prehistoric world, on purpose! Maybe I could learn to control whatever this was.

The creatures I'd seen were swimming south in the same direction as the river. Follow the fossils, find Mama? It was a better plan than no plan.

"We're almost to the Breaks," I told Harry. "Let's keep going."

I wasn't supposed to go there by myself, but I wouldn't stay long. I'd be up higher, so I could see farther, and maybe I'd spot her.

Besides, I wasn't alone. I had Harry.

The clouds had evaporated, and the sun was out in full force. The ground rose gradually, and at the next bend in the river, I was there.

The Breaks. This was where the Brazos sliced through the land and the banks turned into steep red bluffs. I could look across the river and see the striations on the other side. The clay cliffs swirled with rusty reds, oranges, and golds. Like they were made from a jar of sunset.

The drop was ten, twenty, or fifty feet to the river, depending on where you stood. Gorgeous and deadly. I stayed away from the edge.

Small trees and bushes grew right to the edge of the river. I could see at least the next mile, but there was no sign that a woman, or any person at all, had been here. Like, ever. They were so still you could look around and feel like you were the only person alive. The last one left.

The sun was really burning now. I knew I should head back before I roasted my skin so bad I'd be peeling it like tissue paper. But I didn't want to give up.

While I'd been looking around, Harry had gotten too close to the bluff. I sugared up my voice. "Harry, come here, honey. Don't be a silly bird and fall off the edge."

He ignored me.

I patted my pocket as if I had food in it and cooed at Harry. "Come on, sweet sweet."

He began to scratch after me, and I turned to head north.

Keeping up the charade, I slipped my hand inside my pocket. "Yum yums, Harry bird, I have yum yums."

The fossil. My fingers brushed it before I realized.

Harry screamed behind me.

I spun around just as a massive dimetrodon dove with wide, gaping jaws toward Harry.

"Nooo!" I lunged for my bird, but the dimetrodon got to him first.

His snapping jaws closed on air. Harry walked through him and spread his tail.

"Oh. My. God." I tried to catch my breath. He was okay. The prehistoric ghosts, whatever they were, couldn't hurt us.

But this world could.

The ground beneath my feet crumbled, and everything disappeared.

19

MY BODY SKIDDED DOWN THE bluff. I reached out to grab anything—a root, a stone—but there was nothing. Then my feet caught a ledge. The force of the fall slammed me onto my knees, and it hurt so bad I said some words even Grandma West would look sideways at.

Harry's head stuck out over the void to stare at me.

"Get away from the edge! You could fall too."

He cooed and looked unconcerned that I was now stranded halfway down the bluff.

"That's the thanks I get for saving you from a dimetrodon!" I said.

I wanted to scream. I'd gone out to find Mama, and now I was the one who needed rescuing.

I eased down to sit on the ledge. The incline continued another ten feet down to the rocky river's edge. I could've died, just like my parents had always warned.

The sun burned into my raw skin. I was getting so thirsty I wished I could drink my own sweat. I couldn't wait here. I'd have to go up or down.

Up was impossible. There was nothing to hold on to. I looked down and jerked back.

A familiar prehistoric spade-headed creature crept down the opposite riverbank. I'd only ever seen it in a museum. *Obviously.*

I'd loved it because it was a "transitional" species. For a long time, scientists had thought it was a reptile, but it turned out it could live in the water too. It was a surprise amphibian.

Seymouria baylorensis. I only remembered because my dad had burst out with the song "Suddenly, Seymour" while we were in the natural history museum before a guard hushed him. I guessed the guard wasn't a fan of the musical *Little Shop of Horrors.*

Thinking about that movie made me wish I'd never come out here. I didn't want to be hallucinating pseudo-amphibians and wondering when I'd be found. I should be with my family waiting for Mama to come back to us. The family that she should never have left in the first place.

What was so great at the end of the river? It wasn't like she had friends down in Galveston or Freeport. She'd been homeschooled until high school and was, as she'd told me, *too much of a weirdo to fit in*. She'd married Papa really young, and they'd moved here. Her whole life was us. Right?

Seymour dipped its head as if to drink from the river. The water didn't ripple around its jaws, so it was drinking some ghost water, I guessed.

The more I sat under this hot sun, it sure didn't make sense for Mama to travel on foot along the river, and I couldn't imagine her getting in someone's car and driving away without a word to us.

She must've gotten turned around outside in the pastures.

I tried to cheer myself up. Maybe Mama was already home and this whole thing would be over when I walked in the back door. Maybe she'd, you know, be *really* back and sorry for having frightened all of us. She'd smile like she used to, and I could finally stop being scared all the time.

My chin drooped. Maybe if I hadn't destroyed the bone garden, she wouldn't have gone off in the dark. It's easy to get lost out here even when the sun's up.

Seymour slipped into the water and disappeared. Gone. As if it had never been there.

Because it wasn't really there, I reminded myself. My throat ached for water.

The river looked more appealing by the second. I traced its edges with my eyes until I gasped.

Just at the edge of the water, there was a human footprint. I couldn't know for sure, but it looked like it could be Mama's size.

Finally! A real clue. I had to get down there.

I studied the bluff—it was steep, but there were footholds. I could do it.

Leaning back against the clay wall, I took one tentative step down. The bluff collapsed underneath me. I yelped and slid to the bottom on my butt. Clods of dirt rained around me and exploded into fine, dry dust.

"Owwww." I coughed and held up my bloodied hands. My jeans had torn on this second fall, and my sunburned arms were crisscrossed with new scratches. But it would be worth it if I got closer to finding Mama.

I pushed off the ground and then stared in disbelief. The footprint was gone. The dirt avalanche had covered it up.

My stone exterior finally cracked.

"No. No, no, no! I'm just trying to find you!" I yelled. "Why are you making it so hard? Where are you?! You're supposed to be HERE! With me!"

A scraping noise came from above me, and I spun around to look up. "Is someone there?"

The babble of the Brazos was the only answer I got. That, and Harry, pacing at the edge. No Mama, no dinosaur ghosts, no nothing. Maybe I'd hallucinated the footprint along with everything else.

I stared into the water. Then I looked. I really looked.

The riverbed told a different story.

Most of the riverbed rocks had a light covering of algae. But there were regular patches of stones that were dark with wet. If they'd all been exposed to the sun for the same amount of time, they'd have the same green on them.

But if they'd been disturbed—say, by someone walking fast—the stone could've flipped over, turning the riverbed side up toward the sun.

My instincts, the rocks, the footprint—they all said she'd been here.

The river *shhhhhhhhhh*'d at me. I weighed the desire to investigate the river against my instinct that the way it made me feel—how I wanted to slide into it and never leave—was too intense to be trusted.

But I'd been outmaneuvered, and I thought I could hear the river laughing at me.

"Fine, you win. I'm coming in."

Harry crowed from the top of the bluff. I rolled my jeans to my knees and slipped off my boots and socks. I needed to get a closer look at the river rocks.

"This feels like such a bad idea," I said to the water.

I stepped into the salty river to follow her trail. And then . . . I cracked open.

20

IT STARTED IN MY RIBS.

A cracking.

A snapping.

Every bone in my body broke at the same time. I stumbled out the river. It hurt so bad, I couldn't think. Couldn't see. And I was hot, way too hot. Burning. Hotter-than-a-Texas-sun hot. Like there was an engine inside of me steaming. I pulled my shirt off—something was really wrong with my back. The shirt fell into the river and sank. I looked down at my ribs, searching for broken bones jutting out.

My skin was gone. Completely gone.

I nearly passed out.

In its place were dingy scales. They rippled over my stomach and chest. My arms too. My heartbeat tripped as I tried to figure out what I was looking at. Not myself. This wasn't me. I opened my palms and then balled them back up.

These couldn't be my hands, but that was Margie's nail polish on the claw-looking nails.

People didn't have flaps of mesh between their fingers. They didn't have scales that were different ugly colors. People didn't look like an avocado gone bad, all brown and green and rusty red.

Something was really hurting at the top of my butt. I tore my eyes away from my impossible body so I could wriggle out of my pants.

That was better. My insides cooled down, but I wasn't cold. I could feel the sun like a heat lamp on my back. With the pain gone I was able to catch my breath.

"Hay-ulppp!" screamed Harry.

I turned to check on him, and when I did, I *felt* something behind me. Something physically attached that moved with me.

Oh no. Please no. I dared to look over my shoulder.

And saw a tail. Right where my back had been aching since this morning.

"Thisss is imposssssible," I said out loud. I gulped when I realized my words were hissing. Just like Mama's had the night she left.

I spun around, and the tail lifted itself off the ground. A tail? A freaking *tail*?

I'd hit my head on the way down. That had to be it. I was

hallucinating again, and I'd finally snapped. But everything was completely normal except for me. The water murmured past. The birds called to each other. The grasshoppers buzzed nearby. If I was having a breakdown, why wasn't everything else broken too?

I put my hands on my waist, and the scales smoothed down. When I tried to stroke up, the scales caught, and I whimpered. It felt like pulling fingernails back.

Like a snake or a lizard, I thought.

My breath caught. *I'm a girl*, my brain protested. But my skin was scaly, my spine too flexible, and my bones too soft—I wasn't a girl. I wasn't even human. I had turned into a hideous creature.

I squeezed the tears back. Home. I just wanted to go home. I started scrambling up the bank. I needed to run, to get home.

The ground crumbled beneath me with every step I tried to take. This wasn't working.

I reached up to wipe away my tears, then my hand jerked away—my own hand rejected the feel of my face.

Catch trouble with open eyes and hands, Grandma West would counsel.

"Don't be ssscared," I told myself. I wouldn't get out of this situation by wishing it away.

The skin on my face was slimy like I was coated in Vaseline. I explored my body like a map of horrors. Quirky angles, soft buttery skin in my joints, scales everywhere else. The curve of the tail from the base of my spine.

There was nothing I recognized about this body.

I looked around in case Normal Haven's body was nearby and my mind had jumped into an alien's instead, but there were no spare bodies littering the ground.

I stepped to the edge of the river to find my reflection. Leaning closer, I tried to see my face. I pushed my hair behind my ears just as a cloud passed over the sun and changed the river surface into a mirror.

That's when I screamed. The reflection screamed too.

Its jaw distended so far that it scared me silent. My terrified eyes looked back at me across a wide, flat face I both did and didn't recognize. A ridge of finlike skin extended from my ears. I watched the monstrous girl's reflection start to cry.

I'd seen a face like this before. A couple times. The Rubik's Cube pieces were snapping into place, and I didn't like the picture they made. The monster I'd seen who knew my special lullaby, who knew how to put me to sleep, that was my mother. I'd been right. I'd wanted it to be a dream, but I'd known the truth all along. I hadn't dreamed it.

But Mama was wrong about being the only one.

I was a monster too.

21

"STOP CRYING," I TOLD THE monster.

She sniffled, hiccuped, and then stopped.

I looked at the wobbly reflection. I was still in there, right? The real me. Not this horror.

I curled up into a little ball on the narrow riverbank and covered my head with my hands. I hadn't known a body could feel like home until I was shoved out of one shape and into another.

I counted to five and opened my eyes.

Then I closed them and counted to ten.

Still covered in scales. Still monstrous. Still had a *tail*.

I tried to find a silver lining.

Sure, my jaw opened too far, but it didn't split my face in half like Mama's. My eyes were farther apart than normal, but not on the side of my head. Maybe I was only half monster.

A naked half monster. I stepped into the river to retrieve my T-shirt, but the moment my feet entered the water again, I stilled.

My body might not feel like home, but the river did.

An old memory stirred of being in the bath and Mama wrapping me in a towel before carrying me to bed. It felt like that. The kind of safe you remember your whole life. I was where I was supposed to be.

"Hello?" a voice rang out. "Whoa, a peacock."

Hide. The instinct was immediate. I spun around and stared at the edge of the bluff far above me. This couldn't be happening. Who else would be out here?

I balled up my clothes and boots and shoved them under a bush. Could I fit too? No, the bush wasn't big enough to cover me.

I could dash across the river to where the trees overhung the water, but I didn't have time. From the tops of the Breaks, you could see almost everything.

One part of the river looked a little deeper than the rest. I didn't think. I dove for it. The water closed over my head.

This is so stupid! I screamed at myself. *You'll have to come up to breathe, and then they'll see you.*

Only, I didn't.

I'm breathing underwater, I realized. My ribs opened up, maybe like gills? I wasn't sure, but I felt my back gaping to pull oxygen in from the water.

My tail—I couldn't believe I'd just thought those words—swished like it wanted to propel us through the water. I had no idea how to control this new limb! *Stay still*, I thought at it. The tail twitched, but it stopped splashing.

Sound traveled underwater. I could hear the person yelling, and I thought I could even feel their steps. I would just hide here until they moved on. It was so hot, no one would stick around for more than ten minutes, I figured.

I decided to count up to six hundred seconds. I blinked—was that two sets of eyelids? Minnows kissed my toes, and I kicked at the ticklish fish.

All around me I saw the blurred outlines of fish, but they weren't really here—I knew that, somehow. They'd swum here over 200 million years ago. I reached out to touch them, but my hands passed through them. They were a silvery shadow underwater.

The longer I stayed underwater, the fuzzier my memories got of why I was hiding. The sky was so blue. What number was I on? . . . 598, 599, 600.

I pushed myself up to a sitting position. My head broke above the water's surface, and I took a deep breath.

The moment air hit my lungs, my thoughts cleared. I was a girl, and I definitely should not be able to breathe underwater. Except I didn't look like a girl; I looked like a . . .

Monster. I pushed my stringy wet hair out of my face. The sunlight glinted off my bracelet and the nail polish, like it was laughing that my nails could be so pretty while I was this revolting.

Prehistoric creatures flickered out of the corners of my eyes. They were everywhere, like gnats. Not just dimetrodons or seymouria, no. Ancient fish, flying reptiles, and insects blipped into and out of sight.

"What are you?"

I looked up. Rye was staring down at me with wide brown eyes, his blue umbrella over his head.

I screamed and dove back under the water.

"No, wait! Sorry, I won't hurt you—just, I never, ughhhh, damn it!"

I stared back up at the sky where the thunderous clouds were rolling back in even though it had been clear a minute ago. I needed to get home. Papa and Margie were probably already wondering where I was, especially if the storm was about to hit.

Mama had kept herself safe and secret there this whole time. I could do it too.

"Are you a mermaid?" he called out. "I didn't know mermaids wore nail polish."

I paused. Mermaid was a much nicer name than what I'd been calling myself.

"Or an alien?"

Ugh. Never mind. I wanted to yell, *Figure it out, Mr. Puzzles!* But I made the mature choice to just mumble it instead.

In a flash, I realized that he hadn't said my name. My heart lifted. He didn't know the alien mermaid girl was me! Then my heart sank. That meant I really was completely unrecognizable.

I felt the river beginning to fog my brain again. I needed to move. I tried to plant that idea in my head. *Move.*

Action time. I crawled on my belly across the river, the rocks scraping against my skin.

"I see you," he called out. "I don't know if you can hear me, or if you speak English—¿Tú hablas español? No?—but you don't have to be scared of me. I'd never hurt you."

I ignored him and kept moving until I got under the overhanging trees. The shadows they cast on the water would make me invisible. I hoped.

He was still talking. "Maybe you're like me, and you feel like you don't belong anywhere."

There was so much sadness in Rye's voice. Even through my river-dream state I could hear that. If he was trying to befriend an alien mermaid creature, maybe he really did have trouble making friends.

Without resurfacing, I turned to see if Rye was tracking me. He was looking my way but not at me. That was promising.

Harry was still scratching too close to the bluff's edge. My sweet silly bird.

Tears filled my eyes, and I blinked my four sets of eyelids to clear them. I had to leave him behind. Hopefully he could find his way home.

22

WHEN I CAREFULLY EMERGED TO look back, the boy was still watching the area where he'd last seen me. Who was that again? His name felt just out of reach. I couldn't remember.

I glided up the rocky riverbed. My other body—my real body—would've hurt. But this thick skin slid over the stones without any pain.

In some places the river was deep enough to stay below the surface, but a lot of it was shallow. I stayed low and hunched over myself as I ran upriver.

At last I saw the bridge overpass. Our property started on the other side. I clung to the thought of home like a raft. Go home, get inside my room, and deal with this from there. Possibly never come out again.

The bridge was only fifty feet away when the ground rumbled.

This was not good.

A red pickup truck barreled down the road. The ground here was flat—if I could see it, they could see me.

Crapadoodle. I dropped down and got as low in the shallow river as possible. Like a salamander, I pulled myself forward, arms and legs working together. Every muscle ached. Every thought screamed, *Hide*.

This could be bad. If they'd seen me, they'd probably stop and investigate. Something about living so close to the land kept folks curious.

The rumbles got louder.

Ten feet. Five feet. One foot.

I slipped into the shadow of the bridge and down into the deep spot. The water closed far above my head, and I curled into myself. My tail wrapped around me like armor.

I listened to the truck slow down and idle on the overpass right above me.

The rumbles shook the ground like tiny thunder, but it was cool and dark down in the mud. I could outwait anyone down here.

My body shivered. I hugged my knees to my chest. My heart rate slowed down. So did the racing thoughts.

The engine picked up, and the truck took off.

I still didn't move. I was totally, heavily, dangerously sleepy.

I knew I had to get home before Papa called the cops because I was missing too. But all I wanted was to stay here. My head nodded down on my knees.

A pale shape moved in the water beside me.

"Hi, Ssseymour," I said. This larva was a lot smaller than the full-grown one downriver, and it had frilly gills on the outside of its head. Sweet baby. It was pre-metamorphosis.

It swam a little closer and nestled next to me.

Was it really cuddling with me? I thought the ghosts couldn't see me at all. I shook my head. I was sitting at the bottom of a river and not drowning. Snuggling with a baby seymouria was the least strange thing about this.

Maybe it was lonely. I sang Mama's lullaby to it. "Seymour, my daughter, come in from the water . . ."

The song, which had always put me right to sleep, had a different effect underwater. An image of home sharpened in my mind. I remembered my bedroom with Grandma's quilt stretched across the bed, and I could smell something good cooking in the oven. Margie's laughter rang in the living room, and Papa drank his coffee on the back porch. And Mama smiled and held her arms out to me, ready to scoop me into a hug.

Home. It was so real I wanted to cry. I had to get home.

"I have to go," I told the little seymouria. "Sleep well, baby."

I swam up to the surface and emerged on the other side of the overpass.

When the sun hit my face, it was like a light turned on.

My body warmed up and my head cleared. This was West land. I was almost home.

I stepped out of the water and stared up the six-foot slope. Once I was on top, there'd be no hiding.

I looked back at the river with a mix of desire and dread. I didn't like how it made it hard for me to hold on to my thoughts, but hearing nature so clearly had been wonderful. Not to mention the Permian cuddles.

If luck is a lady, don't keep her waiting, Grandma West had said. Wise words from a memory.

With my tail holding itself out to help with balance, I crawled up and over the edge of the red bank.

23

I WAS NEAR THE VEGETABLE gardens that stretched from the river to the house. In a better year, they might've helped me hide, but not this summer. The only things thriving were the pepper plants, and I might as well hide behind a string of Christmas lights. If I ran straight home, it would be a half-mile sprint over open ground. Too risky.

I decided to hike a little farther upriver and retrace my steps across the pasture. That way I could get to the house from the backyard instead.

Keep low. Go fast. Blend in—actually, the scaly skin was doing this on its own. It had turned a gold brown, the color of thirsty grass, camouflaging me like a chameleon I'd seen once at the Fort Worth Zoo. If I wasn't careful, someone might try to put me in a cage next door to it.

When I was finally parallel to the wheat field, I braced

myself to run. *Here's the plan, West*, I coached myself. *You're gonna run to the cottonwood tree, and then . . . you'll figure out the next plan.*

I definitely needed a new plan committee.

On three. One, two—I took off like a roadside firecracker.

Going fast was harder than it seemed. My bones felt rubbery out of the water, like they couldn't hold me up without help. And my webbed feet didn't like the hard soil and scratchy grasses. The tender between-skin tore against the dry rocks and roots.

Limping, I ran as fast as I could manage across the pasture toward the wheat fields. I passed the rattlesnake carcass. The vultures flapped up into the trees.

Fifty feet, twenty feet, ten feet, three, two, one—I scrambled over the fence and dropped into the wheat field. My sides heaved, but I pushed my legs to run farther.

The cottonwood tree was just ahead, but I couldn't make myself hide in the bone garden. With all those fossils scattered everywhere, I was afraid I'd be swarmed by Permian creatures.

I ran past the tree and collapsed in the wheat field behind our house.

Almost safe.

The wheat knocked heads above me as I gasped for air and scoped out my own backyard.

Please be home, I begged Mama. *I need you to help me*

understand what's going on with me. But the back porch was empty, and there was no movement behind the windows anywhere.

Papa's truck was missing, which probably meant he was out on the property somewhere. Hopefully Margie would be under her headphones with her door shut, and I could walk right on in.

Bent over so low my hands brushed the grass, I scuttled across the backyard and onto the porch. I stared through the storm door at the dirty dishes, the TV on a local channel playing an ancient black-and-white comedy, and piles of library books. Normal was on the other side of that door.

If I could just get to my room, I'd figure out how to turn myself back to human, with or without Mama.

A breeze brushed my ear and tickled farther back on my head. I looked up at the sky; I was beginning to hate those heavy clouds that came and went but never dropped any rain.

The kitchen was clear. I slid the back door open and scooted under the kitchen table.

And immediately started shivering. It was frigid! Margie must've thought that AC stood for Arctic Circle. My brain fogged.

Focus. My bedroom was so close. I had to keep moving.

My feet were heavy and loud on the hallway floor. Blood oozed out between my toes.

The door to Margie's room opened. "Haven? You back?"

24

I JUMPED INSIDE THE BATHROOM door and twisted the lock.

River water dripped from my hair and ran down my naked, scaly back.

"Yeah, it'sss me!" I called.

The medicine cabinet door over the sink had swung open, and without thinking, I closed the mirrored door.

Big mistake.

The mirror showed me everything I didn't want to see. My webbed hands pressed over my huge mouth to keep from screaming. It was even worse than I'd thought.

This wasn't me. If a fish and a snake and a lizard had a baby, the creature in the mirror looked like that.

Fins behind the ears. Webbing between fingers. Gills opening and closing on my rib cage. A long, tapering tail that bumped into the towels behind me.

The scales were already camouflaging to the peachy-pink bathroom walls. I blinked, and a second set of eyelids closed from the sides.

Resolution hardened in me. No one could see this. No one could ever know.

I was still shivering. Cold air pumped into the room through the vents, and my thoughts got slower, foggier, sleepier. Sleepy was dangerous. I stumbled over to the bathtub and turned on the hot water.

An ache filled my chest as I wished on every star I'd ever seen for Mama to come make this stop.

Margie's voice was muffled by the bathroom door. "Hey, you okay? Your heart is beating super fast."

No, I'm not okay, I never will be again, I feel like throwing up, and STOP listening to my heartbeat!

"I'm fine," I croaked over the sound of the water. "Any newsss about Mama?"

Margie groaned. "Nothing. I mean, how is she even gonna call us without her phone? Whatever. I called Dr. Kay, and she said she'd keep an eye out for her, just in case she heads her way."

"Ssssmart." My now pink-scaled arms shook as I leaned them on the tub's edge. I tried not to look at them. When the steam reached my face, I switched the knob on the faucet to plug the tub. It slowly filled with hot water.

The doorbell rang, and Margie stomped to the front door.

I couldn't stop shaking. So cold. The tub was only half-full, but I couldn't wait any longer. I plunged my feet into the hot water and sat down, and—

Crunching, breaking, cracking. A furnace of heat. It was like the sun fell out of the sky and imploded inside my body.

My fingers gripped the edge of the tub as my back snapped, straightened, tightened. My skin shifted from peachy pink back to my farmer's tan. A last wave of impossible heat fled my body, and I felt like someone pulled fifty stitches out of the back of my skull as my face loosened.

Gasping, I slid down into the tub. There was no tail to get in my way. The water covered my face, and I couldn't breathe.

I'd never been so happy to drown.

I sat up—ouch—and stretched my hands out in front of me. No webbing. No scales. Just a patchwork quilt of scrapes and bruises from my fall.

I'm back, I thought, tears of relief streaming down my face. Human. Normal.

But even as I took a few deep, shaking breaths, I wondered if I'd ever really feel normal now. What if it happened again?

I washed the cuts so they wouldn't get infected and pushed out of the tub. A pang of longing to stay in the water ripped through me, but I wasn't letting this body boss me around anymore. The human was back in charge. I wrapped a towel around myself and pulled the plug.

Mama took baths all the time. Did it keep her looking human, or did it just feel good? I wasn't sure.

Margie stomped back and huffed through the door. "That was Ms. Johnson."

I opened it. I didn't have anything to hide anymore. "My kindergarten teacher?"

Margie leaned against the doorframe. "Yep. She dropped off a casserole and said she was so sorry about Mom."

"But how could anyone know she's missing? It's only been a few hours."

My throat felt like I'd swallowed a bucket full of dirt. I grabbed my toothpaste cup and filled it with water from the sink to gargle and spit.

"You know how it is. *Sneeze in a corner of your basement on Saturday, and the preacher will ask how your cold is doing on Sunday.*"

I caught myself smiling in the mirror. Margie didn't quote Grandma West very often, and that was one of my favorites.

My smile grew larger as I saw that I really was back to normal looking. Straight, wiry brown hair. Pale blue eyes. Sun-browned white skin. No scales, no extra eyelids.

Margie continued, "Our door will probably have a dent in it by tonight thanks to the good people of LaVerne, Texas. I know they mean well, and it's nice, but, like, if they really wanted to help, they could go *look* for her. I swear, I'm gonna go to college in a big city, where nobody knows anything about me or my life."

My smile faded. I hated when she talked about moving away.

"You probably won't like city life," I said, and put the cup back on the shelf. "It'll be too loud for you. Your ears will hurt all the time."

Her silence became something I felt as much as heard. She walked away without another word and shut her bedroom door behind her.

Gosh darn it. I didn't mean to go and hurt her feelings. But I wasn't wrong! She was too sensitive. Literally and figuratively.

I'd try and fix it later, but right now I needed to get dressed and head back out to find Harry before that bird got so turned around, he ended up in Mexico. At least I could locate one family member, even if it was a feathery one.

In my room I pulled on a tank top and my only remaining pair of jeans. The stuff at the bottom of the bluff would stay there till it fossilized. No way I was going back down there.

I kept glancing at my skin to make sure it stayed normal. My body felt like it could betray me at any moment and trap me again in the shape of a monster.

I was almost out the back door when the container of petit fours on the table stopped me in my tracks. I was starving. One minute wouldn't make a difference one way or the other, right?

I took a sliver of the pineapple one and let myself feel very sorry for myself. Mama missing, Harry somewhere between here and the Brazos, and me having fallen off a cliff and bruised every bone in my body. Not to mention the prehistoric hallucinations.

"It's not a real pity party until you have yourself some cake," I said. It sounded like something Grandma West would've said, but that one was me. I made it up as I crammed the rest of the petit four into my mouth and washed it down with a glass of tap water.

I pushed the back door open, and the kitchen filled with the scent of warm wheat and freshly turned dirt. And just beyond that, the *shhhhheeeere* sound that wouldn't leave me alone.

I closed my eyes and listened. Someone was talking. What if it was Mama trying to reach me?

There once was a sea here.

Once there was a sea here.

Here there once was a sea.

Child of the—

Margie snapped me out of it with a terse "Haven, go out front and help your friend."

The distant words vanished.

"What? Who needs help?"

"Outside. Out front." Her eyes were extra green as she waved me forward like she was directing traffic. She was still mad at me.

I looked out the window and saw the first good thing to happen today. But like everything else, it was complicated.

25

RYE WALKED BACKWARD DOWN OUR driveway with his blue umbrella open, spinning it slowly. Following a few feet behind him was Harry with his beak gaping and his throat wobbling. He seemed to think the umbrella was another male peacock. That, or he thought Rye was a threat.

Which he kind of was, if Rye figured out that what he'd seen in the river was me. But right now, I was just so relieved to see Harry that I didn't worry about the other half of it.

I ran out the front door just as Harry leaped up and flapped his wings, trying to land on top of the umbrella.

Rye backed out of range and kept spinning the umbrella.

"Hey!" I called.

"He's yours, right?" he called without taking his eyes off my bird.

"Yeah! Harry, what are you doing? Leave him alone! HARRY. Stop. That."

Harry circled around Rye before running past me to the chicken coop, where he was met with much clamor and squawking.

Rye shaded himself with the umbrella.

I fumbled for what to say. "Thanks for bringing him home. That's very, uh, neighborly."

Why had I said that? Neighborly was an old-person word. My conversation skills had not gotten any better while underwater. "Where'd you find him?"

He pointed west. "He was on our land for some reason. Over by the canyon."

"The canyon?" I stopped and thought. "Oh, you mean the Breaks. Where the big bluffs are. That's a pretty area, isn't it?"

As if I hadn't just fled it an hour ago.

"Yeah. I've been seeing some pretty interesting wildlife. Today, actually, I saw something really special." He shot a look at me, then stared up at the umbrella.

I tried to laugh, but it came out strangled. "I guess if you're not from the country, turkeys and deer are special."

He shook his head. "No, I think it was some kind of amphibian. A big one."

My heart was running faster, and my feet were getting the same itch. This conversation felt like a net closing in on me.

"Those catfish can get pretty big," I said. It was weak.

He scratched the back of his head and squinted. "Yeah, no, it was weird. It was, like, human-ish?"

At this point, my plan committee up and quit. I had no idea how to handle this! What would a normal girl who *hadn't* just been a monstrous creature say?

Maybe she'd be freaked out? I went for it. "Geez, that sounds scary. A humanish thing in the water? So weird."

Or maybe a normal person would react this way . . .

"Oh, wait, you're probably joking." I hit myself in the forehead. "I'm so slow sometimes. You're being funny, and I just didn't—didn't get it. Ha, ha, funny."

He frowned. "No, for real."

He was sticking to his guns. *Be normal*, I reminded myself. "Sounds like sunstroke. Known to cause hallucinations. You should be more careful out here in the wild." *The wild???* What was I saying?

"No, I was hydrated. I always bring a bottle of water with me," he said a little self-righteously.

Time to exit. I slipped my hands into my back pockets. "Okay, cool, well. Thanks again for bringing Harry back. It's already been a, uh, it's been a day, so I'm gonna head back in."

He stamped the umbrella tip into the ground. "Haven, I'm not stupid. I know it was you. I saw you, you know? You walked with Harry from the overpass to the canyon—I mean, the Breaks. And I would've seen you walk back, but you didn't. Instead there was this, I don't know, water girl!"

"Shhhh, keep your voice down," I said, looking around to make sure no one had overheard him.

My own voice rose even as I tried to keep him quiet. "So what, you were following me? Why? Are you a stalker?"

He looked distressed. "No! I just—I saw the cop car this morning, and then when I was on the roof, you acted really strange by the overpass, and I thought maybe something was up."

"So, spying," I hissed.

"No! I mean, look at me." He waved his umbrella above his *Minecraft* T-shirt, his skinny jeans, and his Spider-Man sneakers. "Do I look like someone dressed for danger? I hate it outside! But I thought something was wrong, and then I heard a scream, so what was I supposed to do? Just ignore it?"

I was shaking by now. Fear and anger boiled in my veins. "Yes, Rye, just freaking mind your own business, okay? I don't need help."

He looked at the ground. "I kind of think you do."

"You're wrong."

"Can I ask a few questions?" he asked.

"I'm not a puzzle for you to solve," I spit at him.

"Yeah, you are. But everyone is," he said. "Not in a game way. People are just—it's hard for me to make friends. I'm not like my dad, who could make friends with a dumpster."

He scratched his head. "It was silly, but when I saw you in the river—"

"I don't know what you saw, but it wasn't me."

"—I thought, *That looks like someone who needs a friend. Maybe I can do it this time.*"

My heart pounded. "So, this is actually about you. You just want to help the poor alien mermaid girl so that you'll have a friend."

He shot me that quick smile that made my insides feel funny. "I didn't think free donuts would do the trick with her."

"Everyone loves free donuts!" I yelled. What was I even arguing about anymore? And how did he shift from being nerdy-awkward to smooth as seamlessly as I'd gone from human to monster? Not fair.

"Haven," Margie called from deep inside the house. "Stop asking him for more desserts."

"I'm not!" I yelled back.

I turned around to tell him off, but he was climbing up on the porch. "We can talk quieter if I'm next to you."

My heart fluttered. The traitor.

"It's like I said at the river." His voice was feather soft. "You don't have to be scared, at least not of me. I just want to help."

I opened my mouth to deny everything, but the words that came out surprised me. "Sometimes things happen to a person and all of a sudden everything changes and you don't recognize yourself, you know?"

He blinked and nodded. "Yeah. I get that."

I thought about Mama. My heart ached with how much I missed her, but underneath that, I still felt how angry I was that she'd shut us out. That she hadn't ever told me why she was so sad, that I'd had to guess.

She'd certainly never told me that she sometimes didn't look like a human.

I didn't want to be like her. But maybe, to be different, I could start by telling someone what was going on. Someone who was asking, who had already seen me at my ugliest, and who didn't seem scared.

I grabbed his shoulder, having decided. "Do you absolutely swear that you will not repeat any of this to anyone, ever? Not unless I say it's okay?"

He nodded quickly. "Swear on my life."

I slumped back against the porch wall. "The first thing you have to know is that I think it runs in the family."

In a quiet, flat voice, I told him about what I'd seen last night, about Mama having been gone when I woke up, and how I'd gone looking for her.

"And then I stepped in the river. One moment I was this"—I waved a hand in front of my body—"and the next, I was . . . not."

"Is the river magical?" he said in an awed voice.

I shook my head. "If everyone who waded into the Brazos got gills, we would've heard about it by now."

"And this never happened to you before?" he checked.

"Never."

He pulled his Rubik's Cube out and twisted it. He muttered to himself. "You could stay underwater for ten minutes without coming up for air, you had a tail, you looked totally different but somehow still like you. What are you?"

He'd said it like a riddle, but I turned to look him dead in the eye. "A person. A West girl. Someone in a bad situation right now."

"You really don't know what you are?"

"I really don't, but I need to. I want to make sure it never happens again."

He held my gaze, but his eyes were full of questions.

I paused. "Do you believe me?"

"Yeah." A slow smile stretched across his face. "And lucky for you, I'm one of the best amateur puzzlers in Texas. If there's anything online about this, I can find it."

My head knocked back against the wall. "I hope you're right."

We listened to the sounds of the grasshoppers. It had felt good to unload the strange story of the last twenty-four hours, but now worry began to creep in. I'd just shared the most vulnerable, scary stuff ever with someone I'd just met. I hoped I wouldn't regret it.

"I'm sorry about your mom," he said.

"Thanks. I'm really worried about her."

"I bet."

There was one question I had to ask. "Why do you want to help me?"

His grin was impish. "I love a good mystery."

I shook my head. "There's got to be more to it than that."

He knocked the umbrella against his shoes. "Uhhh, well, back home, there was always something to go do. Here the most exciting event so far has been the mesquite bean sculpture contest."

I bumped my shoulder into his. "Just wait, Longhorn Cattle Painting is next. Painted horns, still attached to the cows."

"Great, something to look forward to," he deadpanned. "I just, you know, don't want my life to be nothing."

I glared at him. "So, you're helping me because you're bored."

His eyes widened in alarm. "No, that's not what I meant! Ugh, like I said, I'm not great at this."

I smiled. "I'm kidding. You're right, I need the help. It's nice to have, uh . . ." All of a sudden I felt self-conscious, which was weird, 'cause he'd seen my tail, and that was way worse than hoping he was—

"A friend," he finished, saying what I was afraid to. "Yeah. It's nice."

I let the warmth of that settle in my stomach for a moment. Then I stood up and brushed my hands off as I said, "Oh, I also see prehistoric creatures that aren't really there."

"Wait, what???"

I laughed and walked inside. "You coming?"

26

"SO THE DINO HUNT WAS real!" he said as he followed me inside. "I knew something was up! Do you see anything right now?"

He looked around like a dimetrodon might come breaking through the door. And maybe it could, I had no idea.

"Nothing. It helps if I'm touching a fossil. Then it's like I'm in a 3D movie."

"Whoa." He leaned his umbrella carefully against the doorframe. "All right. Where's your computer?"

"Behold, the ancient artifact," I said, pointing him toward the outdated Mac we had in the living room. "We mostly use my mom's phone for the internet, but I don't know where that is right now."

Papa had taken the phone with him when he talked to Officer Bryant, and it wasn't on its charger. He must've kept it.

"I'll try this first." He sat down in front of the computer and wiggled the mouse to get it going. "Okay, so you shape-shifted or something. And you were underwater for, like, ten minutes without scuba gear. That's impossible, unless you're superhuman."

He had a way with words. Mermaid. Superhuman. They were all nicer than anything I'd called myself. But he was still being too loud.

"Keep it down, okay? Margie doesn't know about what happened in the river," I said in a low voice. "No one does but you."

"But she's gotta be the same as you, right? I mean, her eyes aren't natural," he said.

He must've seen my face, 'cause he course-corrected immediately. "Wrong word. They aren't, uh, commonly seen in nature."

Nice save, I thought. "I don't think she's the same thing. I watched her walk in the river, like I did, and the only thing that changed was that her eyes got brighter. Although, she's got super-sensitive hearing and stuff, so, maybe?"

"But she was with you on the dino hunt." He looked confused.

I shrugged. "I'm pretty sure she was just humoring me."

"Ah, gotcha. That kinda sucks."

"Could be worse. She could ignore me." Like Mama had, even if she hadn't always meant to.

"That's fair."

He asked me a bunch of questions about where Mama was from ("somewhere on the gulf near Galveston, I don't know for sure"), her parents ("from the Orkney Islands in Scotland. They moved to the US before she was born, lived off the grid, ate a lot of fish, and didn't talk much ever"), and exactly what happened right before I transformed.

I even pulled up the photo of the strange face in the water from my email. "This is from my grandparents' home."

He studied it. "Can you send it to me? I want to try and find this location."

"Sure. I know it's about ten miles from Randy's Tackle." I watched as he entered his handle. "AustinBurgerMan?"

"That's me."

"You must really miss it there."

"You have no idea." He typed, waited for pages to load, scanned them, and started over with new search phrases.

The words poured out of him. "It was the best. Dad had this food stand that was straight out of a movie, ya know? And I got to work the register and stuff. It was always a party in the kitchen 'cause everyone was super cool and loved food and . . . I don't know. It was the best."

"What was it called?" I asked.

"Strange Burger!" He punched the air as he said it.

"What made it strange?"

"The toppings. We'd add a new option every week. Papaya, carrot, whatever."

He went back to searching and muttering.

"Texas . . . cryptid . . ." He typed.

"What's a cryptid?" I asked.

He exhaled loudly. "Fairy-tale creatures, that's what. Mermaids, krakens, water horses—creatures that no one actually believes are real, but could be. Like Bigfoot, or unicorns, or Nessie, or yetis, or—"

"I get it," I said, a little sharp. "Real human girl, sitting next to you."

He side-glanced at me, looked away, then made the joke anyway. "I mean, my dad would say a girl sitting next to me on purpose was as hard to believe as all the other stuff."

"I like you better than your dad," I said. "Petit fours are obnoxious."

"Obnoxiously good," he said, and we giggled.

After ten minutes of watching over his shoulder, I remembered his mom's Tupperware. "Oh, hey, I'll be right back."

I emptied the crumbs and scrubbed the plastic container with a sponge. Then I worked on the pile of mugs and dishes in the sink. It felt good to do something useful on a day when everything had felt useless, especially me.

Rye walked in a few minutes later and scratched the back of his neck.

"Here." I handed him the Tupperware. "Dish towel's right there."

He dried the container, then set it down and said, "Look, I know you don't know me, not really. And I'm guessing what I saw was not something you wanted anyone to see."

"*Ever.*"

"But I did, and now, you don't have to do this alone. Whatever it is."

He was gonna make me cry. Or maybe I'd just held so many tears back that this was one kindness too many. I dug deep to find stone again and managed to keep the tears inside a little longer.

"Thanks," I managed. "When you put it like that, it doesn't sound so terrible."

"You wanna know how I knew it was you for sure?"

He didn't wait for an answer. He hooked his fingers through my silver bracelet and pulled my hand out of the hot water. Brushed his fingers over my nails.

"These. When you looked at them in the water, I remembered the color from yesterday, when your hands were in the dirt."

"I must've looked like such a weirdo," I said, embarrassed to remember it.

He shook his head. "Nah, you looked like you were part of nature somehow."

I smiled but pulled my hand away.

"Come back to the computer," he said, that mischievous smile returning to his face. "I found something."

In the living room, I pulled up a chair beside his. We were on some kind of academic journal website.

There were only two entries. I read aloud, "'A Feminist Interpretation of the Chupacabra—'"

"Not that one."

The one underneath made even less sense. "'The Evolution of Myth: Adaptation in Transplanted Fauna.'"

"That's it." He clicked on it. He drummed his fingers on the computer table like he could get my computer to load faster if he gave it a beat.

Margie stalked into the living room just as the paper loaded. "What are you two doing?"

I blocked her view of the screen. "Nothing."

"Congratulations, I totally believe you," she said, and plopped down on the couch. "Actually, I just don't care."

"We're researching mythical creatures," Rye answered.

"Sure," she said, not buying it.

Rye and I caught each other's eyes and grinned.

The paper was twenty years old, cross-referenced to folklore and cryptozoology. The theory was that cryptids existed in relationship to their environment, and when they changed environments, so did their appearance. Camouflage was their best defense. That, and isolation.

"This isn't very scientific," I grumbled. "All the claims are based on, like, other fairy tales and an anonymous source. This could be a total conspiracy theory."

Margie sat up and spotted the empty Tupperware by Rye's feet.

She said to me, "You ate the last one?"

"You had the other two!" I shot back.

"Yeah, but I'm the super-taster," she whined. "And I had planned on eating all of my feelings."

"Haven, look at this part," Rye said urgently.

Kitskaras, I read, *are a new cryptid to evolve in the Texan landscape along the Gulf Coast. A mutated form of the Finfolk found in the Orkney Islands, this bipedal humanoid creature lives near bodies of salt water. Amphibious as their predecessors, the kitskaras have adapted to life on land as well as in water.*

As I kept reading, my pulse picked up.

Kitskaras and Finfolk, while essentially the same cryptid, present very different physical characteristics. The Orcadian Finfolk are known to appear as fishlike creatures, or sometimes seals. However, the kitskara's appearance is influenced by native Texan fauna such as alligator gars, bullfrogs, and water moccasins in order to blend in to the natural environment of the gulf. On land, they shift to pass as human.

"But how? How do they shift? What causes it?" I scanned the rest of the article, but it didn't say. "Can we google the author? Maybe we can email them."

Rye googled the author's name, and a photo popped up.

My breath was knocked out of me, and I dropped back in my seat.

"Dr. Kayla Minner," Rye read out loud.

"Dr. Kay?" Margie said. "What's she got to do with anything?"

I looked at her. "We need to find out."

27

I DID A BUNCH OF math in my head to add up how honest I should be with Margie. On one hand, Rye was brand new to me, but he'd been super cool about my transformation. Maybe my big sister would get it too.

Or maybe *because* she was my big sister, she wouldn't believe me at all.

I decided to test the waters by only outing Mama and not myself. "I'm ninety-nine percent sure Mom is not completely human, and I think Dr. Kay knows it," I said.

Margie's eyebrows lifted to the stratosphere. "And I thought I was bitter."

"I'm serious! I saw something last night—"

"Another dimetrodon?" she said dryly.

"Technically, yes, but that's not the point," I said.

Rye waved his hands to get our attention. "Wait, wait, who's Dr. Kay?"

"Our godmother," Margie said.

At the same time, I said, "Mama's best friend."

Rye let out a low whistle. "Yeah, that's suspicious."

"What's suspicious?" It was Margie's turn to look confused.

My feet began moving on their own as I paced through the living room. "M, can you take your sunglasses off, please? I want to know you're taking me seriously when I tell you this."

"You're so dramatic."

"Please!"

She lifted her chin at Rye. "He'll stare."

"No, I won't," he said.

She slid her sunglasses up on her head. "Yeah, you will, but fine."

Her eyes were cycling between gray and brown. She was cautiously curious.

Rye's mouth dropped open.

"Stop staring," I told him.

He closed his mouth and turned stiffly back to the computer.

I turned to her. "So, last night, right before Mama went outside, I saw her face. It looked like her, but not her. She didn't look human, Margie!"

"When you say not human . . ." she drawled.

I lowered my voice. "I mean her eyes were on the sides of

her head, and her skin was cold and scaly, and even her voice was different. Like a monster in a horror movie."

Rye made a disagreeing noise and mumbled, "You weren't that bad . . ."

I shushed him with a look.

Margie's eyes warmed to amber. "Look, Haven, I get it. I really do. Only a monster would leave her kids, right? Real moms aren't supposed to do that. But they do. It happens all the time."

I perched on the arm of the couch and immediately jumped back off. "But what if she left because of what she is? Dr. Kay wrote a whole paper about a mysterious Texan cryptid that sounds a lot like what I saw last night."

Margie's mouth flattened into a line.

"This could be the key to understanding her," I said. "Because she's a . . . what's the word?"

"Kitskara," Rye said. "They're shape-shifters and weather sorcerers."

Kits kits kits karra, the grasshoppers seemed to echo from outside.

I refocused. "If she's not human, then you and I are half something else too! Maybe this is why you're different, like how tight clothes bother you and you can hear heartbeats!"

Margie's whole body tensed. "Are you serious right now? You just compared my sensory processing disorder to being a monster."

"No, that's not what I meant." I was saying this all wrong.

"You can hear heartbeats?!" Rye said. "That's new information."

Her eyes flushed with golden anger, but she kept them trained on me. "What is he even doing here right now? This is private family stuff."

"He's trying to help us find Mama," I said. "He's using his problem-solving powers for good."

Rye interrupted. "It doesn't have to be a monster. What if you're magical?"

Her glare was potent. "You've known me. One. Day. And you think I have 'powers' or something? That is the most inane thing I've ever heard."

But her voice wavered a little.

Rye shrugged. "Nobody solves a puzzle by assuming they already know what is or isn't the answer. That's why they're puzzles. The answers can surprise you."

Her eye roll said it all. "Thanks, oh wise one."

"Wouldn't it be nice to be magical?" I pressed. "To be different, not because there's something wrong with you, but because you're something else. Something . . . new."

The only way I'd convince her was if I really put all my cards on the table and told her what had happened to me in the Brazos. If it got her on my side, it would be worth it.

Margie folded her arms on the back of the couch and said, "Look, if I thought I was anything like Mom in any real way, I'd march myself into therapy right now."

I winced and swallowed my confession. "Therapy?"

Therapy was for people who did yoga and had the money to pay someone to listen to them. It wasn't for people like us—we handled our own problems. *You git what you git and you don't throw a fit.* That wasn't Grandma West; it was the accepted wisdom.

If Margie knew I really was seeing prehistoric creatures, or that I'd turned into a monster, would she think I needed therapy? Or, I don't know, a psychiatric ward? Would she want to lock me away?

Margie continued, "Besides, you're normal. My eyes? They're just a *charming* genetic mutation that lets the whole world know what I'm feeling ALL the time. Nothing fairy princess sparkly about it."

Rye looked at me with *Tell her you're not normal* written on his face.

I looked at him with *You promised not to tell anyone until I said it was okay* on mine.

Back to plan A. Keep this focused on Mama.

"Your eyes are very hazel right now," I observed. "Which means you're annoyed, but you're intrigued. You don't hate this idea."

"Yeah, but I hate you right now." She pulled her sunglasses back down. With a touch of condescension, she said, "Listen, Haven, if there was something different about Mom, whether magical or monstrous or whatever, Dad would know, right?"

I thought back to Papa's reaction when I told him what I'd seen. He hadn't told me I'd made it up—he'd just said that she wasn't a monster.

"Right," I agreed.

"Okay, so just ask him." She lifted her hand like she couldn't care less. "It doesn't have to be so hard."

"I wish I could ask Mama," I said, and as if grief was a time bomb, it went off.

My need for Mama exploded into a supernova of longing. I didn't just need her 'cause I'd fallen in the river, transformed, and I had questions. I needed *her*. I needed the sounds of her moving around the house, the smell of her shampoo on the days she remembered to use it, and the way I knew that even underneath all her sadness, she loved me.

With her gone, that love didn't feel as real. I turned to the computer so I wouldn't have to look at anyone in the room.

Rye tapped his fingers so erratically it sounded like Morse code. Knowing him, it probably was. "I'm gonna head out, okay? Y'all are definitely dealing with some stuff, and I'm in the way."

"No, you're not," I automatically said, but he was right, and I didn't try to keep him here.

He tucked the Tupperware under his arm and picked up his wounded umbrella. "I'll work on the location in the photo from home, and I'll let you know what I find tomorrow."

"Sure." I walked him to the front door. "Tomorrow."

"What photo?" Margie asked as he hopped off the front porch and stumbled.

"I'm okay!" he yelled. "Bye!"

Closing the door, I went back to the computer and pulled up the picture from my email again. Maybe this would convince her. "See that face in the water? It's something."

She pushed her sunglasses up to look at me sidelong. "It kind of looks like a fish, or a weird rock. It could be glare off the water. There's like a thousand things that are more likely than a kisskaract."

She walked away and crashed back down on the couch.

I closed the screen and muttered, "*Kitskara*. And that's the whole point; she didn't look human."

Before Margie could insult my intelligence any more, there was a loud knock on the door.

"I'll get it," I said. "Maybe Rye forgot something."

Instead of Rye, I was met by one of the great forces of nature. A farmer's wife.

Mrs. Cedlik lived on the other side of town, but here she was, thrusting food in my arms before I'd even started to say hello.

"Hi, sweetheart, I had some extra muffins just lying around, and I thought, why don't I just take 'em on down to those sweet West girls? And this is just some leftover venison chili we had in the freezer—no, no, don't thank me, it ain't nothing—gotta keep our folks fed, you know? You heard anything yet from your mama?" Her question mark was more like a comma, 'cause as soon as I started to say, "No, not yet," she was talking a blue streak again.

"No matter, it'll all come out in the wash, darlin', you'll see. Now, I don't wanna take any more of your day, I know this must be a tough time, a real tough time, so I'll be heading on, but you just give me a shout if you need something, all right?"

She left as fast as she'd come.

I felt like I'd been run over by a well-meaning semitruck. I turned back to Margie, reminded that even if she didn't believe me, at least I wasn't alone in this. "How do people know Mama's missing? Do you think Officer Bryant told someone?"

Margie didn't even look up. "The way things are going, I think he called his report in on public radio."

28

THE REST OF THE AFTERNOON, Margie and I took turns answering the doorbell and receiving comfort foods from people all across our community. We saw another teacher, a few church members, and even a cashier from our nearest grocery store who showed up with a couple cartons of milk and some cereal.

Everyone seemed to assume that Mama had abandoned us. There were little comments like "Well, she was always a little different, but you know it takes all kinds."

I got tired of reminding them we didn't know what had happened yet. I knew they were just trying to take care of us. Margie might hate everyone knowing her business, but the food felt like a hug.

Still, a nagging thought ate at me. If the townsfolk knew the truth about me, or Mama, would they still think of us as their own? Or would we become outsiders?

Maybe Mama had always felt like an outsider, and I just hadn't noticed it.

Papa's truck roared up toward the house from the fields. I ran to the back porch to squint at the cab just in case he'd found Mama on the back acres, but the seat beside him was empty.

My heart wobbled. I tried to imagine asking Papa about kitskaras, but I hadn't even told him when I got my period for the first time. That had been strictly girl talk only. Tell him that I had a *tail* a few hours ago? Absolutely not.

But maybe Papa would have some answers—if I asked the right questions.

"Margie, he's back. Let's go see if he found anything."

She sighed and rolled off the couch. We trudged across the yard toward the old wooden barn that Papa used as a garage. We had a nice big steel pole barn too, but that was for storing the wheat.

We slipped inside, and a motion light sensed us and turned on. It cast everything in an overbright yellow light. Seconds later, Papa's truck slowed and rolled inside.

"Hey, girls." He climbed out. He looked exhausted, but his face brightened when he saw us. "Been a long time since y'all met me out here."

I'd always wondered if it made Papa sad that neither me nor Margie had the farming itch. The West family wheat tradition was gonna end with him. The look on his face made me think that I'd been right.

But there was no time to ponder that now. "Any sign of Mama out there?" I asked.

He shook his head. "No. Any calls?"

We shook our heads no, and he slammed the truck door with more force than it needed.

"Hay-ulppp!" Harry protested from outside the barn.

"Harry! We're in here!" I called.

A blue-and-white face peered around the door entrance before my bird puttered inside making low clucking sounds. He hopped up onto the bed of Papa's truck, and Papa stroked his head gently with a gloved hand. "Hey, buddy."

Without lifting his eyes from Harry, Papa said, "Go ahead, spit it out. I know y'all are here for a reason."

"I told Margie about what I saw last night before Mama disappeared," I said.

Papa nodded. "Your nightmare."

"It was real," I said. "I know what I said before—that it was a dream—but I didn't make it up. I saw what I saw."

Papa met my gaze, but his face was unreadable. That was unsettling because Papa's face always seemed so open. Sad, happy, mad, worried—you could see it all play over his face like a storm moving across flat land.

Margie sat down on an empty ice chest. "Dad, I'm getting a little worried about Haven's imagination."

"What?!" I turned to look at her.

Margie said, "Well, I am. She's talking about seeing dimetrodons in the garden, and that Mama looks like the creature from the Black Lagoon."

"I didn't say that about her!"

She waved me off. "And she seems to think that the reason my eyes change color is because of Mama being something inhuman."

Papa still didn't respond, but he looked at me a little closer.

Margie said, "So, tell her the truth. Is there anything different about Mom? I mean, besides her complete lack of interest in being our mother."

I was so mad at my big sister right now. She didn't just not believe me—she thought something was wrong with me. I'd been totally right not to tell her the whole story.

Papa knocked his knuckles on the side of his truck. "Girls, I'm tired. It's been the longest day of my life, and I don't have the energy for this."

Margie looked surprised. "You don't have the 'energy' to confirm that Mom is *human*?"

"Is she a kitskara?" I asked. "Dr. Kay wrote about them in her paper."

Papa looked like he wanted to be anywhere but here. He ran his gloved hand over his short haircut and got bits of grass stuck in it.

"Dr. Kay got thrown out of grad school for that paper," Papa said with a forced laugh. "It's why she's a vet and not a fancy professor somewhere. That should tell you how serious to take it."

"So you know what a kitskara is," I latched on. "It's real."

"We are not talking about this without your mother," he said. "Save all your questions for when she gets back."

"Why are you so sure she's coming back?" Margie said.

The blunt question hung in the air like a challenge.

Papa's face opened up for the briefest moment, and it made me ache to see the raw fear in him. "'Cause she's got to."

Margie frowned. "She really doesn't. She might not ever. We don't know, because she left. Without. Saying. ANYTHING."

"It's her story to tell," Papa said. "I'm sorry, Margaret, I don't know why your eyes change colors. Maybe it's genetic. Maybe it's 'cause she ate too much sushi when she was pregnant with you even though there's no fresh fish for miles and I told her it was dangerous. I can't tell you."

"Can't? Or won't?" she said. "If I am not actually one hundred percent human, don't you think I have the right to know?"

"Oh, now you believe me?" I said, still feeling hurt.

Harry squawked and hopped out of the truck.

Papa ignored her comment and grabbed my hand. "Haven, what are we having for dinner tonight? I was thinking we pull out that frozen pizza we've been saving for a rainy day. Unless Margie already has something up her sleeve, like she usually does."

He winked at her, and with that, he dug the evening's grave.

"I see," Margie said, slow but sharp. "You want us to stick to the routine. It works so well for you. If your sad wife can't make dinner, or hang out with you, your freakish daughters will step up. Cool. Cool. How nice for you."

I pulled my hand from his and wrapped my arms around my waist. I didn't like where this was heading.

His face reddened. "That's not what this is about."

Seemingly out of nowhere, she asked, "When you look at us, what do you see?"

Papa's mouth tightened. "I see my daughters, who should listen to their father, because I'm just trying to keep everyone safe. Including Maureen."

"Because you know everything."

He yelled, "I know more than you do!"

I cringed. Papa never yelled.

He stalked away into the house. I watched him through the window as he pulled a beer out of the fridge and grabbed one of Mrs. Cedlik's muffins.

My stomach growled. I realized I hadn't eaten anything but cake.

"That was so messed up." Margie sounded disgusted.

"I'm not making this stuff up, Margie," I said in a small voice, but she wasn't listening to me.

"It's the ssssecrets," she said, pulling out the *s* sound in a disgusted hiss that reminded me uncomfortably of my own speech impediment that morning. "That's what's wrong with us. He acts like we're one big happy family, but meanwhile, no one is being real with each other."

"Maybe Dr. Kay will help us," I said. "Let's call her, see if she can answer our questions about Mama."

"No," Margie said. Her eyes blazed orange, but I knew from the way she held her body that she'd reached a decision.

"Someone in this family has to start being honest about who they really are," she said. "And I guess it's gonna be me."

The motion light clicked off. We stood in the darkness, Margie stewing, me noticing the silver-white shapes that were forming over the ground in the wheat fields.

We were too close to the bone garden. Things were waking up that I didn't want to see right now. "Margie, let's go. I wanna get out of here."

She was still seething as we walked out of the barn. The motion lights clicked on and threw our shadows in front of us.

Margie's jaw was tight. "You wanna get out of here? Me too."

Her gaze turned to meet mine, and she said, "Eleven p.m. You pack road snacks; I'll get Mom's keys."

I turned my back on the dinosaur ghosts. "Are we going somewhere?"

"We're going to see Dr. Kay."

29

MY FINGERS SHOOK AS I buckled my seat belt.

The light from the waxing moon made everything look shaky, and the car smelled like Mama. Empty water bottles cluttered the back. An old coffee cup wilted in one cup holder, and grimy coins collected in the other one. Every breath I took in here was an ache.

I whispered, "Shouldn't we call Dr. Kay first?"

Margie held up Mama's phone. "I did. Twice. Left a message. Not my fault she puts her phone on silent."

She handed me the phone, and I immediately opened the photo app to look at the picture from the bungalow again. I was sure, even if Margie didn't agree, that there was a face in the water. Not a rock, not a fish, and not a glare from the flash.

We'd left Papa a note on the kitchen table telling him where we were headed so he wouldn't completely freak out in the morning. After the fight, he'd crashed out on the recliner in front of the weather channel, still dressed in his dusty work wear. Mama's phone was back on the charger, so we'd grabbed that and then tiptoed around him to get her keys off the hook by the front door.

Margie eased her car door shut. We wore matching Rangers baseball caps and had canvas tote bags with snacks, toothbrushes, and a change of clothes. We were ready. She'd taken a nap and drunk some green tea. I'd tried to sleep too, but I'd been too wired.

She slipped the keys into the ignition. Turned them. The starter clicked, but the engine didn't turn over.

She pumped the gas and turned the key again, but nothing.

"The battery's dead," she said, and leaned her head back.

"What are we going to do?" Panic clawed my throat. We had to get to someone who could tell me what was going on.

"Nothing. We go back inside and call Dr. Kay again in the morning."

"Maybe we could take Dad's truck?"

Margie fixed me with a look.

"No, I know, we can't." We might as well take his arms and legs at the same time. He couldn't work the farm without his truck.

A heavy hand knocked on the window by my head. I jumped, and Margie screamed.

"Hey, it's just me," Rye said. He pulled open the back

door and slipped onto the bench seat. He set an overstuffed navy-and-white-striped duffel bag across his lap.

"Hey," I greeted him.

"What are you doing?" Margie asked, twisting around in her seat to stare at him.

"I'm going with you," he said, looking to me for confirmation.

"What? How—are you spying on us?" she asked.

He tucked his chin. "Only a little. I was just sitting on the front porch in our new rocking chair when I saw y'all about to ride for adventure, and I always have a go bag packed, so here I am."

We were both staring at him now.

"That's really creepy," Margie said.

His eyes crinkled. "Wow, no, I'm joking. Haven emailed me and said y'all were going to ask Dr. Kay some questions in person, and she said I should come too since I'm on Team Kitskara."

He pumped his arm in the air, then looked at us worriedly. "Is it still cool for me to come?"

"I totally did invite him," I told her. "I didn't mention it 'cause I didn't think he'd actually want to."

Margie looked more upset than I would've expected. "Okay, no, you're not coming. And secondly, we're not going anywhere either. This car is deader than disco, and we can't exactly ask Dad for a jump."

"Disco will never die," Rye observed.

"Not the point! And why do you even want to come? You don't know our mom. You barely know us."

He shifted a little in his seat. "I wanna help."

She looked doubtful.

He added, "And this is the only interesting thing that's happened since I moved here over a month ago. I don't want to miss out."

He only then seemed to hear the rest of what she'd said. He added fast, "And I've got a ride."

"You do?" I jumped on it. "Margie, let's do it. He'll be a big help, I'm sure! And you said you wanted to start living life honestly, so let's go get some answers."

Rye hedged, "My vehicle isn't exactly conventional, but—"

"Fine. Whatever. Let's go!" Margie grabbed the keys and stalked out. I made sure I still had our totes, and Rye lugged his duffel bag back out.

The silence of the night had a heaviness to it, as if the dark had turned liquid and I could swim all the way up to the sky. As we walked toward Rye's house, questions floated like air bubbles in my mind.

Why was Margie so willing to drive us all the way to Dr. Kay's house? I mean, we both knew we'd get better answers in person than over the phone. Dr. Kay was like a cactus— she absorbed everything around her and didn't give much up. You can read stuff from body language that you can't get over the phone, even on a video call.

But still. A midnight road trip was a big deal.

My heart warmed. Maybe she really believed me now about Mama being a kitskara, after Dad acted so weird about our questions.

We crept up Rye's gravel driveway and behind the house to where Mr. Wilson-Ruiz's gleaming chrome coffee truck shone in the moonlight.

It looked different than the last time we'd seen it. Now there was a splashy logo in big letters on the side—SUNRYE'S COFFEE AND DONUTS. Photos of coffee, donuts, and burritos ringed the truck like a garland.

Margie stopped. "Wait, we can't take your dad's truck."

"No, it's fine," he said. "I swear. We'll be back tomorrow morning, right? They're not even gonna notice the truck's gone, or me either. He's testing recipes all morning, and my mom's away on a site visit."

"Do you have the keys?" I whispered.

"They're in the cupholder," he said. "He leaves it un-locked."

I opened the door and looked inside. The cabin was sepa-rated from the cooking area by a partial wall, with a bench seat in front of it. I knew without being told that I'd be in the middle. I scrambled in and started looking for my seat buckle.

"Wait, how good a driver are you?" Rye asked, suddenly

sounding nervous. "This wrap job is brand new. My dad'll kill me if we scratch it."

"I guess you'll find out," Margie said, sounding cranky, as she settled herself in front of the steering wheel.

"She's really good," I assured him. "She's been driving Papa's truck since she was ten years old, and the tractor since she was thirteen, *and* she has her learner's permit. She knows what she's doing."

"Thanks, sis," Margie said.

Rye ran his fingers along the side of the car door where the coffee truck's logo was printed. "Okay, cool. Yeah, it'll be fine."

He sounded like he was reassuring himself, but he slid in beside me and buckled his seat belt. The bags went under the seat.

"This is cozy," Margie said. By cozy, she meant tight. We were right on top of each other. "Gimme a second to see how it's set up, and then we'll go."

After fiddling with wipers, turn signals, and adjusting the mirrors, she put it into drive, and we started down the driveway. I kept expecting someone to burst out of the house and stop us, or flashing lights to stream across the road in our direction. But except for one lonely peacock scream, the night stayed quiet.

30

THE TRUCK RATTLED LOUDLY ALONG the road. Even though Rye assured us everything was tied down in the back, metal stuff jangled and clanged anytime Margie took a curve a little fast or hit a literal bump in the road. The sounds made us all tense.

Margie had put her Rangers hat on Rye with a terse "Keep it low."

With the headlights on bright and our faces in shadow, hopefully no one would notice a teenager driving a massive coffee truck with two kids in tow. We didn't want any extra attention.

The moon lent a bit of light, but the country roads were so dark it was easy to imagine we were the only ones awake in the whole world. Except for the wild things.

Our headlights reflected off the eyes of coyotes, deer,

and cattle. Armadillos scuttled at the edges of the road, and more than one armored carcass memorialized a valiant but failed attempt to cross.

I nodded off somewhere outside of Olney. It had been an impossibly hard day, and the ache in my muscles won out over the dread that had kept me in motion.

When I woke up, everything felt jumbled. With a heart-sinking dive, I remembered that Mama was missing, and that we had so many more questions than answers.

But my first question was: *Why am I curled up next to Rye???* My whole body froze—apparently I'd used his shoulder as a pillow. There was even a tiny drool spot on his T-shirt. Oh my gosh, this was almost as embarrassing as him seeing me as a reptile girl. Or a *kitskara*, I tried the word out in my mind.

Rye's face was pressed into the window, and he was snoring softly. Moving inch by inch, I removed myself from his shoulder and sat upright.

He kept sleeping. *Phewww.*

"What time is it?" I asked, rubbing my eyes.

"About one thirty a.m. We're thirty minutes away from Glen Rose," Margie said. She took a sip of green tea from her travel thermos and glanced down at Mama's phone, where a map app was illuminated.

We were passing through a small town, but close enough to a city that Margie had a decent FM country music station playing.

We drove beside a large artificial lake with massive look-alike homes lining its shores. McMansions, Papa called them. The moon reflected off the surface, and the houses cast lights on the moving water.

"Pretty," Margie said.

"Yeah."

The scene felt surreal. Last night, Mama had gone outside and hadn't returned, and now I was a hundred miles from home riding in a coffee truck with my big sister and the neighbor kid from down the road. I'd thought nothing would ever change, but now things were shifting so fast the ground felt like it was crumbling under my feet all over again.

In the dark, I couldn't see the color of Margie's eyes, but I saw how her hands gripped the steering wheel and the way she perched forward on her seat.

"Does driving at night make you nervous?" I asked her.

She hesitated, then said, "Yeah, I guess."

Since I couldn't read her feelings by color, I had to ask instead. "Is something else bugging you? Besides all the mom stuff."

She glanced at me with surprise, and her expression made me realize that for the past three years, I'd used her eye colors as a shortcut—that I'd rarely asked or let her tell me herself how she was feeling. There was something wrong about that.

"I mean, everything bugs me," she said with a sigh.

"Sounds, vibrations, the way my clothes feel, the taste of silverware, social injustices, bad poetry. Lots of stuff."

"Bad poetry made you grip the steering wheel that hard? Must've been a limerick."

She laughed.

Encouraged, I improvised, *"There once were two girls from LaVerne who . . . had secrets they wanted to learn."*

"This is atrocious," she groaned.

"In a truck made of silver—no, that's too hard. *In a truck made of chrome . . ."*

Grudgingly she added, *"They sneaked from their home . . ."*

"Uhhhhh . . . What rhymes with learn? Burn? Earn? Stern? Shurn?"

She was grinning now. "Shurn is not a word."

"Scurn?"

"Oh my god."

"Fern! Durn!"

She finished, *"Because life as they knew it adjourn . . . ed."*

I clapped. "We are so terrible at this."

She looked more relaxed now. That was a good thing, right? But as she changed to a classical radio station, I wondered if maybe I'd done the exact thing that drove me bananas whenever Papa did it. I'd tried to make things funny and comfortable, instead of listening to what was troubling her.

Maybe I could try asking her again. But as I stared out the window at the lake, all thoughts were banished.

Something was moving in the dark.

A small pointed head on a long silvery neck crested out of the water. It submerged for a moment, and I doubted my own eyes, until it broke through again and floated at the water's surface.

A plesiosaur! My favorite dinosaur! At least, it had been until I'd learned it wasn't a dinosaur, and then it became my favorite extinct marine reptile.

"What are you looking at?" Rye asked sleepily.

"Oh, sorry." I was leaning on him again. "I was imagining what it would be like to see a plesiosaur in the lake."

"Imagining?" He yawned and rubbed his eyes before he turned to look out the window. "I wish I could see one."

His wistful tone reminded me that there were perks to turning into a monster. Like watching my favorite not-dinosaur splash around in the middle of a suburban lake.

Margie said, "Mom had a story about the Loch Ness monster."

"Our grandparents saw it," I told him. "True story."

Rye blinked himself awake. "Okay. I'm hooked. Tell me."

"You tell it, Haven. You've heard it more times than I have," Margie said.

I never took my eyes off the plesiosaur. "This was before Mama was born. Our grandparents came to Texas from Scotland, remember?"

"From Hoy, in the Orkney Islands, right?"

"Right. Grandpepper and Grandmer wanted to say goodbye to all their favorite places, so they went on one last tour of the archipelago and then off to the Highlands."

I could almost hear Mama telling it to me, and the way she'd slip in and out of the Orcadian brogue as she soothed me toward sleep.

"They didn't have a lot of money, so they camped everywhere. One night they'd set up their tent on the shores of Loch Ness. It was the middle of March, and the skies had been cold and gray, but that night the clouds opened up, and the sky turned electric pink and green and blue. *The Merry Dancers*," I said in my best Scottish accent, which wasn't very good.

"Ahh, the aurora borealis," Rye said.

"Yep. Grandpepper and Grandmer stood on the shore staring at the lights dancing overhead when the water churned in front of them. They said the loch's surface boiled like a pot on a stove.

"And then, there she was. Nessie. Her long neck spearing up through the water, her humpback a shadow against the night. She lifted her small head to the sky, as if she were trying to reach the lights herself."

I stretched my hand up high, like Mama had always done at this part, until I knocked into the cab ceiling.

"They watched her until she sank below into the depths."

The plesiosaur in the lake dipped underwater and vanished. *Goodbye, friend.* My mind reached out for it.

I finished, "The way Mama tells it, Nessie'd come to say goodbye. Like she knew they'd never make it back to Scotland."

I shivered at my own words, but Mama was no Nessie. She hadn't said goodbye.

"Wow. The Loch Ness monster. You believe it?" Rye asked.

If anyone else had asked, I would've thought they were making fun of me. But after what he'd seen today, I knew he was asking a real question.

Other silvery creatures swam through the water, and more walked along its edges. The McMansion owners had no idea the incredible beings that haunted their shores. I watched the moon's reflection and hoped to see the plesiosaur rise again.

"Yeah, I do."

31

SOON WE WERE BACK IN the boonies where the winding roads curved to follow the lay of the land. Overgrown trees made the road seem even darker, and the classical station fuzzed into static. The streetlights tapered out until there weren't any more.

Even so, Dr. Kay's house was easy to find, thanks to the big white sign that Lynne had painted. It read KAY VETERINARY—WE TAKE 'EM ALL, BIG AND SMALL. And in case folks didn't think she was serious, there was an image of a horse with a cat on its back, cuddling up to an ostrich. It really brought home the "all" part of the practice.

Our truck rattled up the long drive past a small barn and paddocks. A light turned on inside the house.

"Oh, good, she knows we're here," Margie said.

Rye asked, "She knew we were coming, right?"

"I called her, but she didn't answer," Margie said.

Rye dropped his voice. "Do you think she's gonna be mad we're here so late?"

"She might be," Margie said.

"Yeah, she's not the warm and fuzzy type," I said.

Rye gulped.

We'd just pulled up in front of the house when the front door opened, and a pack of barking, tail-wagging dogs poured out. Dr. Kay stepped into the floodlights wearing a hunting jacket, sweatpants, and a scowl that would've turned a bear around.

My breath stopped. "Margie, she's got a gun."

Margie hit the brakes and rolled down the window. "Dr. Kay! It's me and Haven, and a friend."

Dr. Kay's shoulders relaxed, but she didn't look happy about this. "It's awful late to be out at night, and unless my memory fails me, Margie, you don't exactly have a license yet."

"We're sorry, Dr. Kay," I said, "but this couldn't wait. We had to come right away."

"Get on in, then," she said.

Wet noses shoved into my hands, my belly, and the backs of my legs as I got out of the truck. Margie locked it up while Rye and I were carried up the sidewalk by the surge of happy doggies.

"I didn't know you had a gun," I said.

She huffed. "Two women living alone in the backwoods?

Hell yeah, I've got a gun. And a security system that woke me up the moment you turned into my drive. Most times if someone comes this late, it's with a real sick pet, but"—she gestured at the coffee truck—"I don't get a lot of breakfast vendors at two a.m., so I felt a little jumpy."

"Kayla? Everything all right?" Lynne appeared beside Dr. Kay. She always dressed super cozy. Tonight she had an afghan draped over her cardigan and sweatpants with chunky socks.

"It's Reenie's girls, Lynne, and their friend—what's your name, child?"

"Rye Wilson-Ruiz, ma'am. I'm their new neighbor."

"And their polite friend, Rye. Go on back to sleep," Dr. Kay said.

"Nonsense, I'm up," she said, and blinked sleepily behind her glasses like a baby owl. "Come on in, kids. Who wants tea? We have chamomile, peppermint, ginger . . . I'm a tea hoarder, so we have pretty much everything."

She shuffled us all into the eat-in kitchen—after we all took turns using the bathroom, 'cause three hours on the road meant our bladders were fit to explode—while Dr. Kay went to lock up the gun.

Lynne pulled down what she called "a tea chest." We only drank sweet tea at home, so these herbal teas were a whole new world to me.

"Which one's the sweetest?" I asked.

"You," she said with a nose tweak.

I laughed and pushed her hand away. Lynne was the opposite of Dr. Kay, open instead of closed, soft where Dr. Kay was hard. I adored her.

Dr. Kay's heavy footsteps announced her return. "So, what's this all about? Does Zeke even know you're here?"

"Well, we—" I started, but Margie interrupted.

"Can I talk to you alone?" she said, her voice pitching high with urgency.

I glanced at my sister. "M, what are you—"

"For once, this isn't about you, or Mom, this is about me, okay?" she said, her eyes gleaming orange through anxious gray.

"Okaaay," I said, feeling hurt and bewildered. Hadn't we driven here with the same goal?

Dr. Kay's eyes narrowed like a hawk's, but her voice was kind. "C'mon, kid. Let's go to the exam room. It's the most private."

They walked away toward the front of the house where Dr. Kay did her business stuff. I heard her low rumble, "At least you can *tell* me what's wrong, unlike my usual patients."

A heavy door swung closed behind them, and Rye and I exchanged confused glances.

Lynne pulled out mugs and said nothing.

Elsewhere in the house, there were small movements. I could hear light bird feet shifting on wires from underneath covered birdcages. A ginger cat prowled into the room, hissed at the Good Dogs, and stalked away. Out of sight, a hamster wheel spun. Some of the animals were patients, I assumed, and others were rescues waiting for homes. A few were forever pets.

In the living room, a saltwater tank bubbled, and a few colorful fish swam inside.

I didn't realize I'd been staring at it until a gentle hand touched my shoulder. "Fish are so relaxing, aren't they?" Lynne said as she set two mugs of steaming raspberry tea in front of me and Rye.

"Um, yeah." I tore my eyes away and brought them back to the table.

Rye and I reached for our mugs at the same time, and our hands touched. Even though we'd been riding in a car smooshed together for three hours, this felt different. I jerked my hand back, and he knocked his into the mug. *Very smooth.*

I looked around the kitchen to hide my blush. Two empty sardine cans sat at the top of the recycling bin.

"Oh, do you like sardines too?" I asked Lynne. "Dr. Kay always makes fun of my mom for eating them."

Lynne shook her head. "No, too salty for me."

I frowned. Maybe they'd been for the cat.

A few more minutes passed before the exam door creaked open, and voices spilled out. I watched the hallway for my sister to appear.

Dr. Kay's words got clearer as they approached. "You don't have to, you know. It can just be for you. It doesn't make it any less real or true."

Margie came through the doorway, wiping tears from her eyes and smiling. "I think I want to."

Dr. Kay gave Lynne a look that I couldn't read, and Lynne rose and pressed a mug of chamomile tea into Margie's hands.

"Are you okay?" I asked. I felt a little scared watching her cry.

"Yeah, I'm good. Sorry to be so mysterious," she said with an embarrassed laugh. She took a sip of the tea, then set it down on the table.

She looked at me, then looked away. "I've been keeping a secret about myself, and after . . . everything that happened today, I realized I didn't want anyone to wonder who I really was. I want people—especially the ones I love—to know." She kicked the chair leg. "I, uh, this is hard."

"Take your time," Lynne said softly.

My heart began to race. Maybe Margie and I had the same secret!

She seemed to stare at a whorl in the grain of the table. "I've known for a long time, but I was scared that if I told anyone, they'd think something was wrong with me, or not want to be around me anymore."

She took a big gulp of tea.

"Of course I'll still want to be around you," I said. "No matter what."

Dr. Kay sat down at the table beside Lynne and held her hand.

Margie tucked a red curl behind her ear and said, "I'm gay." Then, with more confidence, she looked up at all of us. "I'm attracted to girls, and I have been as long as I can remember."

The room—the world—came to a crashing halt. This was not my secret. This was a totally different one that I hadn't seen coming.

Lynne pushed her chair back and ran around the table. She wrapped Margie in a tight hug. "You're perfect, you know that?" she said in a fierce voice I'd never heard before. "Exactly like this. I want you to hear me. You, Margaret West, are perfect. And I'm proud of you for being so brave. I know how hard it is."

Margie started crying again, but it was the hiccuping, smiling kind. "Thanks, I know it's really late, but I didn't want to do this over the phone, and I couldn't wait any longer."

I shook my head in confusion. "But why did you want to tell Dr. Kay first?" I didn't say the other part of my question, *Why not me?*

Without answering, she looked to Dr. Kay.

Dr. Kay slurped from Lynne's mug and said, "It's okay, you can tell her."

Margie scrunched her shoulders. "I guess I just wanted to tell someone like me first."

"Like you? But they're just roommates," I said.

"More than roommates," Lynne said gently.

Rye turned full body to face me. "Seriously? I just met them, and even I know they're a couple."

And in a flash, a puzzle that I hadn't even realized was a puzzle got solved.

"Oh my god, I'm so oblivious," I said. They were together. Of course they were. I dropped my face into my hands in embarrassment, but also to give myself a moment. Things were changing around me faster than ever.

"No, no," Lynne said. "It's not your fault. We don't really spell it out for folks."

"'Cause it's no one's business but our own. And also, 'cause it's safer that way," Dr. Kay admitted.

"Haven?" Margie said.

She turned my name into a hundred unasked questions.

I lifted my face. I was hurt she hadn't trusted me, but I understood why better than she could imagine. I realized that, in a way, Papa had been right. It was Margie's story to tell, when and if she wanted to tell it.

"You're still you, right? This has always been you," I said with a little waver.

She nodded fast and pressed her lips together. "Yeah, exactly."

"Then I've always loved you like this," I said. "I just get to know you better now, I guess."

"Thanks." Her face creased with relief. "I still have to figure out how to tell Dad, and I guess Mom when she comes back."

She gave a little shrug as if to say all of this was no big deal, but from the look on her face and the way her body vibrated with nerves, it was a really, really big deal.

Rye cleared his throat and offered a fist bump. "Not that it matters what this random kid from Austin says, but I think that was badass."

She bumped him back with a grin. "It means a lot to me. And you're not a random kid," she said. "You're on Team Kitskara."

Dr. Kay was tilted back in her chair, but when Margie said that, she slammed down onto four legs. "What did you just say?"

32

I TOLD HER EVERYTHING I'D told Rye, more than what I'd told Margie.

"She didn't look human," I finished.

Rye added, "We think she's a kitskara."

Dr. Kay's eyes widened for a moment, but that was all she gave away. "I see."

"We found your paper on kitskaras," I said. "Well, Rye found it. He's helping us look for Mama, and knowing what she is"—*what I am*—"could help us understand where she might've gone."

Dr. Kay looked at him. "Is that why you're here?"

He flashed a wide smile. "I just want to go on the adventure, I guess. It's my dad's coffee truck, and I said they could use it when their car died, and I've been helpful so far finding clues and stuff."

Dr. Kay cleared her throat. "No, that's why they let you come with them, but that's not what I asked. Is that why you're here?"

Rye faltered under her level gaze. "I, uh, I wanted to get out of LaVerne."

She nodded like she'd expected as much. "Doesn't feel like home yet, does it."

"No, ma'am."

She looked at me, and I shrank away from her gaze. "Why are you here?"

"To find Mama."

"Nope. Next answer."

I gulped. "I want to know what I am. If Mama is something else, so are we."

She nodded. "Okay, and we know why Margie's here." Dr. Kay reached out and squeezed her hand. "You need anything, we're here for you. Just like before. Nothing's changed there."

I scowled at Margie.

Her face dropped. "Are you mad at me?"

I didn't want to take away from her moment, but I really was hurt. "I thought you came all this way because you believed me. About seeing Mama."

Margie frowned. "I believe you think you saw something, just like you've been seeing dinosaurs. I mean, you don't really think the dinosaur ghosts are real, do you?"

Hurt hollowed out my stomach. "Yeah, I *really* saw a dimetrodon, and I *really* saw a diplocaulus, and lots of other things that don't exist anymore, and it's really stressful? Actually? But I *also* saw Mama looking like a reptile in the middle of the night."

"I hear you," Margie said, "but what if it's a coping mechanism or something? Like, a trauma response."

I reeled back. "I'm not making this up!"

"They're called fossifae," Dr. Kay interrupted. "Maureen told me about them. And if Haven's seeing them, then she's got a touch of kitskara magic herself."

"More than a touch," Rye muttered into his mug where only I could hear.

"Wait, what?" Margie looked quickly between Lynne and Dr. Kay. "You're saying this is real?"

"It's real." Dr. Kay leaned back in her chair.

Margie gaped, and it was tough not to say *told you so*, but I had bigger fish, um, burgers to fry.

"Do you know where Mama is?" I asked.

Lynne shifted in her seat as Dr. Kay took a sip. "No, I don't."

"Okay. But you know what she is." It wasn't a question anymore.

Dr. Kay set the mug down, crossed her arms, and narrowed her eyes. "Yes, I do."

She wouldn't say more until we all moved outside. "I

don't believe mythology should be discussed under electric lights," she said.

"I'm right behind you!" Lynne called. "There's some blankets and a basket of scarves by the door. Grab one on your way out. There's a bit of a breeze tonight."

Shhhhheeeeehhhhheeeere.

The moment I stepped outside, the river song was back.

"Is the Brazos nearby?" I guessed.

"Yep. It clips a corner of our land," Dr. Kay said. She threw a match on some fire starter, and the logs crackled to orange life.

Just over twelve hours since I'd crawled out of it, and the river was already calling me back. I didn't want to be different. I didn't want to transform again. But a really big part of me wanted to run toward that voice and fling myself into its arms.

Instead I sat myself down in a folding chair beside the brick firepit and tried not to wince as the heat dried my skin.

Margie spread a big blanket out on the ground, and as soon as she sat, she was covered in dogs. They wove around her and nestled into her lap, and I watched how she cuddled into them, like there weren't enough hugs in the world.

Getting out of my chair, I walked over and plopped down on the blanket beside her. I didn't say anything, just wrapped my arms around her. She pulled me in tight. A wriggling dog yelped and scooted out of the way.

Margie pressed her forehead against mine and held on

to me in a way that made me realize she'd really been afraid she'd lose something by telling me about this part of her.

I squeezed her tighter. There was no way she could get rid of me.

We broke apart when a black-and-white wiry terrier tried to lick both of our faces, but I stayed on the blanket with her by the fire.

Lynne sat down in the chair I'd abandoned with a basket of knitting and started clicking away in the firelight.

I watched her hands and wished I could do something like that. I wanted a thing, something I did that was just for me. Mama had her fossils and her cairns, Margie had poetry and literature, and Papa had his weird movies. I did all of those, but none of that was really for me.

Most of the dogs settled down to sleep, but one scrawny reddish-colored dog lay against Rye's legs and nuzzled her face into his lap. He scratched behind her ears.

"You've got a friend." Lynne smiled.

"Who are you?" he baby-talked the dog. "What's your name?"

It was like watching sugar in a hot pan. He was melting in front of our eyes.

"That's Good Dog," Dr. Kay said as she tended the fire. "They're all Good Dog until they find a home."

"You look like a Ginger," he cooed. She licked his hands. "Or a Red, or—"

"Careful. You name her, she's yours," Dr. Kay warned.

"Good Dog." Rye tried to sit back and pet her from a distance, but moments later he was rubbing under her chin again.

Margie hugged her cup of tea. She looked more relaxed than I'd seen her in ages.

But I hadn't forgotten about my reason to be here. "So what are kitskaras?"

Firelight played across Dr. Kay's face. "Imagine science and magic as two dirt roads, and kitskaras are where the roads cross and get muddled, where they're not one or the other. Might be they're a product of evolution, or a transitional species, or a mythical creature. I honestly don't know. I don't think Maureen knows either. Basically, they're a shape-shifting humanoid that needs both fresh and salt water to survive. And when they transform, they're an amalgam of the critters native to wherever they are, even species that've gone extinct."

"Mama is a shape-shifting humanoid?" It didn't sound good when you put it like that.

Lynne said, "Maybe it's like human . . . plus something extra?"

Margie frowned. "Can she shape-shift whenever she wants, or does something trigger it? Like the full moon, or whatever."

Without knowing it, Margie had asked the exact question I needed to know.

But I was disappointed the next moment when Dr. Kay said, "I'm not sure. I always figured she was in control of it because she got through high school without anyone but me finding out."

Disappointment filled me from top to toes. I had no idea what to do to control my shifting. It had just happened as soon as I touched the Brazos.

"Wait, how did you learn about all this?" Rye said. "I'm not trying to brag, but if it's on the internet, I can usually find it, and I couldn't find anything else about kitskaras."

"Because I fell in love with one." Dr. Kay looked to Lynne. "Don't be jealous."

"I never am. Besides, I'm armed and dangerous. I'll defend my love against all comers." She raised a swashbuckling knitting needle.

Dr. Kay smiled, then she spoke slow and quiet, like the words might spook and run off. "I was in love with Reenie. My high school best friend."

It was an odd thing to imagine someone else loving her besides Papa, long before she became my mama.

"Senior year, I got tired of always hiding how I felt, so one day I decided I'd go tell her. I knew her parents were reclusive, but she'd told me whereabouts she lived on the coast, and I'd just pulled up in my truck and was practicing what I was gonna say, when I saw her jump into the gulf, and she didn't come back out.

"I dove in after her, thinking she was drowning, and that's when I saw her in her other form. Her kitskara self."

She laughed ruefully. "She saw me too. She didn't feel the same way I did, but we could hold each other's secrets. And it turned out we both really needed someone we could be ourselves around. Sometimes the scariest thing in the world is just letting someone know who you really are and what you're feeling. Right, Margie?"

Margie beamed, but her face shifted quickly. "So, we really are half kitskara."

I didn't feel so glowy. "What about the fossa—fassafees—"

"Fosse," Rye deadpanned. "The dancing dinosaur."

"Fossifae," Dr. Kay said. "You know me, I'm practical as dirt, but to me that's the coolest thing. Seeing prehistoric creatures like they're still walking the earth? Absolutely amazing. Are you seeing any of 'em right now?"

"Yeah." I looked away from the fire, and immediately the prehistoric world lit up like a drive-in movie. Silvery fish swam through the air. A shark hunted in eternal circles. A mosasaur snapped at unseen prey. An *Edaphosaurus* slunk beside a watery shore. Trilobites swarmed over everything. "Are they real? Or ghosts? They don't seem to see me, most of the time."

"You'll have to ask Maureen. I never really understood it. Something about the earth remembering." She stirred the fire.

"I can't believe you really saw a dimetrodon in the tomatoes," Margie said.

"You owe me an apology," I said. "You thought I was making it up."

"Sorry," she said, not sounding sorry at all. "Nobody would've believed that story. You can't blame me."

There she was. The annoying Margie I knew and loved.

Dr. Kay startled me with a laugh. "You know, it's funny. Your mother thought the kitskara genes had skipped you entirely 'cause you didn't have any of the color-changing characteristics like Margie. But here you are, watching species from hundreds of millions of years ago behind our heads. Any other unique qualities you got we should know about?"

I knew I could tell her the truth. She already knew about Mama, and she wasn't scared by it.

But I wasn't ready. It was still too scary, too new, too strange.

And maybe a little, I was angry that Margie and Dr. Kay and Lynne had all been keeping their own secrets for a lot longer than I had. Maybe it was my turn to have one. It wasn't the same, and I knew I wasn't being fair, but still. I didn't want to.

"No, that's all," I lied.

Rye looked at me over the red dog's head, but he held my secret.

"Here's the thing," Dr. Kay said. "It's unnatural for a kitskara to live so far from the ocean in the middle of wheat country. The only reason she could manage it was because of the Brazos nearby. It's a very salty river, even though it's technically fresh water. Almost like home."

She straightened her legs in front of her chair and reached for her toes. "The Finfolk were said to be sorcerers, that they could control the weather—"

"Sorcerers?!" Margie said. "Do you—are you being serious right now? This sounds made up."

Dr. Kay lifted one shoulder. "It's just a word, darlin'. But here's the thing, Maureen never could influence the weather like her parents could. Your Grandmer and Grandpepper would make it rain just to show their grandkids a rainbow every morning when they visited."

"The rainbow sunrises," Margie said, her jaw dropping. "I thought that was just a thing that happened at the gulf."

"They did it for you," Dr. Kay said. "'Cause they loved you, in their own kitskara way."

A wave of sadness washed through me. They'd tried to share some of their magic with us, and we'd never even known it was them.

Then I thought back to all that time under the cottonwood trees, the cairns, the strange songs and incantations. "Wait, all this time, Mama was trying to make it rain."

Dr. Kay nodded. "She thought the drought was her fault, since it started the same time her parents passed." She shook her head. "I tried to tell her no, that she'd never had the gift for weather magic that her parents had, but she still blamed herself, and damn burned herself out trying."

I remembered all the strange weather we'd been experiencing at home: the heavy clouds that never dropped, the stormy winds and lightning, but never rain. Maybe Mama had gotten close. Or maybe—I held my breath—maybe I'd been affecting the weather without even knowing it. Could I do that?

Margie gave me a concerned look. I started breathing again, and she looked away.

The crackles of the fire filled the silence between questions.

"Does Papa know about her being a kitskara?" I asked.

"He knows. He's always been terrified someone will find out and take her away, like the government or something."

My skin chilled at the thought of someone coming after Mama, or me or Margie.

Rye crossed his arms and glared. "So why'd you write a paper about it, if it's so dangerous for people to know what she is?"

Dr. Kay laughed ruefully. "I wouldn't want to play darts with you. Each question you throw is a zinger. Let's just say I had aspirations of getting a PhD in folklore, but I got laughed out of my degree and became an exotic animal veterinarian instead."

Her voice went somber. "Maureen forgave me for the paper eventually, but only after I promised to look after any kits she had."

Lynne put the yarn in her bag and folded her hands. "Kayla. Tell them what they need to know."

Margie groaned. "What is there possibly left to tell? My brain is already exploding."

Dr. Kay continued, "Something else interesting—in the Finfolk myths, they were always stealing human men to be husbands, but the Finfolk love silver, so you could throw a silver coin at them to escape."

I looked at the matching silver bracelets on my and Margie's wrists. Maybe that was significant, maybe it wasn't.

"Kayla," Lynne repeated sternly.

Dr. Kay dropped her head into her hands. Her two salt-and-pepper braids circled like divining rods as she rubbed her forehead.

I knew before she said anything more. "Mama was here, wasn't she?"

Dr. Kay nodded. "Last night."

33

I HAD TO GET AWAY from the fire. My skin was dry and itchy, and my insides felt the same. My body was topsy-turvy with emotion.

On top was relief—Mama was alive! She'd physically been here. I didn't have to worry that the worst had already happened.

But fury flipped that feeling. She could've called. She should've told me the truth. Didn't she know how leaving would make me feel?

I strode through the darkness, through the trilobites and the sharks, until I was far enough away from the fire that the stars were brighter and louder than my anger.

Footsteps told me I wasn't alone.

"She's traveling by river, isn't she?" I asked.

Lynne hugged her cardigan a little tighter. "Yes. To the gulf."

I nodded. I'd already figured, but it was good to know for sure. "How long was she here?"

"Not long. About an hour. She ate a little, drank some water, and got on her way."

"The sardines," I said.

"That's right."

My voice cracked a little. "Why doesn't she want us to know where she is? Doesn't she miss us?"

Lynne brushed her bangs out of her face and looked up at the sky. I followed her gaze up to Ursa Minor overhead.

She said, "I'm sure she does, but she's not thinking very clearly. She's more kitskara than human right now, and she's going on instinct."

I remembered how the river had made it hard for me to hold on to my thoughts, and I shivered. If she stayed in there too long, would she forget me completely? That was terrifying.

I wiped my nose on my sleeve. "I wish everyone would just talk to us like we're real people, like you do, instead of treating us like glass figurines or something."

Lynne pulled her sleeves over her hands. "People like to think kids live in a bubble that keeps all the innocence in and the tough stuff out. It would be nice if that were true, but that's not how it works, is it?"

I shook my head. "No."

She worried the end of the cardigan. "When I was a little

girl, my father had a heart attack at work and died on the way to the hospital. The way it felt to me, he left in the morning, and he just never came back. No one, not even my mother, really took the time to explain to me what had happened."

"That's so sad," I said. "I'm sorry."

"Thanks." She smiled at me. "Even after the funeral, when she had to work more, she didn't talk to me about it. I felt like they'd both abandoned me, and it messed me up for a long time."

She shook her head. "I don't want that for you, or Margie, or any child. You deserve the truth every time, even when it's hard. And I know from experience how it helps."

Dr. Kay hollered at us, "Y'all come on back! I'm putting the fire out!"

Lynne and I retraced our steps toward the house. "Thanks for telling me that," I said. "All of it."

She patted my shoulder but didn't say anything more.

Steam hissed off the fire as Dr. Kay doused it with water. "I'll get y'all some sleeping bags. You can sleep on the porch here till morning, and then I'm driving you back to LaVerne."

I felt like I'd been dumped in ice water. We couldn't go back tomorrow—we had to keep going. We'd only scratched the surface with what Dr. Kay knew about kitskaras. I needed Mama to help me understand what was going on with me. I needed to bring her home.

"I can drive us," Margie offered, but Dr. Kay cut her off.

"Nope, you won't be breaking the law on my watch," she said. "Maureen would kill me if I let you do that."

Rye looked at us with wide, horrified eyes. "Sleeping bags? On the floor? Isn't there a couch somewhere I could sleep on?"

Dr. Kay laughed. "It's cooler on the porch, but you do you. You can crash anywhere you like, so long as you don't wake me with your snoring."

Lynne fake-whispered, "Kay snores louder than a congested polar bear, so if you can out-snore her, I will be very impressed."

As we headed back into the house, Rye stopped by the door to pet the red dog. I stooped down beside him.

"Hey, Rye," I whispered, "how mad would your dad be if we kept using his coffee truck a little longer?"

"Pretty mad. Why?"

"I still have so many questions," I said, trying not to sound desperate. "I can't go home yet, and now we know for sure where she's going!"

"So you want to take the coffee truck all the way to the Gulf of Mexico?" He stared at me.

I shrugged. "Yeah."

A slow grin spread across his face. "Let's do it."

"Are you sure? What about your parents?"

Good Dog pressed her face into his chest, and he rested his chin on her head. "This is the puzzle of a lifetime, you know? I get to do what I love in real life. Track down a location, and bonus points, find your mermaid alien mom. But we need to drive through Austin, okay? There's a map store we gotta stop at. Where we're going—"

"We don't need roads," I quoted, and laughed until I realized I was laughing alone.

"What?" His face squinched.

"It's, um, it's a movie. My dad. Watches a lot of old sci-fi stuff." Now I wasn't just a kitskara, I was a kitskara *nerd*.

"Ohhhkay, I was gonna say we won't have internet and the phone app probably won't work."

"Yeah, that makes more sense than what I said. Austin, map store, roger that."

I was glad the moonlight couldn't show the flush on my cheeks. Although none of this planning would matter if I didn't get Margie on board. "I'll work on my sister, and you be ready to go early in the morning, okay? Before Dr. Kay and Lynne are up."

"You got it."

Rye took the couch, and Margie and I got comfy on the porch like we'd done every time we visited. With the ceiling fan on, it was heaven to sleep near the stars but away from the bugs.

Not that I could sleep.

Margie had conked out the moment her head was on a pillow.

I whispered, "Margie. Margie. MARGIE."

From under her sleeping bag, she groaned, "What? Go to sleep. I'm exhausted. You got to nap in the truck, not me."

"Margie, we can't go home. We have to find Mama."

"Mmmmmmm."

"Margie! We can't stop now. Can you set your alarm so we can get an early start?"

She rolled over and opened one eye. "Why? We got what we needed. She's alive, and you were right about seeing dinosaurs. Besides, she left us behind. I'm not gonna chase someone who doesn't want us."

"Of course she wants us!" I hoped that was true. "She's just not thinking straight. And I think Papa was telling the truth—she's going to Grandmer and Grandpepper's place."

Her voice got sleepier and more stubborn. "Which we could never find. They didn't have an address, and the last time we went there, you and I slept most of the way. Like I want to do now."

I didn't need to hold a fossil to feel the pull of the water and something bigger beyond. That voice, I was pretty sure it was Mama, calling to me, pulling anything kitskara toward her.

I knew I could find her. "Can you trust me? Call it my fossifae magic or whatever, but I can kind of sense where she is. And Rye's trying to figure out the exact location too."

She didn't respond. I wasn't sure if she was asleep or ignoring me, so I lay down and rolled to my other side.

Once the house was as still and silent as a house with a dozen animals ever gets, I slipped back outside to the firepit. I held my hands over the embers. They'd gone dark, but they held their heat.

Dr. Kay had mentioned weather magic. Time to see what else a monster girl might be able to do.

Closing my eyes, I thought back to what Mama had done in the bone garden. Guilt wormed into me when I remembered how horrified I'd been to see her out there like that, when she'd been doing what she could to try and save our farm. And not just ours, the whole town. I shook myself—once we found her, there was plenty of time for apologies. For both of us.

There was a little breeze moving already. Maybe I could try to make it bigger? That seemed like a good place to start.

Mama'd been crouching, so I did that too. As soon as my hands and knees touched the earth, I felt an energy circle inside me. It felt a little like sitting on one of those playground spinners when it's just picking up speed.

She'd surrounded herself with fossils. I looked around at the gossamer fossifae swimming through the night. I might not have any cairns, but clearly there were fossils nearby. That would have to be good enough.

I dug my fingers into the ground, and the spinning feeling inside me picked up. My heart rate did too. The blood pumped through me as hard as if I'd run across the open field.

What else? Mama had been saying something, probably in Orcadian. Well, I was stumped there. But I had to try something.

Breathing hard, I hummed another of Mama's lullabies and focused on . . . Wait, what should I think about? How did I make weather happen? How did any of this *work*?

Frustration tore through me. I leaned back on my heels and felt all the zooming energy drain away.

This was all too hard. All of it.

I realized the breeze had stopped completely.

Fantastic. If I'd done anything, I'd broken the little bit of weather we had.

Dusting off my hands and knees, I walked back to the porch and lay down beside Margie. I counted mosasaurs until I finally drifted to sleep myself.

I woke up to the smell of fresh coffee and toasted bread. I rolled out of my sleeping bag, stepped over Margie, and found my way to the bathroom. As I came out into the hall, I overhead Dr. Kay on the phone.

"Yeah, they're here," Dr. Kay was saying. "Don't you worry, I'll get 'em back home to you. Nah, they're all right. They're just worried about their mama, can't blame them for that. Yeah. They're sleeping off the late night. Yeah. Yeah, their friend's here too."

I'd heard enough. I ran to Rye and shook him. "Shhh! Wake up! We need to go!"

I dashed back to the porch and shook Margie. "M, wake up! We overslept. Dr. Kay's gonna make us go back home. C'mon, get up!"

Margie covered her head with her pillow. "We're done. Let's go back and wait for her."

Rye stumbled in with the red dog pressed up against his legs. His curly black hair pointed in all directions. "What's up?"

"Margieeee!" I yanked on her sleeping bag.

Margie rolled over and rubbed her eyes. "Ugh, what do you want me to do? Rye's dad needs his coffee truck back, we can't hitchhike, and I'm not going to steal Dr. Kay's or Lynne's vehicles."

"Wait, you're not giving up, are you?" Rye said. "My dad will be fine."

Margie opened one eye. "Why do you care? I thought you were just coming along for the adventure."

He ran his hands through his hair. "Yeah, and it just keeps getting better. Besides, you need me."

Margie reached for her headphones. She looked frazzled. "Look, I *really* don't want to get arrested. For theft *or* kidnapping."

Rye said, "Everyone loves a coffee truck! No one's gonna look twice at us."

I pleaded with her. "Come on, Margie. Do you really want to go back to our house and just wait for Mama to feel like coming back? I know I don't."

She was listening to me, at least.

I said, "I'm mad. I'm really, really mad. She and Papa kept so much from us, and it's not basic, unimportant stuff. It's literally the stuff of what we are! What if something happens to her while she's out there, and she's gone forever?"

I took a breath. "I've been thinking. Kitskaras are almost extinct, right? What if that's the reason I see all these prehistoric creatures? Like, when you're the only ones left, you see everything else that's gone before."

Margie looked stricken. "That's really dark."

Rye tapped his fingers on his other arm like he wanted to say something, but he kept it in.

I added. "She thinks she's the only one like her. We can show her she's not so alone. Margie, please!"

"Oh my god, fine. FINE," she said. "Everyone pee, and we'll go."

"I already went," Rye said.

"Good for you."

We stayed in the clothes we'd slept in, so we were rumpled but ready. We went out the screen door on the porch and crept to the front of the house.

We ran behind the truck and out of sight. Margie quietly opened the driver's door. "What the—?"

Draped over the steering wheel was a handmade mint-green scarf with a note in loopy handwriting. *So proud of you for being you.* And in the middle seat, a big brown paper bag. Margie's face softened, and she wrapped the scarf around her neck like it was a hug.

We pulled the bag open, and inside were biscuits, mozzarella cheese sticks, a carton of orange juice, and three paper cups. And sardines.

Margie turned up her nose. "Eww. Why'd she pack that?"

I smiled. "Lynne thinks we can find Mama."

Margie made a grumbly sound, then asked, "How's it look?"

I looked at my sister, with her magic eyes, her rainbow fingernails, and the green scarf against her red hair. "You look great," I said honestly. "You look like . . . you."

"It's too hot to wear a scarf," she said a little self-consciously, but she didn't take it off.

"Rye, you get in first," I said. "I'll slide in after you. Rye?" I realized he wasn't beside me like I'd thought.

Margie looked around. "Where'd he go?"

I ran back to the house and found him latching the screen door. The scrawny red dog watched him from the inside with adoring eyes.

"I'll come back for you, Ruby, I promise," he said.

"What are you doing?" I asked. "We have to go before they notice we're awake!"

"She follows me everywhere, so I had to shut her in! What if she ran in front of the truck and got hit?" he said.

"C'mon." I grabbed his hand and pulled him around the side of the house. "And *Ruby*?" I hissed. "Not TARDIS, or Naruto, or something like that?"

"I contain multitudes, Haven. I'm not one hundred percent dork."

"Haven? Margie? Where y'all at?" Dr. Kay's voice traveled toward us.

"Hurry!" We raced to the cab, and Margie took off, the coffee truck rattling along.

"Buckle up, kids," she said, sliding her sunglasses down. "Next stop, Austin, Texas."

34

LIES. FORTY-FIVE MINUTES LATER WE exited I-35 in West, Texas, exit 353. I'd always thought we should get a discount anytime we bought anything here since we had the same last name as the town, but so far nobody had gone for it.

"We should keep going," I argued. "We already had breakfast, and there's still two hours until Austin."

But Margie insisted we stop in the punny Czech town to get the world's best kolaches.

We drove past motels—COME CZECH IN!—and car lots—CZECH ME OUT!—before parking the coffee truck in front of the famous Little Czech Bakery.

Margie slipped her headphones over her ears. "Look, the orange juice was great, but I need coffee. And if we drive by, I will have to live forever with the regret of uneaten kolaches and klobasneks. I don't want that hanging over my head."

She was joking, but also not.

"Fine. Bring me a raspberry strudel and a klobasnek?"

"You got it. Rye?"

"I've never had anything from here, so whatever you think is good."

A wicked grin spread across Margie's face. "Oh. Oh, my friend. I am happy, nay, privileged to introduce you to these pastries."

He gave her some strong side-eye. "Why are you talking like that?"

She placed a hand over her heart. "Because my love for this bakery is Shakespearean. Be right back."

She practically scampered inside.

Rye stared after her. "Which Shakespeare play?"

"According to her, it's a tragedy if we skip it."

Rye and I got out of the truck to stretch our legs. We were on a service road right off the highway. If we'd been there a couple months earlier, the roadside would've been blanketed with bluebonnets. Now it was all long grass.

"What kind of food does that truck sell? It looks made up," Rye said.

"Which one?"

He pointed at a food vendor farther up the road. The Czechxican.

I started laughing. "Say it out loud."

"Suh-zek—wait—oh! It's Czech-Mexican food. Ha. My dad would love that."

We'd had to leave the Brazos River behind to turn southwest toward Austin. I missed the feel of it at my back. There was water nearby—I could sense it—but it wasn't the same.

"So when are you going to tell Margie that you're a 'shape-shifting humanoid'?" Rye asked. He made air quotes around my least-favorite descriptive phrase ever.

I kicked a tire. "It only happened once. Maybe it was a fluke."

"You really think that?"

I wanted to believe it was a one-time thing, a skin condition or an immune system flare-up like I'd found on WebMD when I'd searched "skin changing color," but I knew better. My bones were ready to bend, my joints to unknit, my skin to shed. It was in me now.

"No. It's going to happen again." It was my first time admitting it to myself too. "I just wish I knew for sure what the trigger is."

"Water, obviously," Rye said.

"Yeah, but not all water," I said. "I can drink it, shower in it, sweat. All that. Is it just the Brazos that does it?"

"Maybe it has to be wild water, like, out in nature or something."

I thought of Dr. Kay's fish tank and how I'd wanted to stick my face in it. "I don't think so."

I could feel the answer on the tip of my brain. "Maybe it's . . ."

"Hey, man! Amigo!" A baseball-cap-wearing, brown-skinned man leaned out the window from the Czechxican truck. "You got a license? Y'all can't park your cart here without one. I don't care, but the bakery people, they'll call the cops if they think you're trying to take their customers."

Rye responded in Spanish, and the two started conversing much faster than my basic Spanish could keep up. "¡Sí, sí!" Rye said with a grin. "El camión que vende café (y donas) está vacío."

"Estás loco," the man laughed.

"What are y'all talking about?" I asked.

"That we're road-tripping in an empty truck. He thinks we're out of our minds, but I'm gonna convince him it's epic."

After a minute of more conversation, the vendor motioned him over, and Rye trotted across the parking lot.

The vendor pointed to me and handed him a plastic bag.

I blushed. Even with my elementary español, I understood "Para tu novia." *For your girlfriend.*

"Gracias, Gael," Rye said, and walked back toward me.

I was pretty sure my cheeks were as red as one of the salsas I'd seen Gael tuck inside.

"We have a feast!" Rye said. "Potato and egg breakfast burritos."

"Yum," I said, and then yelled across the street. "Thank you!"

"Good luck!" Gael called as he withdrew back inside his own truck.

I pretended not to have understood his earlier comment, or that Rye hadn't corrected him.

Margie waltzed out of the bakery moments later with paper bags already showing grease stains.

"Sweets for the sweet!" she called.

Rye struck a theatrical pose and held out the burritos. "To eat, or not to eat." He dropped it and said, "That guy over there gave us some extras. He's pretty cool."

"Nice," she said when Rye showed her the burritos. "Does this truck have a fridge? 'Cause you're about to have a come-to-Jesus moment involving pastry and sausage, and I think we should save the burritos for later."

Rye smiled. "It sure does."

"Hang on," Margie said. "I'm gonna text Dad real quick. Even though I am technically not speaking to him, he should know where we are."

She pulled the phone out of her bag. She stared at it for a long second.

"What is it?" I asked. "Are there a million missed calls from him?"

"No," she said. "It's dead. And I didn't pack the charger. Did you?"

Crap. "No, I forgot. And the car charger is—"

"Back in Mom's car," she finished with a grimace.

I ventured, "I heard Dr. Kay talking to him, so he knows we're alive."

Margie sighed. "I can get us to Austin, and we'll buy a charger there, okay? Let's get these burritos inside."

Ignoring for now the thought of Papa worried sick and not able to reach us, we unlatched the back door of the truck and climbed inside.

It was my first time in the back of the truck. "It's so shiny and clean," I said. "And smaller than I thought."

Stuff had fallen off the shelves while we drove. There were bags of coffee and paper cups in a box on the middle of the floor. One of the milk crates had overturned, spilling bottles of flavored syrups onto the floor.

Rye looked at the mess guiltily. "I guess he was about to start experimenting on the coffee stuff too."

He flipped a switch, and the cooler turned on. "It's running on a battery now, but it'll usually be powered by the generator."

"This is really cool," Margie said. "A whole café in a truck."

Mr. Wilson-Ruiz had taped laminated instructions all over the walls. As Rye shoved the spilled items back into drawers, I read one that hung in between the grinder and the coffee maker.

DRIP COFFEE & JAPANESE ICED COFFEE

1. Pour 1 bag of whole beans into espresso hopper.
2. Make sure grinder's dial is set to proper # before pushing "on" switch!
3. Drip coffee grind setting: 14
4. Japanese iced coffee grind setting: 11
5. After grinding, place grounds in filter of coffee maker.
6. (Make sure coffee urn's spout is in "off" position—or things'll get messy!)
7. Write "drip" or "JIC" + time brewed on coffee pot with chalk marker.
8. (When serving Japanese iced coffee, make sure you pack cup FULL of ice!)
9. Make fresh batch every 2 hours.

I blinked. Who knew coffee could be so complicated?

Rye unhooked the bungee cord that held the fridge door shut so we could open it. We tucked the burritos inside, and a small packet fell out of the bag.

I picked it up. "Anyone use salt for their burritos, or should I toss it?"

"Not me," said Rye.

"You can toss it," Margie said.

I stared at the packet, and pieces started to fit together.

Mama's bath salts by the tub. The salinity of the Brazos

River. The saltwater aquarium at Dr. Kay's.

I brought the salt close to my face, and my body felt electric with knowing.

Margie said, "Ooooohkay, you can just hang on to that super-special salt, if you want, but we're gonna head back into the cab and have us some klobasneks."

Moments later, I dimly heard Rye and Margie appreciating the Czech pastries and sausage rolls, but I was overwhelmed by the realization.

Salt water was the trigger. That's what turned us kitskara.

And the bath I'd taken back home . . .

Fresh water changed us back.

35

I WANTED TO TELL RYE that I'd figured out what made kits-karas shift, but there was no good way to do that with Margie around, so I just stared at him with big, buggy eyes trying to communicate, *There's something I need to tell you.*

He stared back at me. "Do you want the last bite of my kolache or something?"

"Never mind," I huffed, and sank back against the truck bench.

Two hours later, we had the cranks.

Maybe it was too many pastries, or not enough potty breaks. Rye's elbow kept catching my ribs, and Margie had developed an annoying habit of clearing her throat every ten seconds.

"Could you not hack for, like, five minutes?" I asked.

"Do you see all these cars? Highway pollution gives me

postnasal drip. I'm too sensitive for interstates," she said. "It's the kitskara in me."

I rolled my eyes. "It's probably just allergies. You're not that special all the time."

Traffic was getting worse the closer we got to the city. The truck's big windshield meant the sun blasted us, and even with the air on high, we were sweaty messes. Any time I tried to get more comfortable, my skin would stick to the seat and make a disgusting squelching sound whenever I moved. Rye kept laughing and calling out "Skin fart!" which made me feel like the grossest girl on the planet.

Margie kept changing the radio station because "they all suck," Rye was whining that she was skipping all the good songs, and I had a terrible headache.

"Switch places with me," I said, unbuckling my seat belt.

"That's really dangerous," he observed. "We're on a highway."

"I can't sit next to her anymore, and your elbow is about to rupture my spleen."

Margie said, "Actually, that's your appendix. The spleen is on the left side of your body."

"Oh. My. God. You see? Switch with me! Just do it!"

"Okay, okay."

We unbuckled and moved—"Skin fart!"—and I settled down by the window. Rye buckled back in and fought with

Margie as she tried to put on classical music but he wanted indie rock.

"All those bands are terrible!" she protested.

Extinction was more appealing than staying in this hot truck.

Last night I'd tried to affect the weather, and I'd failed. Maybe I was like Mama, and I didn't have the knack. But if I could do something about this heat, it would be worth trying again.

Closing my eyes, I thought about gray skies and a strong, steady breeze. I was pretty sure incantations needed sound, so I hummed a few notes along with the punk-pop song on the radio (Rye was currently winning the station wars).

Clouds . . . clouds, clouds, clouds, clouds . . . wind . . . wind, wind, wind, wind . . .

I opened my eyes. Nothing had changed. Except the station, which was now playing Tchaikovsky.

Useless. I leaned my forehead against the cool glass window and stared outside.

Strip malls, banks, and fast-food places passed in a blur of beige. I listened for Mama and the ocean—*shhhhheeere*—there. It was strange how it made me feel lost and found at the same time.

As I focused on the sound, the prehistoric world became clearer.

It was swampy. Lush green vegetation grew around pools

of water. I held my breath as a giant sloth ambled across a mound of grass.

I blinked, and it was gone. I was seeing a different time. Now the world was dark, and ammonites propelled themselves through the water.

It was a little like clicking through photos online, but cooler by a million percent.

Blink. Oysters grew on rocks.

Blink. A dire wolf stalked a smaller, rodent-like mammal.

Blink. A herd of iguanodons gathered at the edge of a pond.

I tried not to blink—iguanodons were one of my favorites. My eyes watered as I tried to hold on to it, but a semi-truck zoomed by, and they were gone.

A woolly mammoth lifted its tusks toward the sky.

Blink. The swamp was back.

"What do you think, Haven?" Margie demanded.

It took me a moment to refocus back inside the cab, in this plane of time.

"What are y'all talking about?" I asked.

"Wait, are you okay?" Margie asked. "Your heart is racing."

"I'm fine. What's the question?"

"Whether Dad should lease our land to Rye's mom for wind turbines," Margie said. "I think it's a great idea, but I don't think he'll go for it."

I considered the question. "I don't love the idea of those

big things in our backyard. We'd hear them all the time."

Rye said, "You mean the sweet, sweet sound of saving the earth from over-relying on fossil fuels? And you get paid for it."

Fossil fuels. I looked back out the window at the fossifae whose remains had probably contributed to Texas's huge supply of oil. Climate change hadn't been their fault— it had been asteroids and volcanoes that destroyed their atmospheres—but we weren't so innocent in our era.

"That's a good point," I admitted.

"And the farm could really use the money," Margie added.

I asked, "Would he have to stop farming wheat?"

Rye shook his head. "That's the cool thing; studies show that most crops actually benefit from wind turbines."

"Huh." I liked the idea of wind energy, and those turbines had to go somewhere. Why not our land? It was our planet, so why not our responsibility?

"I think it's a good idea," I agreed. "Let's talk to him about it."

"Yesssss," Rye said. "Now maybe my mom will forgive me for running away with Dad's coffee truck."

"Speaking of fuel," Margie said, and looked to Rye, "this traffic is eating up the gas. And I bet this truck takes diesel, right?"

He held his hands up. "You're the one who drove tractors at age five or whatever! How would I know?"

She scoffed. "What, so, you can identify the different license plates from around the world to pinpoint a location, but you don't know if your dad's truck takes unleaded or diesel?"

"It hasn't come up," he said.

Picking up on the undertone of her question, I asked, "Are we okay for money, M?"

She grimaced. "Ummm, maybe? I brought everything I had left over from tutoring this year, but it's not a lot."

"Meaning . . . ?"

She scrunched her nose. "I probably shouldn't have bought so many pastries."

"You didn't have a choice," Rye assured her. "They're that good."

"You're an enabler," she said with a grin.

He leaned forward and put his hands on the dash. "Here we are, folks. Austin city limits."

36

ACCORDING TO MARGIE, CITY DRIVING was like scraping her skin off slowly with a vegetable peeler dipped in lemon juice.

She jumped as a car honked next to us. "I hate this. We should've gone around."

"No, no, no," Rye said, tapping his fingers on the dash like it was a keyboard. "It's gonna be worth it. The map place is right by my dad's old burger joint. We can swing by Strange Burger for lunch, pick up the map from down the block, and head out."

Margie groaned. "We don't have money for burgers."

He shook it off. "They're like family. I'm sure they won't charge me; they never did before."

I squirmed in my seat by the window. *This is taking too long.* Mama had never felt farther away than she did in that sea of cars inching toward the center of town. I scratched at my shoulders, miserable at still being so far from the gulf. I tried to listen for her, but I couldn't hear anything.

"I could use a break," Margie admitted. "And a Dr Pepper, but that's probably all we can afford."

"It won't take too long, right?" I asked, but they talked over me.

Rye said, "I'm telling you, they're gonna give us so much food you'll wish you had a third stomach. Take this next exit."

Her cheeks got blotchy with stress. "You say that like it's easy. I've never done this before!"

She put on her turn signal and waited until a little VW Bug slowed down enough for her to pull over.

"I think they're afraid the big coffee truck will squish them," I observed.

"Sshhhh!" she ordered.

She crossed into the right lane and kept the blinker on as she eased her way onto the exit. I raised my hands in a silent cheer for her.

We came off the highway into streets lined with houses and yards landscaped with succulents and small rocks.

"What's next?" she said, her jaw tight.

Rye directed us away from the capitol and the university. Houses spread out, and there were lots of food trucks and picnic tables everywhere. Our coffee truck didn't look out of place at all.

"It's on the next block," he said. He sat back hard in the

bench and knocked his shoulder into mine. "You're gonna love it. Name your topping, you can get it."

I didn't have the heart to tell him my appetite had dried up the farther away we got from the Brazos, but Margie was game.

"How about pineapple?" she said.

"Yep!"

"Mango?"

"Totally."

"I bet you don't have a chocolate burger," she said.

"It's the mole special," he replied with an air of triumph.

We crossed the intersection, and even though the thought of eating right now made me feel nauseous, I was curious to see the place I'd heard so much about. But as we slowed, I didn't see it.

I frowned. "You said it was next to a vintage clothing store, right?"

"Yeah," he said, looking worried. "Between Vivi's and GelatoRio."

I saw Vivi's Vintage—it had racks of clothes on the sidewalk and lava lamps in the windows—and I saw GelatoRio, which looked like an Italian ice cream place with specialty flavors like churro and Mexican hot chocolate.

But in between the two places was an empty lot. It was nothing but brown dirt and rocks with a construction sign in the ground.

COMING SOON! HUMBOLDT'S BEANS AND BREWS!

"Are you sure it's this block?" I asked.

"It's gone," he said, but he wasn't talking to us. He was blinking, staring at where Strange Burger was supposed to be, and saying, "They tore it down. It's gone."

"Oh no," I said. It wasn't eloquent or helpful, but that's what came out.

He turned away from the window. "Let's go."

"Rye, I'm sorry—" Margie started in a soft voice.

"Just keep driving," he begged, refusing to look at either of us. "The map store is one block away. *If* it's still there."

We left the empty lot in the rearview mirror. Rye pointed ahead at an old brick house with a retail sign that read LONGLOST MAPS.

"There's a parking spot just past it," I said.

Margie hung in the intersection a few extra seconds than normal. "That's not a pull-in parking spot."

"Yeah, you'll have to parallel park." Realization hit me. "Oh, can you do that?"

She grumbled, "I've done it, but only in Mom's sedan, and only a few times."

She crossed the street and positioned herself beside a parked blue Volvo, then slowly backed in.

The first time her angle was too sharp, and we stuck out into the street. "Don't say a word," she warned.

The second attempt she nearly scraped the side mirrors off the Volvo.

I made the mistake of encouraging her. "That was better!"

She barked, "I need. TOTAL. Silence. Third time's the charm."

This time she slid into the spot seamlessly, her bumpers inches away from the Volvo in front of her and the Range Rover behind.

She pumped her fist overhead. "Woo! I just parallel parked a food truck," she said. "I feel like I should automatically get my license now. Like, poof, here it is! 'Congratulations, you exited off an interstate and parallel parked without killing anyone. We assume you can use turn signals.' "

She turned the truck off, and quiet filled the cab. Nobody moved toward the door.

"Sorry about lunch," Rye said. His fingers curled into his jeans.

"I wasn't hungry anyway," I said.

"What kind of name is Humboldt?" Margie wrinkled her nose. "That has to be the worst name I've ever heard for a coffee and beer place."

Rye answered. "It's German. Humboldt was a famous geographer and naturalist. That's why his name is all over the country."

Margie shook her head. "Only you would know the answer to that."

"Yep. I'm soooo special." He dropped his head in his hands. Without looking up, he said, "He told me he'd sold the business to one of his employees. To Luciana. Said she'd carry on the Strange Burger legacy."

"Maybe she sold to developers?" Margie suggested.

"Or maybe he lied."

"Why would he lie about that?" I asked.

"'Cause he knew how much I loved Strange Burger. He knew. He *knew*."

Rye sat up and wiped his eyes with the backs of his hands. "It's not just the food, you know? It was home. I ran the register; I knew everyone's name and what they ordered."

His shoulders slumped. "I was part of something special. And now it's gone, and it's like I was never here."

"No," I said, knowing he was wrong but not knowing how to convince him. "That's not true."

He half stood and crawled around me. "I need to move. I'll see y'all inside."

He pushed the door open and hopped out, walking straight into LongLost Maps without looking back.

37

To get inside the map store, we had to walk past a steel sculpture of a globe that took up most of the lawn. A small neon sign glowed against the dark brick entryway with the words NOT ALL WHO WANDER ARE LOST.

"So does this place want us to buy maps or not? I'm getting mixed messages," Margie said as she pulled the door open.

The moment we walked in, I spun to the right. I could feel it before I saw it.

A large burbling saltwater fish tank stood a few feet away against the wall with bright orange-and-white clownfish inside. There was live coral and a treasure chest that opened and closed with bubbles.

Under the tank was a shelf marked TREASURE MAPS with preprinted coloring sheets and crayons for little kids.

The setup was cute. And totally dangerous for me. I didn't know if it took one drop or a dunking, but I couldn't turn into a kitskara in front of everyone in the store.

Although that didn't seem to be an issue. The place looked deserted.

"Let's go this way," I said, nearly pulling Margie behind me.

There were no surprises in the first room. It had Austin souvenirs, city street maps, and travel gear like packing cubes and headphone splitters. Travel guides shared space with prepper how-to books and survivalist literature.

"Where do you think Gulf Coast maps are?" I asked.

Margie shrugged.

We walked farther into the house, and the more I saw, the odder it seemed. All the rooms were small. Some were stuffed with maps, but others held only a few.

Margie started sneezing from all the dust. "Keep looking," she said. "I'm gonna go back to the truck and grab one of my masks."

"Wait, don't leave me—" But she was gone.

"Rye?" I called. No response.

The rooms were connected by short hallways, and they were all hung with colorful cross-stitched art featuring peace symbols, succulents, the hemp plant, and llamas, plus lots of quirky phrases and strangely specific quotes.

Home is where the harp is.

Keep Austin Kind. And Weird. Kinda Weird?

Squeeze the Day 🍊

Girlboss

Don't 💩 *where you live.*

I know karate.

They were kinda cool. Maybe I could take up cross-stitching. Grandma West had some good one-liners I could memorialize.

Love is love is love is love in rainbow colors. If I got good at cross-stitching, I could make something like that for Margie.

Or maybe she'd prefer one of the literary ones. I held one that said *Metaphors be with you.* Papa would think that was funny.

Out of nowhere, I missed Papa so hard it hurt, but I shooed the feeling away. If he'd been willing to talk to us, we wouldn't be here at all.

A voice close behind me said, "You want the pattern? I sell the finished ones, but I give the patterns away for free."

I spun around and spotted a plump, older Asian American woman with mischievous eyes watching me from the "Vancouver/Alberta/Siberia and Other Very Cold Places" room.

She studied me. "Or maybe you want the poop one."

I stuttered, "Umm, no, that's okay."

"Can I help you find something?" she asked.

She looked older than Dr. Kay, but she was dressed a lot flashier. She wore drapey black pants with orange elephants on them, mismatched with a bright green blouse dotted with white four-leaf clovers. It was a barrage of colors. I liked it.

"I'm trying to find my friend? He's in here somewhere. We're looking for maps of the coast near Galveston."

"Ah, Rye. Yes, he's in the back. I'll take you. This place can feel like a maze the first time."

She led me through Kingdoms of Africa, took a right through Oceania, and passed through a low-ceilinged room filled with cartography tools like pens, rulers, compasses, stencils, protractors, and different kinds of paper.

"Is this your store?" I asked.

"It is," she said, flashing me a red-lipstick smile over her shoulder. "I'm Ms. Jeanne. I collect maps, sell them, and occasionally make them. And you are?"

"I'm Haven."

She smiled wider and led me through a door to the left. "Even if I weren't a mapmaker, I would love your name. How did you—?"

"What's this room?" I said, stunned enough to interrupt.

It looked like a greenhouse, but there were no plants. Just stoppered glass bottles that hung from hooks on the wall or sat in wooden stands on a long potting table. The sunlight bounced off the glass to reflect on the walls.

Ms. Jeanne tapped a long nail against a dark blue one.

"They're all filled with sand, or ocean water I scooped up, or notes I scribbled to myself from places I've been. Places and people change, but these are stuck in time. I like that."

She turned on her red flats. "This way. The workroom is back here."

Two rooms over we found Rye standing behind a big brown table with a stack of road maps beside him. "Hey, Haven," he said. "I think I've found what we need."

There was no sign that he'd ever been upset. His curls were sticking out all over, and he had bits of dust and paper caught in them from all the old maps. He looked like a mad scientist, if the scientist was stitching together a route instead of a monster.

He held up the kind of map I'd seen in the dash of my dad's truck. "This is just a general Rand McNally's road map, but it's pure gold."

He held up another one. "And this looks like the same thing, but it's actually from thirty years ago, which I'm guessing is when your mom was living with her parents. So, we need that in case there were roads that don't exist anymore. And this one is really neat—it's a fishing chart of the coastal areas."

I waited until Ms. Jeanne slipped out of the workroom. Once she was gone, I said in a low voice, "Rye, I'm so sorry about Strange Burger. It sounds like it was really special."

He tried to smile, but the usual light in his face was

dimmed. "Whatever, it's fine. If you look at this one—"

I took the road map out of his hands. "Rye. It's me. You know stuff about me no one else does. Come on, talk to me."

He pressed his hands down on the table and took a deep breath. When he looked at me, the pain was back in his eyes. "To be real with you, there's nothing to say. I thought this would be like coming home. I was wrong."

I hesitated. "Don't laugh, but—"

"No promises," he said. "Sometimes you're really funny."

"No, seriously," I said. "Something I'm learning from the fossifae—and I *know* how weird that sounds—is that nothing's really gone forever. We're all made from what came before us. So, you'll always have Strange Burger with you, and so will everyone who loved it."

He stacked the maps, then restacked them a different way, not looking at me. "Yeah. I guess. I just wish it was still here."

"Me too."

A thought hit me like a gut punch. "Hey, did you want us to keep looking for my mom after Dr. Kay's just so we'd bring you to Austin?"

He shook his head, and his eyes widened. "No! I really did—do—want to help." He paused and considered his next words. "But maaaybe I've gotten super involved because I don't want to think about the truth."

"What truth?"

He shrugged. "Where's my home now? LaVerne? Not yet, and maybe not ever. But it's not here either. I don't really have one anymore."

Ms. Jeanne chose that moment to pass back through the workshop. "If only home could be found on a map. That would be something indeed," she intoned.

She winked at us and exited without another word.

Rye caught my eye, and we giggled.

He straightened up. "Maybe *my* home can't be found on a map, but your grandparents' can. Here's what I've been working on."

He drew a circle with a pencil around a point on the older road map. "We know they lived within a ten-mile radius of Randy's Tackle, Bait, and Candy Shop. And we know the bungalow is on the coast."

He marked off the borders. "It must be in between these two points. Anything else you remember? Islands in view? Sandbars? Anything?"

"No. No islands."

"Okay, that's helpful too." He crossed out a couple sections. "So probably not here or here."

A cozy feeling spread through me, like I was wrapped up in one of Grandma West's quilts, but it was seeing Rye working so hard to help me find Mama that warmed me up.

"Thanks, by the way," I said, kicking the floor with the toe of my shoe. "Thanks for doing all this."

His quick smile flashed at me. "We can do this, Haven. We really can."

I grinned back at him. "Lemme find Margie and see how much money we can spend on maps."

Rye startled and began sorting the maps into piles. "Okay, these two are the must-haves. And this one, 'cause I drew on it. These are the probably-should-haves. And these are the it-would-be-nices. And these—"

"I'll be right back," I said, and tried to retrace my steps, but I wound up in the first room again.

The saltwater tank burbled an invitation, but I tried to pretend it was more like a growling dog. Danger. Stay out. Beware of fish.

I found Margie crashed down in a sagging armchair in a corner of Antarctica. With her mask and sunglasses on, her whole face was hidden.

"Hey, M? What's our budget for maps? Rye found a whole bunch, and I can't tell them apart, but he seems to think we need at least five."

"It doesn't matter," she said.

I scratched my shoulder. "So, five's okay?"

"No, I did the math. We only have a quarter tank of gas left." Her shoulders slumped. "We can't get home; we can't get to the gulf. If we keep going, we'll break down out on a country road in the middle of nowhere. We're stuck."

I wanted to press my hands to my ears like Margie used

to when she was little to keep the noise out. But the map store was completely silent—her words were loud enough to tear my world apart.

"We can't stop," I said. "We have to go find her."

She sounded miserable. "I'm so sorry, Haven. I know how much it means to you to get there."

We couldn't give up now. No, we were so close to a way forward! Panic shot through me, but it came out as anger.

"No, you don't," I spewed. "You barely listen to me, and you only believe me when someone else backs me up. You have no idea how I feel!"

Her eyebrows lifted as if I'd ignited something in her. "You're right," she said. "'Cause you're just as bad as Mom. I watch you bottle everything inside. Stone-cold Haven. Won't shed a tear, won't admit you need help. But you actually need help for *everything*. I make sure you have dinner, that your clothes are clean—I freaking chauffeured you across the state!"

"*Halfway* across the state," I shot back.

She sank back into the seat and folded in on herself. "I'm sooooo sorry I'm not everything you want me to be, Haven. I can't fix this for you. We're gonna have to call Dad and get some money so we can get home."

"Sure, give up. Like you gave up on Mama a long time ago," I said, and stomped away.

Furious tears burned my eyes, but I wouldn't let them

fall. Not because I thought I didn't need anybody or whatever she'd said, but because there was no way I'd let Margie think she'd won the argument.

I raced through the rooms, looking for the workshop. This store really did feel like a maze as I made one wrong turn after another.

Tears blurred my vision as I stumbled into the greenhouse room and walked straight into the table filled with colorful bottles.

One of them wobbled.

"No no no no no!" I lunged for it, but I was too slow. The cobalt-blue bottle hit the floor with a *CRASH* and broke into jagged pieces. Water spilled out and splashed on my legs.

Ocean water.

38

I COVERED MY MOUTH SO I wouldn't scream. The change happened so fast.

My hands, webbed.

My joints, soft.

My bones, cracking bending snapping shifting.

My spine, gliding.

My eyes, blinking four eyelids apiece.

My scaly skin registered the warmth of the sun through the glass. The warmth made me fast. I spun around, my tail slamming into the door.

My tail! It had pushed out above my shorts. I tried to tuck it back in, but it was too rigid and wouldn't curl.

"I'll be right there—watch your feet! Don't step on any glass!" I heard Ms. Jeanne's voice from across the store.

I couldn't let her see me! I needed fresh water.

Quickly, I glanced at Ms. Jeanne's other bottles. Maybe one of them had fresh water in it? I reached for a brown bottle, ready to pop it open and pour it out, but I couldn't do it.

It was too much like destroying Mama's cairns. I didn't want to damage Ms. Jeanne's memories. But I needed to shift back to human before someone saw me. Austin was weird, but it wasn't *this* weird.

I'd have to find the bathroom in this labyrinth of a store.

I plunged into Kingdoms of Africa, but my tail was a dang menace. It bumped into everything. I ran into the cartography room, and my tail knocked into a shelf with quill pens. Feathers tumbled to the floor.

Thud, thud, thud. The halls were too narrow. My tail tried to balance me, but it hit the walls with every step. Cross-stitched art rained down.

Where is the bathroom???

I came out into Antarctica, spotted Margie still sunk down in the armchair. Her head lifted, and I spun around to race back the way I'd come.

For a second I considered, *Would it be so bad to break the news to Margie this way that I'm a shape-shifter like Mama?*

I caught my reflection in an evil-eye mirror that hung over the Greek Isles nook. I looked like a deranged crocodile in a dirty T-shirt.

Yes, this would be a TERRIBLE way to let her know.

Rye would know what to do. If I could find my way back

to the workshop, maybe I could hide under the table until he brought me a bottle of water.

But Margie's words had stung when she said I always needed help.

I could do this myself. All I needed was to find the bathroom, splash some water on my hands, and I could change back.

Darting through a room called Maps of Imaginary Places (my tail crashed into a box of maps of Middle-earth), I found myself on the other side of the entryway. I could see through to the front door. But still no bathroom.

"You should get a map to thisss sssstore when you walk in," I grumbled.

Through the front door, I spotted the coffee truck parked on the street.

The solution snapped into place. The truck! It was loaded with water. If I got inside, I could change myself back. I just had to get there without anyone seeing me.

Staying hunched over, I scurried into the entryway. The fish tank hummed beside me, and since it didn't matter anymore, I stuck both hands in the salt water.

"I'm sssorry my handsss aren't clean," I whispered.

That same sense of rightness that I'd felt in the river washed over me. Except I wanted to climb inside, and it wasn't that big a tank. I needed something bigger. Something like an ocean.

No, I needed to focus! I pulled my hands out and dried them on my clothes.

The street was clear. I burst out the front door, just in time to see a dad and his toddler turn on to the sidewalk.

"Daddy! I saw a dinosaur!" the little girl screeched.

I jumped behind the globe and crouched down. Did the little girl see fossifae too?

"The dinosaur was wearing a shirt!" the little girl said, her voice going into a squeak on the final word.

Ooooohhhh. She means me. It didn't feel good to be compared to a dinosaur. They weren't anyone's preferred beauty standard.

"Mm-hmm," the dad said, not looking up from his phone as he tugged his daughter forward. "Oh, look, I think I see Allison already on the slide."

"ALLISON!" the toddler screeched, and took off running.

A car drove by, and then another. And another. Time felt like it was made of razor-sharp seconds, and I felt the cut of each one as they passed.

I wasn't going to get a perfect moment to run. And the longer I waited, the riskier it got to stay where I was.

A blue-and-green car drove past. Its colors reminded me of Harry—that was a good enough sign for me.

I raced for the coffee truck.

"Mommy! Mommy! An alien!"

A different kid, this time a little boy in a Lightning McQueen shirt, was pointing at me. This was bad bad bad.

Why did we park next to a playground???

I reached the back of the truck and yanked on the bolt latch.

"C'mon, c'mon, c'mon," I muttered as my too-flexible fingers tried to get a good grip on the shiny metal latch.

Finally, I got my webbed thumb through the finger hole and pulled the bolt up and out.

The door swung open, and I jumped inside into the shadows. I yanked the door shut behind me.

"Owwww!" I yelped.

I'd closed the door on my tail.

"You dope!" I said through tears of frustration. I was talking to myself AND the tail.

I opened the door enough to get my aching tail in, then shut it hard and slid the interior bolt to lock it.

It should've been pitch-black in there. Instead I could see the inside of the coffee truck almost as clearly as if the windows were open. Must be my kitskara eyes. I could even see color. It wasn't as cool as breathing underwater, but still. Pretty cool.

Moving fast, I found the seven-gallon water jugs with the spigots under the counter and slid one out. My hands shook as I pushed the button down.

Fresh water streamed out. I cupped it in my palm, planning to splash myself with it, but just that handful was enough to start the change.

From inside my skin, I felt the scales recede, my joints stiffen, and my eyes move closer together. I blinked one set of eyelids.

Now the truck was completely dark.

I leaned forward on the prep table and tried to calm down. That had been way too close.

BANG! BANG! BANG!

Someone was beating on the coffee truck door.

39

NERVOUSLY, I SLID THE INSIDE latch to the side and opened the back door.

I blinked in the sun. The mother with the Lightning McQueen kid was standing there. His face looked stormy.

"Hi," she said, her voice strained, "are you serving coffee? Please tell me you are."

Over her head, I saw Rye and Margie walking out of LongLost Maps with their hands empty. I guessed Margie had told Rye the trip was over. I waved to get their attention.

A plan to get us to the gulf was forming in my mind. And all it would take was everyone's favorite beverage.

"Yes, totally. We do coffee." I spoke loudly so Rye and Margie could hear me. "Just give us a few minutes and we can get that coffee for you."

The mother's face creased in worry. "You look very young

to be working." Whatever else she was going to say, she stopped because her son started wailing.

"I *saw* it! I saw the alien!" His face flushed with the indignation of not being believed.

Trust me, buddy, I understand. Leaning forward, I got closer to his level. "I saw it too," I said. "It ran right past my truck. Funny-looking skin, right? Kind of greenish?"

He nodded as a smile cleared his face. "Yeah! And it had brown hair like yours!"

The mother scolded him. "Sorry, he doesn't mean you look like an alien. Fletcher, say you're sorry."

Fletcher looked at me. "I'm not! She does look like the alien."

I felt a surprising thrill. Even when I was a kitskara, this kid thought I looked at least a little bit like human Haven. And no one would actually believe a toddler.

Except Rye, who was coming up behind them and overheard the kid. His eyebrows shot up.

The mother sighed and shrugged her shoulders, seeming to give up on reforming her toddler. "Is it possible to get an iced coffee?"

"I don't think—" I started.

"Yeah, we do iced coffees," Rye said, jumping into the truck beside me. "We can get you a hot one in ten minutes, or an iced one in fifteen, if that's okay."

The mother rolled her eyes. "Oh, I will be living at this

playground for the next two hours. Trust me, I can wait fifteen minutes."

Margie stalked past the knot of us and climbed into the cab of the truck.

The mother looked from me to Rye, and again, her face got worried. "Are y'all okay? You're just so young. Is anyone forcing you to do this?" She dropped her voice on the word "forcing" and narrowed her eyes in Margie's direction.

I said, "Oh, no, we're fine. Think of it like . . . a lemonade stand!"

"We're very entrepreneurial," Rye added.

"Color me impressed," the woman said. "I'll be back in fifteen."

She walked toward the slides, and Rye turned on me.

"An alien?" he repeated in a low voice, then fixed me with a look. "When were you a kitskara?"

I wrapped my arms around my waist to make myself smaller. "It happened in the store—it was an accident. Don't worry, nobody saw except a couple little kids."

"A couple kids?" His face shifted to disbelief. "Your dad has kept your mom's identity a secret for who knows how long to keep her safe. And you're running around in the street? Do you *want* to get caught? You should've come got me so I could help!"

"I can take care of myself," I protested.

"It's too risky!"

"What are you two talking about?" Margie asked, appearing at the door with her sunglasses on her head.

"How to make coffee," I said, covering the conversation.

She groused, "I'm already driving, let's admit it, a stolen coffee truck, without a driver's license, and now we're going to actually sell coffee?"

"Just enough to buy a tank of gas," I said. "I'm not giving up and neither is Rye. Right?"

Rye was still scowling, but he turned to Margie. "We'll need ice. If you go to the end of the block and take a right, you'll see a convenience store with a big freezer out front. Bring back two bags of ice. Haven and I will do the rest."

Surprise turned Margie's green eyes pink, but she pushed her sunglasses onto her nose and marched down the street.

Rye looked like he wanted to say more about my kitskara escapade.

I cut him off before he could start back in. "Let's get to work."

Together we figured out how to unlatch the metal windows of the truck and prop them open. Now we had heads turning in our direction.

"Okay, let's get brewing," Rye said. "We gotta turn the generator on first."

Again, time seemed to have teeth as he figured out what needed to be connected, what buttons to push, where things went.

Rye's dad had taped signs all over the truck with instructions. Good thing, 'cause this stuff was really complicated. The generator lived in a compartment under the truck, and I would've been scared to even touch it otherwise.

We had to make sure all the equipment was off, then turn the tank on. Rye put the generator in something called a "half choke" position, and then he pushed the power button. I nearly jumped out of my skin—it sounded like we were starting up a cranky car. He did it a few times until the generator fired.

"Now we let it run for a bit," he said. "Let's get stuff set up."

We pulled out cups and lids and got the flavored syrups within reach. We found SUNRYE'S COFFEE AND DONUTS stickers in a drawer and slapped them onto cups.

The truck had power now, so we turned on the equipment one by one. First the grinder. We opened one of the big bags of coffee and poured it in. We set it to eleven for Japanese iced coffee and hit the button. It cranked away.

"Now the water," he said. We poured one of the big jugs into the truck's water tank. It was already connected to the coffee maker, and Rye measured out the freshly ground coffee.

"Here goes nothing," he said as the coffee maker started to brew coffee into its carafe.

"How are you so good at all this?" I asked. "I mean, I see

the directions, but I can mess up making hot chocolate from a packet."

"I read instruction manuals for fun," he quipped.

"No, really."

He pulled on one of his curls. "My dad. He taught me how to do everything at Strange Burger, and when he knew he was gonna sell that and do something new, he took me with him anytime he checked out a truck for sale. We learned how to do all the stuff together."

I ventured, "It sounds like your dad was hoping you could love the coffee business the way you loved your burger place."

"Yeah. Maybe."

Margie burst back into the truck with two big bags of ice, a quart of half-and-half, and almond milk.

"Good thinking, Margie," Rye said with admiration.

"You gotta spend money to make money, right?" she said. "Okay, I'll handle the customers and the cash, you two make coffees. If I say we're done, we're done, okay?"

I was still sore from our argument in the store, but I had to admit she was stepping up.

"Thanks for this," I said.

She muttered, "Yeah, I'm amazing. If only child labor and grand theft auto sounded good on college applications."

Rye filled up a plastic cup with ice and carefully poured the hot coffee over it.

"Doesn't that melt the ice?" I asked.

"It's Japanese style," he said, then yelled, "Your iced coffee is ready!"

The woman waved to acknowledge she'd heard us and scooped Fletcher off a spinning seat.

"Quick, give me an empty cup," Margie said.

Rye handed one to her.

She set it up in the window, dug in her pocket, and dropped in a five-dollar bill and some change. "Tips." She shrugged.

The mother held a wriggling Fletcher over her shoulder as she swung a backpack-style diaper bag to her front. "How much do I owe you?"

"Four dollars," Margie said.

I nearly gasped; that seemed outrageous, especially since I was the world's least-experienced barista.

"Do you have change for a five?" the mother asked.

"We don't," Margie said, sounding convincingly sorry. "We're exact change only."

The woman looked like she was about to protest, when Margie pushed her sunglasses up. They were turquoise with orange gleams. Scheming and irritated.

The woman gaped. "Your eyes are stunning."

"Thank you so much," Margie said sweetly. "It's a genetic mutation. I'm lucky it only affected my eyes."

The woman handed over the five-dollar bill without another word. She took the iced coffee and began to walk away.

But when she sipped it, she turned around with a grin. "This is fantastic. Thank you!"

A huge smile broke across my face, and when I looked at Rye, his mirrored mine.

"See?" he said. "It feels good when someone loves what you make, right?"

"Yeah!"

"And cheers to Margie for that eye-color power move," Rye said.

"They gotta be good for something," Margie said with a flicker of true-blue happiness.

Other parents began lining up, and Rye and I were busy with iced coffees and hot coffees. Anytime someone wanted to add a flavor, Rye would yell "Flavor shot!" with the same glee he'd yelled "Skin fart!" in the cab.

I saw what this did for him. He lit up when he was solving problems. Having something to do with his hands made it easier to talk to people, and he chatted with strangers as if they were old friends. No wonder losing Strange Burger had felt like losing a part of himself too.

"Are you going to be here tomorrow?" a guy in a UT shirt asked. "We need a good coffee spot here."

Rye hesitated, then said, "There's a new one going up down the block. You should check it out when it opens. Called Humboldt's."

"Thanks for the tip," the guy said, and walked off with

his almond milk iced coffee with a splash of vanilla.

"That was really nice of you," I whispered to Rye.

He shrugged, but a smile tugged at his lips. "Food people have to stick together."

After an hour, the tip cup was blooming with one-dollar bills, and Margie told us to close up shop.

We lowered the window, and Margie handed Rye some cash. "Here, go get the maps we need."

Rye scampered into LongLost Maps. After all the hubbub, the quiet in the truck felt too heavy.

Margie and I looked at each other warily, like we'd stubbed our toes on each other's unexpected corners.

"You were right," Margie said. "I was giving up. It would be a lot easier to just go home. Every mile we drive, the more I have to accept that Mom is never going to be . . . I don't know, a normal mom? Nobody's normal, but I wish she could really be *with* us, you know? Not locking herself behind a door and leaving us to fend for ourselves."

"Yeah, but . . ." I struggled to find the words for it. "Who she is and what she does are two separate things. She wasn't always so distant, but she *was* always a kitskara."

"True." Margie rolled her shoulders. "But you really see them? The fossifae?"

"I really do," I said. "And there's . . . other stuff too. That's why I need to find Mama so badly. She's the only one who can really tell me what's going on."

"Other stuff?" Margie tilted her head, but when I didn't say more, she didn't push it.

Instead she looped her arm around my shoulder. "I'm sorry I said you always need help. It's not true, and I should've talked to you before just deciding that the trip was over. Selling coffee was a really smart idea."

"Thanks, M," I said. I wrapped my arms around her waist. She hugged me tight.

"We'll get through this," she said.

Rye rapped on the back door. "Got 'em!"

Margie broke the hug. "Okay, load up. I wanna get gone before anyone gets too curious."

Before Rye climbed in beside me, I saw him run his hand along the hood of the coffee truck the way my dad sometimes did with his beloved tractor. Maybe he could learn to love the coffee business after all.

Margie turned on the truck. "We'll get gas and potty breaks once we're out of Austin. I'm not paying city prices for gas."

As LongLost Maps faded in the rearview mirror, I thought, maybe we were always a little lost, always trying to find where we fit.

Margie turned on the radio, and Rye immediately started arguing with her.

I smiled.

Maybe home was found moment by moment.

I let my eyes drift half-closed and watched the iguanodon on the other side of the windshield munch on low-hanging leaves.

Time to find Mama.

40

RYE WAS THE KIND OF car passenger who fell asleep almost as soon as the motor was running. Margie had learned to let him win the argument about the radio stations because ten minutes later she could do whatever she wanted without him protesting with more than a snore.

As we headed out of town, I noticed Margie eyeing a college girl with pink hair, headphones, and tattoos lounging in front of a fancy-looking bookstore. We drove past, and Margie sighed.

"Did you like her?" I asked, trying to understand her mood.

"Her? Oh, no, I mean, she was pretty, but I just felt like, that's what I want. Not to be her, or to be *with* her, but to be here."

"In Austin," I clarified.

"Eh, this city is a lot, but someplace like this would be nice. Where there's different kinds of people, more people like me."

I pushed the skin around on my kneecap. "How does it feel?"

"How does *what* feel? Being gay?" she asked a little sharply.

I felt a flush of embarrassment, but she'd misunderstood me. "No, how does it feel now that it's not a secret?"

"Well, I still have to tell Mom and Dad," she said, "and that'll probably be it for now. I don't know if I'm ready to be out at school, but I want to be able to be myself when I'm at home, you know?"

She pursed her lips. "But to answer your question, I feel like I've taken off a costume, and now I'm just me. And that feels . . . easier, and exciting, and a little scary, but mostly it feels good."

Her hands were trembling on the wheel.

"Are you okay? You're shaking," I pointed out.

She laughed at herself. "Yeah, I get these shots of adrenaline when I talk about it, even though it's a happy thing. It's not easy yet."

I could understand that. I was still getting heart flutters when I thought about how I'd dashed down the street looking all kitskara-y. Rye was right; it would've been smarter to ask for help.

Margie added, "Mom hid her true self from us all this time, and I see what that leads to."

"What's that?" I asked, dreading the answer.

"The people who love you the most don't even know who you are. She's missing, in every sense." Margie sighed. "I don't want that to be me. And I wish she'd just told us."

I was glad Rye was sleeping. He'd be giving me some kind of look about how I should tell her.

And he was right.

"Hey, Margie, there's something important I need to tell you," I said.

"Can it wait till we're out of town?" she said. "The traffic is picking up, and I should focus."

"Yeah, of course," I said, agreeing too easily.

I pulled the newest road map out of Rye's bag. We'd never picked up a charger, so we'd need to rely on paper to get there. According to Rand McNally, I had three and a half hours to tell her before we reached the coast. Plenty of time.

This was the hardest and longest part of the trip. We drove through towns so small you could start a sentence rolling through the only stop sign and be in the next county before finishing your thought. Long stretches of pasture and farmland passed by like in a dream.

I never got bored. Everywhere I looked there were new fossifae to see. Huge crocodile-like creatures snapped at each other, and an amphibian that looked a lot like it had a toad head on a lizard body swam through long-gone waters.

Things got really cool when we drove into Karch, a small town outside of Bastrop that had a natural history museum. A billboard advertised that the museum had fossils from all over the state.

Most of the fossifae I'd seen up to now had been marine reptiles, ancient fish and bugs, and Permian creatures, but these fossifae were honest to goodness dinosaurs!

A *Pawpawsaurus* walked around looking like an over-grown armadillo. A spiny-backed dinosaur—an *Acrocantho-saurus*, if I remembered right from Mama's books—stalked around with mean-looking teeth.

I froze in my seat. A *Tyrannosaurus rex* stomped into the middle of the road! Suddenly I was extra glad that the fossi-fae couldn't see me too. Its jaws opened in a silent roar as we drove through it.

I looked up in the air and gasped.

"What?" Margie jumped.

"Sorry, I just saw a pteranodon. Wow."

Margie glanced up. "All I see is a crow. Not as cool."

"It's a distant relative," I said.

Beside the fossifae in space, if not in time, were white-tailed deer, wild turkeys, coyotes, and some really unusual farm animal choices, like zebu and water buffalo. Llamas, alpacas, ostriches, and emus—it was a wild, wild Texas, but it was spread out over two hundred miles.

For Margie, it was a strain. She'd never driven so far, and none of us had had enough sleep.

Rest stops were our best friend. We ate Gael's breakfast burritos for a late lunch in Columbus, Texas, parked beside semis that had pulled off for the same things we had: potty breaks, cat naps, and Dr Peppers.

I breathed a big sigh of relief when our path matched up with the Brazos River again. It was nearby by once more, even if it wasn't always in sight. My soul was soothed having it close.

By the time we rolled into Brazoria County, the summer sun was still high but dipping toward evening.

I rolled down the windows, and the salt air of the gulf filled the cab, along with the scents of long grass, fish, and factories.

Margie wrinkled her nose. "I think we're near a chemical processing plant."

Rye sat up and stretched out. "Where are we?"

"We're in Freeport," I said. It was a lot of concrete—fish markets, processing plants, a water treatment plant—all crowding the mouth of the Brazos River. It was impossible to get to the gulf without going through those dangerous waters.

I started to feel a little panicked. We were getting so close, but just when I thought we'd be back on Mama's trail, it felt wrong.

"Mama wouldn't have come this way. It'd be too easy to

get caught, or fished, or—" My throat tightened as I imagined the dangerous industrial waters.

"Hang on." Rye held up one of his maps. "Look at this. There are two mouths to the Brazos River. There's the natural one, that one goes through town and gets used by all the factories. But the second one was manufactured, and it's three miles south. That one"—he tapped the page—"is right by a nature refuge."

"That's gotta be it," I said. "We need to get to the river mouth!"

Everything in me was reaching for the gulf. The sooner we got there, the sooner I would find Mama.

41

"No," Margie said. "We're not driving straight to the gulf."

I turned on my sister. "But that's why we're here! That's what we came all this way for! We can't keep wasting time! We need to go there, NOW."

Margie leaned against the headrest. She looked as rumpled as her clothes. "Look, the sun'll be gone in two hours. We have to find Grandmer and Grandpepper's bungalow, or we're sleeping in the truck. And the bungalow's the most likely place we'll find Mom anyway, right? It's not like she'd still be hanging out right where the Brazos meets the gulf."

Rye nodded his agreement.

"Fine." They were right, but it was hard to convince my body when all I wanted was to crawl out of the cab and race to the coastline.

We got directions to Randy's Tackle, Bait, and Candy Shop from a man with a fishing rod walking to his truck, and as we drove by, places started to look more familiar. After so many surprises in the last couple days, it was nice when things didn't change.

"Remember when we had the brisket at that BBQ place?" I pointed it out.

Margie nodded. "Yeah, Dad had to finish yours because the servings were so big."

"And there's the taqueria with the shrimp tacos that were sooo good," I said.

Margie smiled. "Oh, look, that's where we rented the fishing gear. That was a fun day."

I realized that in all these memories, it was Margie, Papa, and me. Mama and our grandparents had never come.

Swimming at the beach, fishing from a boat, going crabbing. We'd done it all with Papa.

"Remember how Papa always said, 'We're gonna let your mom have some time, just her with her parents'?" I asked.

"Yeah?" Margie said.

I said, "I think he was covering for her."

Rye got it right away. "Your dad took y'all to do stuff so she could be all kitskara'd out with her parents?"

"Yeah. Exactly."

Margie's lip corners turned down. "So, they've been lying to us our whole lives. Even 'daddy-daughter time' had a secret agenda. Great."

She pulled into the parking lot at Randy's, and we all filed out of the cab.

When I stepped out of the truck, the salty breezes were hooks in my skin pulling me toward the sea. Mama was there—I could feel her. I gritted my teeth and tried to focus on what Rye was saying.

He looked around, confused. "Wait, this is a gas station? I thought you said it was a bait shop."

"It's all that and so much more. Listen, we don't have a ton of cash left," Margie warned, "so let's look for some cheap snacks we can use for dinner. No more sodas—we can drink the water in the coffee truck."

I walked into Randy's and felt comforted by how unchanged it was. The TV by the front register was playing telenovelas, like always, and the tinny speakers blared old country music.

Rye was weirded out, though. He whispered, "Gas stations are supposed to smell like gas and hot dogs. This place smells fishy."

I agreed. "Yeah, and the smell gets on everything."

I looked longingly at a package of powdered donuts. They were my favorite, but they definitely weren't dinner material. I grabbed a can of SpaghettiOs and made sure it had a pull tab. Didn't want to trust we'd find a can opener at Grandmer's when we couldn't even assume we'd find the bungalow.

As I walked toward the front, I ran my hand over the coolers filled with live bait, glow worms, and all kinds of wrigglers.

Rye raised his eyebrows from the other side. "Yum, yum."

"Eww, no." But I had to wonder, would these look good if I were in the water as a kitskara? Or would I still want the junk food? I'd have to ask Mama.

I reminded myself of the plan. We'd find the bungalow, and then we'd find her. Everything was going to work out.

RANDY'S CANDY ran all the way across the front wall of the store. He stocked every kind of Haribo gummy, most every candy bar I'd ever heard of, plus all the controversial favorites like candy corn, circus peanuts, Junior Mints, and licorice.

Randy was pulling on his white beard as he watched the telenovela play out, so it wasn't until we got up to the register that he even saw us.

"I know you!" he said in his cheery bass voice. If Santa Claus was from South Texas and rode a motorcycle, he'd look and sound like Randy.

"You've gotten so big," he said to me, looking wounded, as if I'd personally promised him I'd stay under four feet tall.

"They just keep feeding me," I said with a shrug.

"And look at you," he said to Margie. "You are the darn spitting image of Maureen in high school. I feel like I've traveled through time, seeing you standing there. But you"—he looked at Rye with bright eyes—"you're new to me."

"I'm Rye," he answered with a low wave. "Their neighbor, friend, and puzzler extraordinaire."

"You don't say? Wow. Hey, where is Maureen?" he asked with friendly curiosity. "She out in the car? Tell her to come in and we'll gab a bit."

Margie shook her head and smiled her prettiest smile. "She's at the bungalow; she just sent us to get snacks. But I got a bit turned around on the way here—do you know how I get back?"

He looked over his round glasses. "Well, I never went there myself, but I know it's down the road a ways. Your grandparents—may they rest in peace—they always complained about the roads. Said they were real bumpy, but then again, they never were much for driving. But yes, your question, you take a left out of the parking lot, turn at the docks, and head south. I don't know past that."

"That's perfect, thanks," she said. "We'll take these."

She pushed across a plastic jar of peanut butter, crackers, the SpaghettiOs, a Dinty Moore beef stew, and a package of hot dogs, no buns.

He rang it up, and she paid for it with the dwindling bills.

"Haven, sweetie, I remember you liking these," he said, and reached over the counter to snag the powdered donuts and added them to the bag. "Just make sure you share 'em. Ain't no fun getting a tummyache."

"Thanks, Mr. Randy." I smiled, even though he was talking to me like I was six years old. For free donuts, he could ask me about my favorite character on *Sesame Street*, and I wouldn't mind.

And for the record, it was Grover. I liked anxious monsters that tried really hard.

We got back in the truck, and Margie said, "Okay, Rye. You got it figured out yet? Where are we going?"

He held the maps in front of him and said, "I'm ready, but if anything looks familiar, let me know."

Randy's directions got us out of Freeport and headed toward the salt marshes. We drove slow and let the minutes tick by, trying to time it.

The truck rumbled on the bumpy roads. Everything in the coffee truck rattled. When Margie hit a big rock, something in the back spilled out on the floor.

Rye turned to look into the kitchen. "Oh crap, it was the vanilla syrup. That's gonna be nasty."

"We'll help you clean it up," Margie promised.

The *sssshhhhhere* of the water was so loud I barely heard them. How could they think about anything except the gulf and finding Mama?

"We're nearly there, right?" I asked, feeling jittery. "There should be a turn soon, on the left."

"No, it was on the right," Margie said. "I remember for sure."

A few hundred feet later, we got to a stop sign.

The road split three ways.

42

I COULD BARELY SIT IN my seat. The sea was so close, and my skin was hungry for it. Mama was nearby. She was calling to me, I was sure of it. Maybe in the water, or the marshes, or standing in the living room at the bungalow. Somewhere close.

"Left, left, we have to go left," I said.

"I'm telling you, it's right," Margie said.

Margie put the truck in park and hit the emergency blinkers in case anyone came up behind us, although it seemed unlikely. We were alone, and ahead were two national bird refuges. Egrets and spoonbills weren't famous for their driving.

Rye said, "Haven, I think Margie's right. There's an inlet up ahead that could match the coast in your mom's photo. There's no way to get to that beach unless we come up behind it, so, we'd have to go right."

"But—"

"The only thing to the left is water," he said gently.

I slumped down, defeated and grouchy.

Margie turned right, turned off her flashers, and said, "Look, if I'm wrong, we'll just turn around and come back, okay? No big deal."

It felt like a big deal to me. I pulled my knees into my chest and covered my eyes. If I could cover my ears too, I would've.

Mama's voice was everywhere, and she was calling to me. *Hssssshheeeeere. Child of the sea.*

"Are you okay?" Margie asked. "You're reminding me of *me* when I go into sensory overload."

"I'm FINE," I said.

Rye popped his tongue, which said more than words would've.

The coffee truck bumped along. Even I had to admit the road was bad enough to fit our grandparents' description.

"There!" Rye pointed.

How he spotted the bungalow before we did, I'd never know, but Mr. Puzzles had done it. The eaves of the bungalow were just barely visible behind a thick wall of red cedar trees.

Margie pulled the truck up to the higher ground behind the house. Before she even put it in park, I unbuckled and slid out Rye's passenger side. My feet pounded up to the door.

The key was under the mat, like always, but a little rustier. I jiggled it into the lock, and the door swung open.

"Mama?" I called, stepping into the musty bungalow. "Mama! We're here!"

I ran from the living room to the kitchenette, to Mama's old bedroom and into Grandmer and Grandpepper's room. Everything looked the same as the day we'd locked it up after the funeral.

The rooms were silent. Margie stepped inside, and I walked across the living room to pull open the glass sliding door to the deck.

The gulf stretched away in every direction. I scanned the inlet for Mama, but the enormity of the landscape hit me. She could be anywhere. Maybe deep underwater, or soaking in the marshes, or still making her way down the Brazos.

"Where is she?" I asked. "Did we beat her here?"

Margie turned around and left me alone on the deck.

I felt confused. The pull I'd felt at the river, the voice that had called me all the way here, I'd been sure it was Mama. But as I stood on the deck, I realized I'd made a terrible mistake.

Shhhheeeeeeere. The sound was in the rustle of the marsh grasses, the splash of the porpoises as they leaped out of the water like jumping beans, in the hush of the inlet water.

It had never been Mama. It was the gulf all along.

She could be anywhere. If we were wrong about where she was headed, we had come all this way for nothing.

A deep fishing boat went along the horizon with its nets out trawling. I used to like watching them, but now I shivered. It would be terrible to get caught in one of their nets.

I couldn't tell Margie I'd been wrong about my special ability to find Mama. I just couldn't.

Hearing Margie and Rye clattering around inside the bungalow, I forced myself away from the water and went inside.

Margie's sunglasses were on top of her head, and her eyes shifted between orange and gray. Irritated and worried.

"Did you know Mom never packed this place up?" Margie said. "I could've sworn she'd done it before the funeral."

The rooms were unchanged, but instead of feeling homey and familiar, it felt wrong. Even though the bungalow was cluttered with plant pots, deck furniture, and a plastic card table, without Grandmer and Grandpepper, it felt impossibly empty.

All the furniture was plastic. Even the futon couch was covered in plastic. I used to think that was weird since they'd lived off the grid and tried to lead an organic, sustainable lifestyle, but now I saw it probably had more to do with having stuff that could dry fast when they came in wet.

Margie stated the obvious. "She's not here."

"She's probably out there," I said, pointing to the gulf.

"So, if I see a reptilian human-shaped thing crawl on the deck, I should assume it's Mom and not an alligator?" She was trying to be funny, but her eyes told the truth. She was really, really nervous, and that stung. Would she be scared of me too?

"Shape-shifting human-OIDS!" Rye cheered from the kitchenette, out of sight. "Anyone hungry?"

"Let's find the sleeping bags first," Margie suggested. "When the sun's gone, there's not much we can do besides go to bed, and I'm so tired I could sleep for a month."

Rye walked into the living room with a horrified look on his face. "Do NOT open the fridge in there. It smells like death."

Margie groaned.

I returned to Mama's old bedroom. Here, moisture had done some damage. Her white metal twin bed was rusting at the joints, and the posters and photos on the wall were rippled and pulling away from the tape. I pushed the window open to air it out.

I looked at Mama's room with new eyes. A photo of her and Dr. Kay as teenagers was on the wall right by her bed. They looked gleeful and giddy, with hair pulled into high ponytails and bright lip gloss. On the other wall, she had a shelf with seashells and fossils arranged carefully, a lot like the ones we used to have in our living room. Posters of '90s teen heartthrobs were taped to her closet door. I wondered if she'd actually liked them, or if it was just another way to try and fit in.

A watercolor portrait of Mama, painted by Grandmer,

hung on the wall behind protective glass. Even so, mildew dotted the matte. Her blue-green eyes were sad as they looked straight into me from behind her red curls. It must've been hard to be different from everyone she knew.

The portrait got me thinking of Grandmer. She didn't paint often, but when she did, it really made you stop and look. She understood water and light better than anyone.

When we'd walked in, I'd thought the bungalow felt empty, but it was crowded with memories. Like, Grandmer had a croaky laugh, and I'd heard it often 'cause she thought I was pretty funny.

Grandpepper had been quiet, but it was the good kind of quiet, where you could tell him about anything and knew he was really listening. The last time we'd visited I'd talked his ear off about all the stickers I was going to use to decorate my binder for school. Not the most fascinating topic, but you'd never know it, 'cause he'd ask little questions to keep me talking.

An ache spread through my chest. They were gone, and I couldn't get that time with them back.

I dug into Mama's old closet and found the sleeping bags inside plastic zippered bags, but no pillows.

I threw the sleeping bags into the living room and popped into Grandmer and Grandpepper's room, which was totally empty, unsurprisingly. They never spent much time indoors. The closet in here was bigger, though.

"Found pillows!" I said.

"Awesome!" Rye called back.

Nestled under the pillows was a plastic tub of art supplies. Sitting down, I pulled it into my lap and pried the lid off. Gently, I picked up the paintbrushes my kitskara grandmother had used to reflect the world around her. Another pang went through me at not having gotten to know her better. I wished that I'd tried harder.

Then my heart skipped a beat. Behind her paints, in a Ziploc bag, was an embroidery kit. I pulled it out and saw embroidery floss, fabric, needles, a hoop, and a simple seashell pattern half-completed.

Cross-Stitch for Beginners. Had Grandmer been starting a new hobby before she passed? I held it like a treasure. The new knowledge felt like a connection to her.

I brought the kit out with the pillows to the living room and tucked it into my canvas bag.

"Rye, if you want to sleep on the bed or the futon, you can," I said. "We know how you feel about roughing it."

"I think I've toughened up a lot in my one night on the run," he said, "but, uh, yeah, I'll probably take the couch if that's okay with y'all."

"You can have Mama's bed, Margie," I said. "I might sleep outside." It would be easier to slip into the water unnoticed that way.

The evening crept by. I managed to keep myself out of

the marsh by playing cards. We'd found a sealed deck in the kitchen drawer and played every game we knew out on the porch. Rummy, gin rummy, spades, Texas blackjack, and when we got too tired to think, Go Fish.

Margie sighed. "If she's still not here in the morning, we'll go back to Randy's and call Dad. Let him know we're on our way back."

"What?" I straightened. "We can't go back without her."

"We thought she'd be here, and she's not," Margie said, her voice getting testy. "I don't want to stay at mildew mansion, with no electricity, just to wait for someone who may or may not show up.

"Besides," she said, going back to cool and distant, "we have to get Rye's dad's truck back to him."

Rye looked at me but said nothing.

I folded my hand. "This is no fun—Rye wins everything."

He said, "If you study some game strategy, you could—"

"I don't care!" I said, and walked down to the dock.

Margie couldn't understand; she wasn't like me or Mama—even though she looked like her.

Because you haven't told her.

I shouldn't have to tell her, I argued with myself. *She should just trust me.*

Like you trusted Papa?

Ughhh. Did having two physical forms also come with

a double personality? I didn't want to fight myself. I didn't really want to fight Margie and Rye either.

The sun set. The stars came out. I moved back onto the deck and apologized for yelling.

Margie yawned. "Apology accepted. I get it—we're all super tired and stressed. I love you, you're fine, and with that, I'm going to bed."

Rye followed soon after.

I tucked myself into my sleeping bag outside and watched bats fly between me and the stars. When I heard Rye's snores and Margie's even breathing, I moved out of the sleeping bag and tiptoed down the dock.

The gulf beckoned. And beyond the gulf, the ocean.

My bones sang with it as I piled my clothes at the end of the dock.

My heart whirred with the countless minnows, shrimp, catfish, and a few large snook I could somehow sense all around me.

I stepped into the salt marsh and let the Haven I knew melt away.

43

THE CHANGE WAS EVEN FASTER this time, and nearly painless. Webbing grew between all my digits, and my ribs gaped open, ready to breathe underwater. The sand under my feet was coarse. The water looked black under the night sky as I walked toward the moon's reflection in the gulf.

The water was at my knees, then my hips, then I had to start swimming to stay afloat. I looked down, and the floor had dropped below the reach of moonlight. It looked bottomless.

There was so much *muchness*. It made me too nervous—I swam back to shallower water.

I touched my feet down, and the water closed over my head. My brain fought it until my gills took over, then it felt natural. I was breathing underwater! On purpose this time!

Shadowy, silvery figures moved in the dark. I crouched

down until I could dig my fingers into the sand. I was always able to see the fossifae better when I was touching the earth their fossils were in.

The forms filled out, and I saw the long, graceful neck of a brachiosaur arching high above the cedars. I couldn't help it; I laughed out loud underwater 'cause I was so excited. Nearby, the clubby tail of a *Pawpawsaurus* swung from side to side. Mammoths lumbered across the marsh. Ancient fish arced over my head.

Shimmering creatures slithered toward me, and I watched and waited. They swarmed around me, against me, through me. I braced myself for some kind of shock, but it didn't hurt. There was only a sense of bone memory.

Child of the sea.

Remember with me.

They weren't my memories. They belonged to the water and the earth.

"I see," I bubbled. "I'll remember."

A memory of my own resurfaced. It was from a video I didn't watch very often because it made me sad: Grandma West in her hospital bed the day before she passed, and me in her arms, all of age three.

She'd said, "Haven, soon you won't be able to feel me, but I haven't gone anywhere. I'm right here with you, and I will never stop loving you. That's what grandmas and mamas do. They love."

Out of sight on this video, I could hear Papa crying 'cause he knew he was losing his mother.

But Grandma West never stopped hugging me. "I'll live in your heart, and as long as you live, so will I. I love you, baby girl."

"I love you too," I'd told her, and patted her face. After that, in the video, I started telling her about what movie I was going to watch when I got home, so Mama had stopped recording, but Grandma West was smiling at the end. She'd looked happy that I was three and couldn't really grasp what was going on.

Salty tears streamed from my eyes and blended with the brackish waters of the marsh.

I finally understood. The fossifae were earth's memories of loved ones gone. As long as the earth lived on, they'd never fade entirely. And maybe because my form was shaped by the fossils around me, I could remember them, and love them too.

Something large rolled over in the water near me. I blinked. That was not a fossifae.

The long reptilian form of an alligator floated upward.

I looked around in the dim water, but I couldn't see anything else. How many alligators were nearby? And would they see me as friend or prey? Professional colleague?

This was the kind of practical question I would've liked to ask Mama on day one of my kitskara experience. I didn't want to find out for myself.

I paddled quickly toward the dock and hauled myself

out. Just as I did, I heard a strange murmur in the water. A low, bass sound. I twisted around to try and see where it was coming from.

Out in the gulf, outside of this inlet, something slender and silvery splashed into the water. But the moon cast strange lights on the surface, and it was impossible to see what had made that sound.

Another long-extinct mosasaur snapped its jaws out in the deep. It didn't matter how many times I saw them, they were scary. I pulled my feet out of the water. Even if the mosasaur was in a different plane, the alligators were here, and I wanted to keep my feet.

Now to go splash some fresh water on my hands, change back, and get in the pajamas I'd scavenged. Mama would be here in the morning. Right?

I gathered my clothes and turned around.

A shadowy human shape stood ten feet away, watching me.

The moon silvered her red curls, and for a moment, I thought my search had finally ended.

But it wasn't Mama. It was Margie.

"When were you going to tell me?" she asked.

"Umm, it was hard to find the right time, but ssssoon. It was going to be ssssoon." I held my clothes in front of me like they could shield me from her disappointment.

"You don't sound like you," she said, taking a step away from me.

It hurt to hear her say that. I'd noticed the same thing with Mama, but it still stung.

"I'm ssssorry I didn't tell you before, I jusssst . . ." I trailed off and hugged my clothes closer.

"Who else knows?" she asked.

"Jussst Rye. He sssaw me the firsssst time it happened," I said.

"So, Rye has known this entire time," she said. "This whole trip he knew this about you, but I didn't? Why didn't you tell me?"

I looked at my webbed feet, then back up at her. "I didn't want it to be true."

She chuckled joylessly. "A shape-shifting humanoid. I don't think I actually fully believed it until now."

I flinched at her words.

She dropped her head back, and I thought she might cry. Instead she screamed, and I nearly jumped out of my skin.

"Dang, that felt good. Try it."

I opened my mouth—my jaw unhinged, which was a surprise—and screamed as hard as I could. My fear, my anger, my frustration, and my deep, bottomless need emptied into the sky.

The birds in the trees went silent. Even the bullfrogs paused their songs. For a moment, it felt like the tide hung for a second longer on the shore. Then the night music took back over, the tide drew out, and it was just me and Margie staring each other down.

"We both had sssecrets," I said. "I wanted to tell you. I was jussst ssscared."

She let go of a loud breath. "This is just a lot, you know? But, okay. You're a kitskara."

"And you're gay."

She burst out laughing. "You know, I felt pretty alone, but I have a feeling there's a lot more like me than there are you."

I laughed with her, but my heart sank. Unless Mama came back, I might be the only one like me in the world.

"How do you . . ." She waved her hands in my direction. ". . . change back? Not that you have to."

"Fresh water," I said. "I can jussst sssplash sssome water on my hands; it doesn't take much."

She cocked her head. "How about I get the shower going for you instead? That might feel good."

I blinked tears away with my double eyelids. Seemed like I was always on the verge of crying lately. "That sssounds really nice."

She said, "Remember, there's no water heater, so it'll be chilly, and you'll have to use flashlights to see what you're doing."

"I have been here before." I laughed. "I didn't get a new brain when I transsssformed."

But that wasn't entirely true, was it? My thoughts got less . . . human like this. And the more I thought about it, the more I wondered if that was why we hadn't seen Mama yet.

44

WHEN I WOKE UP, A seagull was perched beside my head. I yelped and jerked away from the pointy-beaked bird. It flapped up to the deck railing and cawed something that sounded very inappropriate to me.

"You hungry, Haven?" Rye asked. He slid open the door and left it that way. "I brought you breakfast."

The seagull flapped down to the water at the noise.

Rye held out a small glass plate that held an orange, four Ritz crackers with peanut butter, and a single powdered donut.

That can of sardines that Lynne had packed us was calling my name for the first time in my life. Salty fish would go great with these crackers. But I wanted to save it for Mama.

"Yeah, thanks. This looks . . . edible."

He sat down beside me with an apple. His mouth was

already smeared with white donut powder. "I heard the good news."

"What's that?" I asked. I peeled my orange and threw the scraps toward the seagull. It hopped away, then flew back and scooped it up, swallowing it whole.

"Margie said she saw you last night looking all kitskara-y."

I quartered the fruit. "Yep. No more secrets. Thank goodness."

"None?" He grinned. "That's new."

My stomach flip-flopped at that smile. "I mean, don't tell anyone that I talk to Harry like he's a person."

"They already know." He leaned back on his elbows.

"You just moved here! You don't know everyone!" I argued.

"Trust me, they know."

The coffee truck's motor rumbled, and I turned to see Margie pulling into the drive. "Wait, Margie left and came back already? Where'd she go?"

Rye took a bite of apple. "Yeah, about an hour ago she went to Randy's to call our folks. I gave her my mom's number—I miss her, but I didn't want to make that call. She's not gonna be happy."

My blood chilled. She'd told Papa where we were.

Margie stomped through the house and out to the deck.

Rye shrank in on himself. "Soooo, how'd it go?"

She threw the truck keys onto the deck floor. "We

are, and I quote, all grounded until the second coming of Christ, or until hell freezes over, whichever happens first. We are to stay right here until they arrive. We are not, under any circumstances, to even think about driving anywhere—"

"Wait, they're coming here?" I asked.

"Who is?" Rye worried.

"Dad and Rye's mom," Margie said. "They're on the next plane from Dallas to Houston, and then they're driving here. I think they'll be here by three p.m. or something."

"Why'd you tell them where we are?" I cried.

She sat down heavily on the deck. "Because I couldn't let them wonder about us anymore! It's terrible not knowing about Mom. I don't want to do that to them."

"Grounded," Rye said stonily.

She dropped her head in her hands. "It's fine, my plan was to just stay home and get my grades up so I can try to get into a good school anyway."

"This isn't fair! No one else is even trying to find Mama," I said.

Margie's head snapped up, and she stared at the water. A moment later, I heard it too.

A low, bassoon-like sound rose to a high, siren-like shriek.

It gave me chills to hear it. It sounded painful, and despairing, and lonely.

Rye looked between us. "What the heck was that?"

I looked at Margie. "Would you believe me if I say I think that was Mama?"

She nodded. "That wasn't animal, and it wasn't human. It was . . . other."

I stood up and stared at the gulf. "It came from out there."

"We need a boat," Rye said.

"We don't have a boat," I said. "How are we going to get to her?"

Margie stood beside me. "But we have you."

I looked at her. "I've only shifted three times, and I've never gone out in deep water—I have no idea what I'm doing!"

Margie took my hands in hers. "Heyyy. You're a West girl. Tough as dirt and wildflower pretty, right? But you're more than that. You can do something we can't. You can go find Mama, in *her* world. I believe in you. Rye?"

He shoved his hands in his pockets and nodded. "I'd bet on you every time."

My heart was pounding out of my chest. Margie was right. It had to be me.

45

MARGIE SLID HER SILVER BRACELET over my other wrist and tightened the clasp. "Remember to come back," she said. "If you find Mom, great; if you don't, it's fine. Don't stay out there too long."

I'd told her about how the longer I stayed in the water, the harder it was to remember human stuff, and it had scared her pretty bad. She wouldn't let me go unless I had something more to remind me.

I'd wrapped myself in one of Grandmer's old robes. "Okay, I'm ready."

"Call to me if you need me," Margie said. "I'll be able to hear you farther than you think."

I stepped into the water. My skin shifted to a mottled brown and green, and I blinked both eyelids against the bright sun.

Margie's gasp made me turn around. She and Rye were both openly staring. I got it—they'd never seen it happen before—but it's not like it made me feel good.

I handed her the robe. "Take a picture next time," I said. "Actually, don't."

The shallow water was brown and full of sediment and debris. Branches floated by, and I stepped on little bits of root and old logs. But even though the water wasn't clear, I could see a lot easier than at night, and I wasn't as worried about surprising an alligator.

One hundred feet out, the shallow coast began to descend into the continental shelf. I knew it didn't get super deep until you were about a hundred nautical miles offshore, but it was still three times as deep as anything I'd ever swum in before.

It would help if I knew where to start.

I called back to Margie, "Do you hear a heartbeat?"

"Just yours," she called back. "But I'll keep listening."

Rye's voice traveled over the water. "I wish I could get higher to get a better view."

"Good luck with that," I yelled. "Thisss shore is as flat as a dog's butt."

Maybe if I let the gulf pull me, like it had been since I'd first stepped in the Brazos a few days ago, it would take me to the same place Mama had gone.

I tried again to open my senses, but it was too much. And then it was *much* too much.

I blinked and saw plesiosaurs. Blinked and saw the choppy water. Blinked and saw ancient sharks. The fossifae crowded my vision until all I saw was silvery light. Too much noise, so many memories that weren't mine.

"Margie?" I called back. I could hear the panic tingeing my own voice.

"What's wrong?" Her worried face watched me from the dock.

"What do you"—I gulped air—"what do you do when the sssounds are too much? Right now I'm getting . . . a lot— and I don't know how to ssstop it."

I put my hands on my knees and tried to breathe, but my lungs and gills were fighting each other. Looking down, I saw silvery snakes twining around my ankles, and an alligator gar swam by, and the birds wouldn't shut up their racket, and—

"Haven, you know what I do?" Margie called. "I picture my bottommost ribs, like, I really picture the bones. The last ones above the waist. And I breathe into there."

I tried, but it didn't work. "I can't! My gills are trying to breathe too, and I'm—I can't get enough air, or maybe it'sss too much! I don't know!"

"And then"—she kept talking as if I hadn't interrupted— "I think of one really good thing. And I hold on to it like a rope."

One good thing.

Harry appeared in my mind's eye, and I latched on to him. My good, sweet, silly bird who followed me everywhere.

Harry was a good thing.

I put everything into remembering him. The way he bobbed his head as he walked across the backyard. How soft the barbs of his feathers were. The way the greens and blues of his plumes shimmered in the golden sunlight. He fought snakes for me, and he woke me up in the middle of the night, maybe 'cause he was hungry, or maybe because he missed me.

The world calmed down. My gills let my lungs do the breathing. The silvery fossifae faded to fog.

I took a deep breath and refocused on where I was. The warm water around my waist and the dark blue of the water as the coast gave way to the continental shelf.

The bassoon-to-siren cry shattered the air again. It felt like it was a coming from under my feet. *Mama*.

I couldn't wait any longer. I dove in.

46

THERE WAS SO. MUCH. WATER.

I'd gone from feeling like there was never enough to too much. From feeling like I was too big for the river to feeling so incredibly small.

And the gulf itself . . . I knew in my bones that it went on forever and ever, and if I wanted, I could swim away and not stop swimming for a very long time. I could disappear.

That was terrifying. I touched the bracelets and sank deeper underwater.

Crawling up the Brazos River had not prepared me for swimming in deep water. That dang tail! I knew what I needed to do—but I had no idea how to do it.

I flicked my tail, and the action shot me forward and to the right. Flicked again, and I careened to the left.

I threw my arms and legs out to the sides as if I could

grab something, and my motion stopped. I hovered in the water.

This wasn't working.

A school of striped fish circled around me, probably gossiping about the weird alligator who couldn't swim.

Even though I wasn't built like a fish, I watched how their fins and tails worked together. I was more like a water snake with legs. Which, *duh, Haven*, was a salamander.

I couldn't remember ever seeing a salamander swim, but I'd seen plenty of snakes on the ground. Their spines moved through S curves to move forward. Maybe I could do something similar.

Pressing my arms and legs against my body, I wriggled my spine and flicked my tail just a little.

I shot straight forward!

I tried it again. If I thought too hard about it, I ended up darting from side to side. But if I turned my brain off and let my body balance the propulsion from my tail, the motion came a lot easier.

The looseness of my joints was an obvious benefit now as my spine undulated. *Flick, wriggle, swoosh* smoothed into a steady *swoooooosh* forward.

Now I cut through the water fast. I grinned—it was flying, but in the water.

Catfish and flounders lurked on the floor of the gulf, and jellyfish floated through the water like small clouds. Silvery fish darted by, and in the distance, I spotted a turtle swimming ahead of me.

And there was so much debris. I saw abandoned shrimp cages, old tangled nets, and rusty metal scraps from who knows what. It made me sad to see the fish poking around the trash.

A current pulled at me and promised to take me far out to sea. *Shhhh come with me, shhhhh so much to see . . . to sea to sea.*

I touched the silver bracelets on my wrists again and refocused on Mama. All that swimming practice had sent me in different directions. Had I gotten completely off track?

"Mama!" I tried to yell through the water, but without air, I couldn't make noise underwater.

I swam back up to the surface—the sky was a shocking clear blue—and gulped in some air.

Diving down, I tried to shout through the water.

The sound dissipated into bubbles. Useless. I needed to try something else. Maybe I could mimic that bellowing sound I'd heard?

I swam back up and grabbed more air. "Awhoooooo!"

It came out more as a honk. I was embarrassed; Margie had probably heard that, and I sounded like I was part goose, not part magical creature. I took another deep breath of air.

This time, when I dove under, I kept my mouth shut and hummed as big as I could.

A muscle in my throat that I'd never felt before vibrated, and a big bassoon sound emanated from my body.

"AWHOOOOOOOOO!"

Warm tingles of pride swept through me—I'd figured out how to swim, and now I could make noise too.

But would Mama hear me?

I spread my arms and legs to the sides and stilled my tail. Hovering. Waiting. Listening.

Doubt struck. What if she wasn't here at all, and I was completely alone in the gulf? The vastness of the water was overwhelming.

"*Awhooo!*" a weak call answered me.

There! To the side!

Pressing my arms and legs against my body, I twisted left and flicked my tail.

In the distance I could see a lot more fish clumped together. They surrounded an object on the gulf floor about the size of a horse trailer. *Why are they all in one place?*

I swooshed to get closer, and when I saw it, a shiver prickled down my spine all the way to the tip of my tail. A shipwreck!

It looked like the boat had been there a long time. Coral had built up at the base, and every surface was covered in algae and barnacles. Sea urchins reached their spindles out, and fish swam through the long-gone windows. An eel swished through the water in an effortless version of my swimming style. Maybe someday I'd be that good.

"*Awhoooo.*"

I startled—the sound came from inside the wreck. Diving, I peered into the upside-down boat. It was dark inside, but the same eyesight that had made the coffee truck visible in total darkness illuminated the interior of the wreck. More algae, coral, and fish, but there at the far end was something large. Something reptilian and humanoid.

Mama!

Relief swept through me. I'd found her. She was here. Really, really here. But this was the Mama she'd kept secret. My feelings felt as jumbled and crowded as the invertebrates living on the boat.

She turned her head, and when she saw me, her huge eyes blinked rapidly.

Her face looked like I'd seen it the night she left, with globe eyes and a split-wide mouth. It was nothing like the mother I'd known, but undeniably her.

I stared at her as she stared at me.

My heart thumped so big and loud I wondered if Margie could still hear me.

Why wasn't Mama swimming over, hugging me? Even if she didn't recognize me, I'd thought she'd be excited to see another kitskara.

Picking my way inside the wreck, I floated above scurrying crustaceans and tried not to bump my head on the low overhang of the boat.

As I got beside her, she hummed and thrashed weakly, and I saw why she hadn't come to me. Fishing twine curled and tangled around her arms and legs, pinning her in place under the boat.

She was trapped.

47

THERE'S SOMETHING HEART-SICKENING ABOUT SEEING a parent helpless. Even though I'd come all this way with the idea that if I found her, I could help her, or maybe save her. That maybe she'd feel less alone when she learned I was like her. But now that I was staring straight at her, and she needed my help, I wished I didn't have to.

I wanted her to be stronger than everything that held her down. I wished that she'd never gone so far away in the first place, so far that we'd needed five maps to find her.

I wanted her to take care of me, not the other way around.

She hummed a questioning sound, and it jolted me into action. What I wanted and what was real were two different things.

I needed something sharp.

"I'll be back," I tried to say, but it was garbled underwater.

I swam extra carefully out of the boat—I didn't want to get tangled too 'cause then we'd really be stuck.

Adrenaline made it hard to think. Go back to the bungalow and grab a knife? Or maybe scissors? I couldn't remember what we had in the drawers.

Surely there was something sharp enough to cut twine nearby. I recalled the metal scraps I'd seen, but there was no way I could retrace my steps. Er, strokes.

Curious fish followed me as I poked around the wreck. There had to be something here. Maybe an old glass bottle, like at LongLost Maps? Or a fishing knife that someone dropped off the edge of their boat? That would be perfect. But the invertebrates that covered the boat made everything look like one big reef, and the only things I found were netting and more fishing twine.

A thought chilled me. All the fishing detritus meant that people knew about this spot and came here regularly. We couldn't risk anyone finding us, not in this form. I glanced up, but the water was clear overhead. For now.

Along with the fish, a fossifae shark swam a loose circle around me.

Wait.

To see a fossifae this clearly, I must be near its bones. That gave me an idea.

Staying close to the gulf floor, I ran my hands along the sand. Images flooded my mind—tiny crustaceans, mollusks, ammonites, all moving through the water. Millions of fossi-fae fish pressed on my mind, but I imagined a bubble around me, and I pushed them out. I kept moving, letting the images flow through me. And then, when the shark came into vibrant view, I stopped. I dug into the ground. Sand and silt clouded the water as I felt for hard bits of bone.

There!

I held up my treasure. It was a common find, on land or at the beach, but I'd never been happier to see one.

A shark tooth.

I knew from listening to the anglers at Randy's Tackle, Bait, and Candy Shop that sharks could cut through anything that wasn't metal. Especially fishing twine.

I swam back toward the wreck.

Mama's globe eyes watched me carefully as I approached her. She thrummed at me, but I couldn't understand her.

Slipping the tooth under the twine near her arms, I sawed with the serrated edge. Here, my flexible joints made this tricky. It was hard to keep a good grip on the tooth. But I kept at it until the twine frayed and snapped.

One arm was freed, and she reached out to touch my face. Did she know it was me, her daughter? Or was she just grateful? I tried to hum *Mama* at her, but her expression was unreadable.

Maybe I was already too late, and she'd forgotten she'd ever been human. The shark tooth shook in my hand at the thought.

I moved toward her knees. Mama's tail twitched, but the twine kept it bound to her legs. She wriggled as I began sawing again, and the tooth slipped to the ground. I barked a grumbly sound at her as I picked it up. She stilled.

She also never took her eyes off me.

My mind hadn't gotten fuzzy in the gulf the way it had in the river. Maybe it was 'cause every stroke I took, I saw Margie's and my bracelets. Or maybe it was just that here a kitskara could be fully awake. The river was too shallow for anything but dreams of the ocean.

The shark's tooth worked away at the twine until it finally snapped. I pulled it off her in loops. She stayed still until it all fell away, then darted out of the boat, as quick as any fish I'd ever seen.

I followed behind her until we were both free of the wreck. The fishing junk everywhere made me nervous—I kept checking to see if there was a boat above us.

A shadow passed overhead, and I looked up, scared I'd see human faces looking down. But instead I stared into a mouthful of sharp teeth, and this time it wasn't a long-extinct mosasaur, terrifying but harmless.

It was a big white shark, and it was very much alive.

48

THERE WAS NOWHERE TO HIDE, and I couldn't outswim it—I'd only just figured out undulatory locomotion!

I twisted around, trying to keep the shark in front of me. I had no idea what to do if it attacked, but I wanted to keep my eyes on it.

Mama swam above me and reached her hand out toward the shark. Maybe she could do some advanced kitskara magic thing that would save us!

But if she did anything magical, I missed it. All I saw was her scratch the shark's belly as it swam over her.

She looked at me as if to say, *See?*

I swam up beside her.

The shark circled lower to come back. Just as it passed by us, I reached my webbed hand out and skimmed its rough back.

I laughed, and the sound bubbled underwater. Mama's face split like a frog puppet into a wide grin.

Mama swam around me, humming a kind of song language I didn't know, fluttering her finned hands with excitement.

But her eyes were as cold as the shark's. She was completely kitskara, not human. She didn't recognize me, and it made me want to cry.

"Mama," I tried to say, but underwater, the word didn't carry right. She looked at me funny, as if wondering why this kitskara girl was trying to use people sounds.

I couldn't go back to Margie and leave Mama behind. But I didn't know what to do. I couldn't make her come with me, and I couldn't force her to remember.

I reached out for the shark, who was making its third circle to get belly rubs and back scratches, when a gleam of light from the sun hit the bracelet on my wrist.

Mama turned her head to look at it through her right eye, then swiveled to look at it from her left. Her mouth opened in interest.

Dr. Kay's words from the fire came back to me. They hadn't seemed important then. *Finfolk love silver, so you could throw a silver coin at them to escape.*

Or maybe even catch one. I held up my wrists in front of me and shook the bracelets.

Her hands reached for them, and I darted out of reach.

Kicking as fast as I could, I swam toward the surface and trusted she'd follow me. I needed to get her home and turn her back to human so she could remember me. *Us.* Somehow.

At the surface, I twisted around, searching for the shore.

Mama swam underwater nearby. She popped up and chittered in a worried way—I got the feeling she was trying to get me to come back under with her. I'm sure she was right, that it was dangerous for us to stay near the surface.

But first I had to figure out where home was.

I treaded water and turned in a slow circle. There was no shoreline. Only endless water.

I was lost.

Mama grabbed my hand and tried to tug me down. I yanked my hand free.

Could my sister hear me from this far away? It seemed impossible, but I didn't know what her limits were.

"Margieeeeee!" I yelled, and then I keened as high and long and loud as I could. "Where are you?"

I'd screamed that same question at the Breaks. I'd gotten no answer then. And I realized I wouldn't get one now either.

Even if Margie did hear me, how would I hear her? My senses weren't as strong as hers.

Mama's hand grabbed my ankle and pulled me under the water.

I kicked at her until she let go. But she swam up beside me and grabbed my wrist again, bringing her eyes close to it. It was probably too much to hope that she recognized the bracelets when she didn't recognize me.

Our heads turned at the same instant—to my right, a distant *hoooonnnnk* traveled through the water.

A grin split my face. I knew that horn. I'd heard it in Austin traffic more than a few times.

It was the coffee truck—Margie and Rye were leading me home.

Suddenly the gulf didn't feel so vast.

I turned and *flicked, wriggled, swooshed* until it evened out and I could *swoooooooosh* forward. Mama kept up with me easily, and I tried to copy the easy way she moved. She made it look so simple.

I needn't have worried. She wasn't gonna let another kitskara out of her sight.

The horn never let up. I pictured Rye leaning on the horn and Margie on the dock, watching the horizon and waiting. I wouldn't let them down.

The gulf got shallower, and the sun seemed brighter as we got closer to land. I popped my head up—the shore was in sight. Almost there!

"I see her, you can stop!" Margie was on the dock like I'd pictured her, but her hands were pressed against her ears. The sound must be hurting her, but she'd kept her headphones off to listen for me. My heart swelled with love for my big sister.

The horn faded. I felt the shift from the fully salty water to the brackish waters of the salt marsh as I dove through the inlet. When it got to just a few feet in depth, I stood up.

Margie stood at the edge of the dock. She took me in with one glance, then looked beyond me. "Where is she?"

I turned around. Mama had been right beside me the whole time. But now she was a hundred feet behind me at the mouth of the inlet. She ducked nervously and popped back up.

"There." I pointed. Standing in the marsh between Mama and Margie, I felt like a bridge between the two worlds. I just hoped they'd be able to meet in the middle.

"What's she doing?" Margie asked.

"She's ssstill all kitsssskara," I said. "I don't think she remembers anything yet."

"So what now?" she said, sounding angry and hopeless at the same time. "Why can't our own mother remember us?"

I watched Mama and tried to figure out a way to describe what it was like to go down the rabbit hole of kitskara brain, but I couldn't.

"She's trying," I said, hoping to convince both of us.

Rye joined Margie on the dock. "Can you change her back to human?"

Margie started coming up with ideas. "We need fresh water, right? Haven, what if I get you a bottle of water, and you swim it out to her and dump it on her head or something."

I didn't think that would work. We needed something bigger. Enough fresh water to counter the gulf.

I knew the inlet had a lower salt level—that's why we'd never been allowed to swim in it when we were kids. Things could grow in it that were really dangerous for humans, like flesh-eating bacteria. If we could flood the inlet with fresh water, maybe that would shift the balance just enough to change her back. I had to try.

I held both wrists out and shook them. She followed them with her eyes and swam a little farther in.

"Come here," I said. "If you come closssser, I'll give it to you."

She cocked her head. Considering it.

"What are you doing?" Margie whispered.

"Trusssst me," I said.

Mama swam in until the marsh got so shallow, she had to crawl using her hands and feet splayed to the side to stay underwater like I'd done in the Brazos.

When she was ten feet away, she leaned back on her knees and held out her hands in a clear *throw it to me* gesture.

Making a big show of it, I unclasped my bracelet. As I did, I dug my toes into the ground. Just like at Dr. Kay's, I felt a surge of energy. But it was a clearer and stronger connection to the earth than I'd felt before. Probably 'cause I was in the water, and in my kitskara form.

I still didn't know how any of this worked.

But I was a kitskara, a weather sorcerer, a shape-shifter, and a West girl.

I tossed the bracelet—Mama stood up out of the water to catch it—and I dropped down to dig my fingers into the mucky marsh ground, humming as I did. I'd listened to the river and the gulf call me, and now it was my turn.

I called for a storm.

49

THE SURFACE OF THE WATER out in the gulf got choppier.
The light overhead dimmed as clouds gathered.

I focused completely on my melody. It was something I
made up out of Mama's lullaby and one of the country songs
I'd heard on the radio—and the feel of my body in the water.
The marsh was like me: salt and fresh, land and sea, a place
of shifting both-ness.

Fossifae moved around us in the water. A plesiosaur
paddled past the inlet, and I almost got distracted, but I con-
centrated hard on this moment.

I called, and the earth answered. At first, I felt a single drop.

Rain splattered on the water's surface, and then it poured.

I stood up out of the water and felt my body shift back to
human. Margie—flesh-eating bacteria be damned—jumped
into the water and wrapped a robe around me.

She helped me up onto the dock, and we both turned to look at Mama.

Her lower half was in the water, her upper half still upright where she'd caught the bracelet.

She flickered in the rain. The fresh water kept shifting her toward human, but not completely. I watched her face as it molded into my mother's, then morphed back into the shape of a lizard's. She clutched the bracelet in one hand and held the other hand out as if trying to make the changes stop.

I needed her to remember. I needed *her*.

More, I called. *Wilder!*

The wind picked up and the rain drove down in torrents. The gulf outside the inlet got choppy and white capped.

I saw when it happened. When the rain was heavy enough that fresh water won. The moment when Mama remembered. Her red hair clung to her too-thin pale body, and she stared at us with disbelieving eyes. Joy, grief, longing, sadness—the emotions shifted across her face in as complicated a transformation as the one we'd just watched from kitskara to human.

And I saw, with my breaking heart, how she turned to look at the gulf. That part of her wanted to dive in and forget all over again.

Words gathered at my lips. Promises and apologies. How I'd never disturb her bone garden again, that I'd help Margie with dinner, that Mama wouldn't need to lift a finger, if only she'd come home. That I'd try every day to make her smile.

If she wanted to rock in her chair all day, that was fine. She could teach me the Orcadian dialect, and I'd sing it to her so she didn't feel so alone all the time.

But the words wouldn't come. I realized in a flash as clear as the lightning overhead that it wasn't up to me.

Mama's sadness was like the rain. No matter how far I went or how fast I was, I couldn't catch it for her. And I certainly couldn't hold it all. No matter if I was human or kitskara, I couldn't bring her to land unless she caught the rope.

I was a rope. Margie was a rope. Papa was a rope.

And she hadn't caught us in a long, long time.

Mama turned away so we couldn't see her face.

My tears came then. The ones I'd held back for so long I didn't know what else to do with them. As I cried, the driving rain softened to a steady patter. The winds became breezes, and the waves tossed but lost their white caps.

A strong hand curled around mine—Margie. A softer, slimmer one took my other hand—Rye. We stood three across as the rain drenched us all.

Only Mama could make the choice to come out or stay where she was. Not me. It had never been up to me, and it wasn't supposed to be.

She looked at us from the water, clenching the silver bracelet in her hand.

Mama wiped the rain out of her eyes, smiled, and began to walk in toward us.

50

MARGIE WRAPPED MAMA IN ANOTHER of Grandmer's robes. I made a quick, sniffly introduction to Rye, and Mama shook his hand in a friendly but confused way.

Rye excused himself. "I need to clean up the truck," he said. "Ants'll get into that syrup if I don't. I hate ants."

"They're the worst," I agreed. I knew he was giving us space, and I was grateful. Margie, Mama, and I were all as tender as a powder keg.

Rye disappeared up the dock and into the coffee truck.

That left Margie and me alone with her. For a moment, we all just stared at each other, and then Mama wrapped us up in a big hug.

I melted into her arms. She smelled like mud, rain, and growing things. She smelled like *her*. I drank in that scent and held on tight.

"My girls," she said, her voice raspy with emotion. "My girls, you're here."

"We're here, Mama," I said, and then I broke down bawling all over again. My emotions were as fluid as the inlet we stood in.

"I'm sorry," I blurted. "For destroying your bone garden. I know how important it was to you, and I didn't do it on purpose, not completely anyway, and I felt so bad." The big realizations I'd just had about emotional responsibility and whatever? They vanished in my desperation to keep Mama now that I'd found her again.

My voice broke. "I've tried to be cheerful, Margie's tried to pick up all the slack, Papa just kept hoping—we've all tried so hard, but it's not enough. I don't know how to make you happy, and I wish I did. Please come back home."

The words were barely out of my mouth before Mama wrapped me in the tightest hug. "No, no, no, Haven, you do make me happy. Both of you, so very, very much. Don't ever think that. You could never do anything that would make me leave you."

"But you did," my voice quivered. "And you lied to us about who you are."

"Kind of a family trait," Margie muttered.

Mama's eyes darkened to a worried gray. I realized with a jolt that her eyes were changing colors again! That hadn't happened in over a year.

She said, "What you saw, me, out in the water, that is, I've tried to figure out how to tell you, but it's so hard, and I didn't want to . . . but you should know . . . you see, your grandparents . . ."

"You're a kitskara," I said. "We know."

She stared at me. "How do you know that word? Did your father tell you?"

We shook our heads.

I said, "Papa wouldn't tell us anything helpful. He said you'd probably gone to your parents' place, which did turn out to be true, I guess."

"But Haven had seen you the night you left, when you didn't look human," Margie said, "so she wouldn't let it go. She knew there was more to the story than that."

I nodded. "Rye helped me find Dr. Kay's paper about you, and we squeezed more information out of her on our way here."

"Of course, Haven had another reason for wanting to find you," Margie drawled.

Mama looked at me with questioning eyes, like she still doubted what she'd seen moments ago. "Are you really . . . like me?"

"Yeah, I am. And not to be all braggy"—I felt a surge of pride—"but I made that storm."

Margie squinted at me. "You *made* it?"

I looked to Mama. "Maybe that's the wrong word? I

didn't make anything. It felt more like pulling things together."

Mama half smiled. "You called a storm, and it came. I've tried my whole life and never been able to do it. It must've skipped a generation."

"And all I got were color-changing eyes," Margie bemoaned.

"And super hearing," I pointed out.

"Yippee."

Mama chuckled. "I'm starving. Is there any food in the bungalow?"

We trooped inside, robes dragging through the water. I kept looking at Mama, needing to check and make sure that, yes, she was really here.

Margie said, "Looks like we have an apple, some bottled water, peanut butter and crackers, and a can of sardines."

Mama's eyes lit up.

"You can have it," I said. "Compliments of Lynne and Dr. Kay."

Mama was already peeling the can open. "You sure y'all don't want any?"

"Very sure," Margie said.

Mama looked more like herself than I'd seen in a long time. Her skin had color again, and she didn't look as gaunt, as if being herself had filled out her edges.

After she put on some of her old high school clothes, she looked so much like Margie it felt like I was seeing double.

Mama slurped the sardines down like a noodle soup. "So where is Zeke?"

Margie and I looked at each other guiltily.

"He's on his way," I said.

At the same time, Margie said, "You'll see him soon."

Mama's eyes narrowed, and she looked very mom-like and not at all like a magical creature. "Wait, if he isn't with you, then how did you get here?"

"We drove," I said, hoping she'd leave it at that.

She didn't. "*Who* drove?"

Margie turned stony. "You don't get to be mad. If you hadn't left, we wouldn't have had to follow you, and I never would've gotten behind the wheel of a coffee truck."

"A *coffee* truck?!"

"Why did you leave?" I asked, interrupting whatever mom reaction she was about to have.

Mama had been puffing up like a puffer fish, but with that question, she deflated. "I didn't mean to, exactly."

She sat down on the sofa and shivered. "I always know there's a chance, when I go into the river, that something could happen and I might not come back. Whether it's wild animals, or hunters, or"—she hesitated—"losing myself."

She scratched a patchy spot on her elbow. "I don't re-member a lot about how I got here. I know I swam at night and slept down in the mud during the day, but it's a blur. Until you were there in front of me."

She turned to face me. "You saved me, Haven. I don't know what I would've done if you hadn't found me there."

I deflected. "Yeah, what were you doing inside that boat?"

She narrowed her eyes with a sliver of a smile. "Are you telling me that if *you* were exploring the seafloor, and you saw an old wreck, you'd do the smart thing and stay out of it?"

I grinned, because this was the Mama I remembered from before Grandmer and Grandpepper died. The one who was curious about the world and always exploring.

"I'd probably do the adventurous thing," I said.

Margie said, "Me too. For example, taking a coffee truck and driving it across the state to an unmapped location."

Mama tried to hide her smile. "Touché. But how did you get your hands on this truck?"

We caught Mama up on Rye and how he'd helped us get here. Margie hadn't heard the full story of how Rye saw me when I transformed for the first time, so some of that was new to her.

I told them about falling into the Brazos—I just didn't mention that it had been at the Breaks. I was already grounded until the end of Earth time. I didn't want to be grounded into infinity.

Mama squeezed my hand. "Go get your friend. I owe him a big thank-you for helping me get back to you."

"Okay." I took a long look at her to convince myself she

wasn't going anywhere, then ran out the front door.

When I got to the truck, I saw Rye sweeping little brown specks out the back. I assumed it was coffee grounds until I saw his pained face.

"I was too late," he said. "The ants found it."

"Ewwww," I said, and watched more ants get unceremoniously flung out of the coffee truck.

He wiped his forehead. "Can you make it rain bug poison or something?"

I laughed. "That sounds like some supervillain stuff."

He set the broom down and dug his hands in his pockets. "It's wild, like, you have actual superpowers. You could be one of the X-Men or something."

I leaned against the truck door. "And?"

"I just feel like, you're gonna figure out how cool you are, and how cool I'm *not*, and then I'll be back to zero friends in a town with a population of ten."

I laugh-groaned. "There are more people in LaVerne than that."

"Correction: a sixth-grade class of ten kids, total."

"Okay, that's about right."

He sighed. "'Cause, I mean, as awesome as it is to solve Rubik's Cubes or identify Croatia by its highways—and before you ask for my autograph—it's not really the same thing as being able to summon a storm."

"As awesome as it is," I said, echoing him, "to call up

some weather, I think I'd rather be able to call a friend and know that he'll show up."

He drummed his fingers on his legs. "I guess I'm good at that."

"Showing up at impossibly awkward times in my life? Yeah, you're freakishly good at it."

He pumped the air. "My superpower, unlocked!"

I giggled. I liked him, but right now I was grateful just to have a friend. "Can you take a break? My mom wants to talk with you."

His face paled.

"No, not like that! She wants to thank you."

"Ah, gotcha. Yeah, gimme a few minutes. I have a war to win."

With a determined look on his face, he picked his broom up and returned to escorting ants out of his coffee truck.

I walked inside just in time to hear Margie say, "I don't want you to come back."

51

MAMA SAT ON THE FUTON looking stunned. "What?"

Disbelief froze me on the doorstep. All I wanted was Mama back where she belonged with us—how could Margie say that?

I unfroze and rushed across the room to sit beside her. "She's wrong! Of course we do! We want you to come home."

Margie shook her head and leaned against the wall. "Not if we just go back to the way things were. I *don't* want that."

That silenced me.

It was too easy to picture us getting home and Mama fading. How she'd pull away from us and hide in the bathroom. Horror chilled me at the thought of reliving that.

Margie was right—I couldn't go back to being the girl made of stone. Not when I was water and earth and air and roots and raging fire.

"I think you need help," Margie said. "Professional help, like, therapy."

A little gasp escaped me. Things had been rough, but were they *therapy* rough?

"What?" Margie crossed her arms over her chest.

I squirmed. "Isn't therapy for people who can't handle their own problems?" West girls were tough—we'd had to be.

Margie's eyebrows furrowed. "What? No. Asking for help can be incredibly hard to do. Lots of people need therapy, for lots of reasons, and it takes a strong person to do that."

Margie turned to Mama. "It's not your fault you're depressed, but when you stop talking to us, or taking care of yourself, then something's really wrong. You're hurting us, and that's not okay."

"You're right," Mama said, and rubbed her face. "I kept thinking that if only it rained, or if enough time passed, this feeling . . . or not feeling, the *numbness* . . . would go away. But it hasn't."

"Have you always felt this way?" I asked. "I thought you got depressed only after Grandmer and Grandpepper passed."

Mama paused, then said, "I think I've had this all my life, but losing my parents made it feel too big to handle. You know, I tried to talk to them about it when I was in high school. But a depressed kitskara?" Mama rolled her eyes at the memory. "My parents said that was only for humans. Might as well be a bipolar unicorn."

Margie snorted. "I am going to start a band called the Bipolar Unicorns."

I shook my head. "You only play the piano, and you're really bad at it."

"Wow, Haven, harsh," Margie said.

"I'm just saying, put your energies somewhere else."

"And I'm just saying"—Margie turned back to Mama— "that you don't have to do this alone. That's what therapy is for. And you know, being honest with us."

Some of my hurt resurfaced. "Mama, how come you didn't tell us about being a kitskara? If I'd known, I wouldn't have been so scared when it happened to me."

Mama sighed. "It seemed safer to keep it secret. We didn't even know if we could have children. A human and a kitskara, together? It must've happened before, but I'd only heard of it in Finfolk and selkie stories, and those don't have happy endings."

She reached for Margie's hand and squeezed it. "And then we had you, and you were so perfect, but also *different*, and every thought became about protecting you."

"Ther-uh-pee," Margie chanted.

Mama dropped her hands in her lap. "It's really expensive."

"If money's the problem," Margie said, "there's always . . ."

"Leasing the land for wind turbines," I finished.

Mama scoffed. "Your father would never."

"I think he would," I said. "For you. For all of us."

Rye knocked on the door and poked his head in. "Let's hope you're right, 'cause, uh, they're here."

52

DR. RUIZ WALKED IN LOOKING like a comet on its way to battle—she glowed with anger as Papa followed behind her. But when she grabbed Rye, it was to pull him into a tight hug.

"Mijo, you terrified us," she said with a soft Mexican accent. "What would we do without you? My god. Don't ever run away like that again!"

Mama stood and introduced herself. She talked to her, mom to mom, and apologized that Rye had gotten dragged into our search for her.

"If I were in your position, I'd be furious with us," Mama said. "But please know how grateful I am that he was such a good friend to my girls. You should be very proud to have such a kind son."

Dr. Ruiz ("Please, call me Sonia," she'd said to her) seemed to soften. "Your father and I are not happy that you took the truck"—she scowled down at Rye, then looked up at us—"but I'm glad he's found friends so soon. Moving to a new town is so hard."

And Papa. His heavy hands fell on my shoulders. "You know what else is hard? Keeping a truck clean in such a dusty environment. Fortunately, I know two volunteers who would love to wash that coffee truck anytime it needs it. Anytime at all."

Dr. Ruiz looked at us sternly, but I thought I saw a smile peeking through at the corners. "Good to know," she said.

I saw a long future ahead of burning to a crisp under the sun as I scrubbed the red dirt off Mr. Wilson-Ruiz's shiny coffee truck. But that future had Mama in it, so it was worth it.

And it turned out we didn't have to sell Papa on the wind energy at all. Dr. Ruiz had convinced him in the hour they'd had on the plane.

He was his typical optimistic self about it. "I'll always be a farmer," he said. "It's in my blood. But now I can farm the wind too."

He was not cheerful about our escapade across the state, but he wasn't one to talk about kitskara stuff in front of other people. "We're going to have a serious talk, the four of us, right after they head out."

Margie pinned him with her eyes. "A real conversation?"

He nodded stiffly. "A real one. Nothing but the truth. Probably some limits, but only the truth."

Margie and I looked at each other, and then at him. "We have a lot to tell you," I said.

Dr. Ruiz packed Rye up in the coffee truck and left right after that. He'd tried to tell her that it had been his idea we take the truck, but I figured it would be a long time before she forgave us for taking Rye so far from home.

Margie and I watched them drive away. "She's gonna be shocked when she finds out our idea of a good time usually just involves watching old movies," I said to her. "It's not always highway adventuring."

When we walked back inside, Mama and Papa were holding on to each other like they were each other's oxygen. They eased apart when they noticed us, and Papa wiped his eyes with the back of his hand.

"We should probably head back soon too, right?" Mama said.

She tried to sound cheerful about it, but we all knew the look on her face. The one where she was burying what she really wanted hundreds of feet under her skin.

"I don't know about that," Papa said, leaning back on his heels. "No need to rush back. My buddy said he could look after the cows for me, and the wheat is pretty much a wash at this point anyway."

Papa turned and slowly took in the room.

I saw it all over again for the first time: the discolored walls, the peeling deck, and the haphazard furniture. It wasn't hard to understand why he thought we'd be better off without it.

"What would it take to make this place feel like home again?" he said.

Mama's eyes turned a cautious gray blue. "What are you saying, Zeke?"

He shook his head. "I never should've insisted on selling this place. It's your family's home—it's up to you."

Mama's eyes glowed a rosy-gold color as she looked at him, and I was embarrassed to think what that might mean.

He tugged her hand. "You were right about something else too. Lots of things, actually. The girls need to know what you are."

"We already do," Margie said, acting bored.

"But you don't know about me," I added. "I'm a kitskara too. The, uh, shape-shifting kind. I look like a reptile. Sometimes."

Papa's face looked so pale I thought he might faint.

"We always knew this could happen," Mama reminded him. She let go of his hand and wrapped an arm around my waist. "With two shape-shifters in the family now, this place is even more important."

Papa cleared his throat, and I braced myself for what he might say.

"Let's make it nice for us," he said. "I imagine we'll be spending a lot more time here now. My girls need a place they can be themselves. So what does it need?"

I let out a big breath and relaxed. That hadn't been so bad after all.

Mama blinked, looking a little stunned. "Well, it used to have electricity. If we could reconnect the solar panels, we could run an air conditioner when it gets too hot, or at least a fan."

She smiled at us a little embarrassedly. "I've been living a mostly human life for so long, I don't want to live without AC anymore."

I grinned back at her. "Me neither."

Papa got to work on the solar power right away while us girls went thrifting for the stuff we needed to make the bungalow homey again. Margie cheered when I found a dirt-cheap hand-crank radio—now we could have music while we cleaned and fixed up the house.

At first we were really careful with each other as we eased into being together as a family again, like we were scared we'd tear each other's skin if we said the wrong thing.

But after a couple sweaty days of housework, Papa was back to making silly jokes and Mama was laughing at every single one. At first Margie rolled her eyes at the two of them. But when I overheard her chatting to Mama in the kitchenette like she used to, about everything and nothing, I closed my eyes and just listened to them talk like it was my favorite song.

And me? I was good. For the first time in a long time, I didn't have to lie when I said that.

Early on our third morning all together, I called Margie out on the dock.

"M! Come see!"

She walked out with her sleeping bag still wrapped around her. "I swear to god, Haven, if it's just another egret, I'm gonna—"

She stopped mid-sentence when she saw the rainbow stretching over the inlet as the sun rose above it.

"Just like Grandmer and Grandpepper used to make," I said. "A rainbow sunrise is tricky, 'cause it needs rain and sunshine, and my weather magic is about as good as my swimming, so—"

"It's amazing, Haven."

She watched it for a few minutes before saying, "I'm gonna take that as a sign that it's time for me to tell Mom and Dad about, you know. Me."

"Do you want me to come with you?" I asked.

"That's okay—I want to do this myself."

I stayed out on the deck, but ten minutes later when the glass doors slid open, she was all shaky smiles.

Papa's laugh was shaky too. "Y'all aren't making it easy on me. Look, I'm gonna say it so many times you get sick of me—I love you the way you are, and I want you to be who you are."

His face scrunched. "And I'm gonna worry my tail off 'cause this world isn't always good to folks who are different."

I thought of Rye and all the kindness he'd shown me from the beginning.

"But sometimes it is, Papa," I said.

At night, Mama would take me out swimming, just like I'd hoped she would.

Everywhere we went, we stirred up fossifae. Sometimes Mama pointed them out before I spotted them.

A giant sloth ambled down the beach. A mammoth moved with lumbering grace and elegance. A dire wolf ran past us and opened its jaws as if its hunger were large enough to survive extinction. But the endless surface of the gulf made even the mammoth look small.

She was also teaching me how to thrum-speak underwater, but it was tough for me to hear the differences in the tones. Margie picked up the language faster, although she didn't have the vibrating throat muscle, so it was more like a hum than a thrum when she did it.

It might have been the happiest week of my life. But after seven perfect days of gulf swimming, painting and cleaning, giggling over card games as the sun set, and some hard conversations, we had to go back home. The rental car was too expensive to keep another day, and the farm needed Papa.

But Mama wasn't ready to come back.

After all our stuff was packed in the car, we walked to the

end of the dock where Mama stood halfway out in the inlet.

My body ached to be in the water with her, and because she and I were the same, she knew what I was feeling.

Mama said, "Haven, you can ssstay here with me. At leassst until ssschool ssstarts again. Right, Zeke?"

Papa frowned, but he didn't argue.

My heart hurt. "You're gonna be gone that long?"

Her globe eyes looked sad. "I don't know how long thisss will take, but I promissse you I'll come back. Thisss is therapy too. I need to let myssself be a kitsssskara, after trying to contain myssself insssside a bathtub for ssso long."

I frowned at her. "But you'll be doing real therapy too, right?"

She nodded. "Real therapy too."

It was tempting to stay. Being with Mama and learning from her was what I'd wanted ever since I'd first transformed.

But I shook my head no. "I want to go home."

Her smile was sad, but she nodded like she agreed. "I'll be there before you know it."

She dove under the water, and my heart ached to watch her swim away. Mamas weren't supposed to leave. I wanted to fix her. I wished on every star, above and below, that I could make her better, or at least, make things easier.

But that wasn't how it worked. And it wasn't my job to make her happy.

I was also scared that that kind of sadness was lurking

in a corner inside me somewhere, and once it came out, I wouldn't be able to put it back.

A high-pitched thrum filled the inlet.

Papa waved. Margie hummed, and I thrummed back. *I love you too.*

That's all we could do. Be honest about how her actions affected us and love her the way she was.

A few hours later, we buckled our seat belts on the plane that would take us to Dallas and the long drive home from there.

As I watched Houston drop away below me, panic crowded in. What if Mama never came home? What if she forgot us again? What if we were doing the wrong thing leaving her behind?

My breathing tightened. I repeated Margie's advice to myself.

Focus on one good thing.

Grandma West whispered in my memory's ear. *What can you count on?*

I hadn't heard her voice in a while. I realized that I'd been listening to myself a lot more, and I liked that.

Margie felt me looking at her. She quirked an eyebrow at me, then nestled back into her seat. She was already falling asleep under her headphones. She'd gone through the airport with her sunglasses off and stared down anyone who gawked at her.

As the plane turned around in the sky to clear the city, I watched the sun setting, and I knew it was shimmering pink and orange over the gulf where Mama was trying to recover all the pieces of herself.

At least I could count on my sister and sunrises.

Epilogue

I PULLED MYSELF OUT OF the Brazos and climbed up the red banks to our wheat fields. I tugged the lid off the top of the big metal cooler we'd dug into the ground to hold everything I might need when I went for a swim. We kept glass bottles of water in there, and I grabbed one along with the jeans and T-shirt I'd tossed in on my way out. I always wore my silver bracelet. Never took it off.

There was a set of clothes in there for Mama too, just in case.

As I drank the water, I shifted back to human and pulled on my clothes. I took my time walking back to the house. Tonight Papa was cooking, and Margie'd told me to go to the river.

"Get out of here," she'd said. "You're getting cranky, and you know you'll feel better." She'd been right.

Halfway home, I decided to climb the windmill. It had become a bit of a habit. Mama called us every few days from Randy's, so I wasn't worried, but I liked to keep a faith watch for her. She would come back. She'd said so.

All day long the sky had been holding its breath, ready to exhale a storm. I wasn't gonna take full credit for it, but I might've spent some time incanting in the dirt. I'd been experimenting, and without an ocean to draw power from, LaVerne had had its strangest weather ever.

There'd been rain, sure, but I'd nearly flooded everyone's crops. So then I tried to bring out the heat to dry it all and baked everything to a crisp. After the latest tornado (it stayed in the sky, no damage done), I was ready to give up on weather magic until Mama came home. She might have some tips to help me nuance it.

I glanced toward Rye's house, but I didn't see him. Ruby was lounging on the front porch, though, so he must've been close by. She never let her boy get more than ten feet away.

My own tagalong screamed at me from the ground. My peacock didn't like it when I climbed up here. He spread his tail and turned his eyes on me. We stared at each other, one oddity to another.

"Are you happy here, Harry?" I asked him. "Do you wish you were adorning a palace lawn instead?"

He screeched again.

Do you belong here? I asked him in my mind. I asked myself.

He lifted one leg and hopped to the other.

"What are you doing, bird?" I asked. "You dancing?"

Movement near the Brazos caught my eye. As my heart sped up, so did the weather vane.

A woman crawled out of the river and pulled herself up to standing. Her bones looked wrong, like they couldn't quite support her out of the water, and she walked as if she'd come a very long way.

I cupped my hands and yelled back to the house, "She's here! She's back!"

I knew Margie would hear me. She always kept her headphones off when I went to the river. I dropped to the ground, and my fingers dug into the dirt. My roots ran deep here.

All at once, the clouds opened and deluged us all.

I whooped. Harry strutted and shook.

A peacock, dancing in the rain.

A magical girl, jumping in a storm.

A mother, both monstrous and human, come home.

And still the river called.

Acknowledgments

Endless thanks to my agent, Alexandra Levick—you are the perfect blend of art, smarts, and savvy. To my wonderful editor, Maggie Rosenthal—thank you for your grace, insight, and vision. You grew this small-town story into a Texas-sized tale! Thank you to Abigail Powers, Krista Ahlberg, Marinda Valenti, and Crystal Watanabe for powerhouse copyediting; Lily Qian and Kate Renner for the gorgeous design; and Dion MDB for the perfect cover.

Enormous thanks to Chris Flis and the Whiteside Museum of Natural History. Thank you to Marien Martinez, Melissa del Toro Schaffner, and Michelle Calero for help with the Spanish-language sections. Any errors are mine. Thank you, Ashleigh Davis of Cloche Coffee! You saved me with your coffee truck and iced coffee know-how.

Thanks to the Writers Voice program, especially the magical Beth Bauman. Endless gratitude to my Lesley MFA mentors: David Elliott, for wise words and timeless championing; Michelle Knudsen, for helping me linger in the hard parts; Susan Goodman, for transforming the way I write; Chris Lynch, for listening to my real story; Jason Reynolds, for inspiring a drive toward greatness; and Tracey Baptiste, for helping me thread the needle of writer and mom.

Love forever to the Magick Six: Candice Iloh, Devon Van Essen, Gabrielle Basha, Michelle Calero, and Axie Oh. Thanks to Andrea Vogelsonger and Kathy Karch for rapid-fire beta reads and friendships I rely on. Huge love to the Table of Discontents—Nat Cassidy, Brian Silliman, and Matthew Trumbull—for making this book (and my life) infinitely better. Love to Jørn Otte for keeping the faith for Haven when I lost it. Thanks to Hannah Karena Jones for brilliant revision and story questions. So grateful to Sher Lee for insightful beta reads and well-timed emails. Thank you to early readers Hope Cartelli and Maryanne Olson, to Mili Thomas for writing dates, and to Chris Chappell for puzzle help.

This book wouldn't exist without childcare! Thank you to Samantha Williams, Kathy Karaisaridis, and Holly Sickinger-Bifulci. Forever thanks to SLP's Sheri Legan Lehmann and Claudia Siguenza.

I am indebted to the NYC indie theater community. Love always to the Lowry family, Matthew Freeman and Pam Grossman, the DelGrosso family, the Baldwin-Ancowitz family, Sean and Jordana Williams, Kelley Rae O'Donnell, the Kenin Elias-Reyes family, the Kennedy Stagg family, the Schulenburg-Cohn family, Lindsey and Mark Palgy, Emily and Ned Hartford, and Patrice Miller.

No one can take the place of family, but three women came close: Linda Cutson, Lisa Sayegh, and Donna Fishman. Love to Kristin and Greg Marchilena, Allen Arthur and Caitlin Brodnick, Ben and Caitlin Clever, Katie and Craig Woehr, Doug and Elise Ramsbottom, Sarah and Nat Calloway, Carrie Shuchart, Rachel Perkins, and Bob and Debbie Burhoe.

JoAnna Trumbull—thank you for the love and laughter you poured into us. Thanks to the Willing family: my dad, Michael, who made sure I knew I was loved every day; my mom, Gail, for instilling the belief that I could do everything I dreamed; and Philip, Rebekah, and Jacqueline for so many wonderful memories. Kimberly DesAutels— this book owes an unmeasurable debt to you and your family. May fossils always bloom at your feet. Theo and Ezra—you make me laugh and love harder than I knew was possible. And finally, thanks to my husband, Matthew, for being my forever home.